It Pours

By
CD Cain

A Chambers of the Heart Book

By
CD Cain

Life is short. Break the rules. Forgive quickly. Kiss slowly. Love truly. Laugh uncontrollably and never regret anything that makes you smile."

– Mark Twain

Dedication

To my little family of three.
Each morning I pause to give thanks
for the blessing of sharing another day with you.

Chapter 1

EYES OF DARKENED ruby tortured me with one of the best and simultaneously one of the worst memories of my young adult life. They were lying on a pillow of soft cotton within the tiny white box. Unlike my own eyes, these were protected from the sight of a future I had accepted yet no longer desired. They saw only the white cotton which nestled them softly in the memories they sparked. Had it not been for its contents, the small box would have been hidden among the trinkets of Charlie Grace's over-sized wooden desk. It was from her. There wasn't a card or any tangible evidence she had been the one who sent it, but there was little to no doubt the gift was from Sam. Gift. Such an odd word for the object I couldn't take my eyes from nor tear my thoughts away from since the moment I found it. Had she meant it to be a gift? Surely not, as this was the day of Charlie Grace's long-awaited engagement party. The social event of her one-and-only daughter's engagement. A December night's proposal had been the last contact between Sam and me.

"Dear, staring out the window at your guests doesn't exactly count as attending the party." Charlie Grace had entered the room without my notice. "You do actually have plans of leaving this room and joining us, don't you?"

"Of course, Mother," I said. "I'll be down in a minute."

Charlie Grace turned to leave but stopped shy of the doorway. "See that you do, dear. See that you do."

"Hey, Mother?"

She looked over her shoulder but didn't turn around to face me. "Hmmmm?"

"Did I get a package in the mail yesterday?"

"It's your engagement party. You've gotten many packages this week. I can hardly keep up with all of them." She waved her hand as if dismissing the entire topic altogether. Although we both knew she would have been highly offended if the presents hadn't arrived by the dozen the weeks before the party.

I walked from behind the desk to face her and held up the tiny white box. "This box? Did I get this one in the mail yesterday?"

"Oh, dear Lord, that thing is hideous. Who on earth sent this to you?" She picked the box up from my hand and inspected it to see if she could find a name on it. She handed it back to me. "Who would ever make, or better yet, buy a gaudy cicada charm?"

I looked down at the charm shaped like a tiny locust. The sunlight streamed in through the window and reflected off of the gold to make it look as if it glowed. I suppose some would call it gaudy. Although the meaning behind it made it the most beautiful piece of jewelry I had ever seen. It had been our first kiss. So many moonlights ago, we had sat on the bayou's dock and listened to the cicada's song. We were lost in each other. Had been lost in each other. Even though my heart ached for the loss of Sam in my life, my mind soaked up every bit of the memories of her lips upon mine. This charm took me back to a time when I dreamed of a different life. A life not held to the conformities I faced now. I felt a glimmer of once-felt happiness stir inside of me. I turned my attention back to Charlie Grace before I let those feelings gain strength in me. This is what I had. This day is what I had.

"I don't know who sent it," I finally said.

"Well, dear. Do make sure you never wear it in public or around me." Mother turned her back to me and left the room.

"I'll see you downstairs, Mother," I mumbled under my breath.

I had grown tired of our conversation. Truth be told, I had grown tired of most of our conversations. Without Memaw as a buffer, Charlie

Grace and I held no delusions of our mother-daughter relationship. Memaw had been more of a mother to me than Charlie Grace ever was. Than Charlie Grace ever could be. Without her, the glue to what little relationship Charlie Grace and I had was gone. We were strangers to each other. Strangers who had absolutely no common ground to build a foundation on.

Sure, Mother thought my engagement to Grant brought us closer together. She believed my wishes to let her plan everything in relation to the engagement was a sign we had grown closer. Little did she know, or even care, that it was merely a way to disassociate myself from the inescapable event. If I had my wish, I would sleep through the whole damn thing.

I walked back to the large window behind the desk. Looking out at the setting in front of me, I realized Charlie Grace had her perfect day. Yes, she would finally get her long-awaited wish. In her eyes, a good southern woman was nothing without the gold band that attached her to a fine southern man. It was as if a woman was defined by the type of man she was lucky enough to snatch as a husband. For me the man was Grant Thibodeaux and he was the epitome of her dreamed son-in-law.

I had known Grant throughout grade school. Growing up in a small town, we didn't have the school diversity most of the larger cities had. Therefore, you pretty much stayed with the same kids and attended grades together year after year. It wasn't until Grant came home for the summer after his undergraduate years that our relationship took a path all its own. Charlie Grace worked her matchmaker skills the night of my graduation party and had Grant arrive as the main event for the evening. Of course, she tried to masquerade it as him delivering the jeep she had gotten me but I saw beyond the diversion.

She had tried for years to attach me to a young man of an influential family but I had always managed to dodge the connection. Grant was different. He was easy to be around. He never pressured me or tried to make our relationship be more than it truly was at heart. More importantly he loved our town as much as I did. Looking back, I realize this was one of the key elements in my relationship with him. We had common dreams—common goals to connect us to one another. I could be with him and never change what I wanted in life. He slipped in under my radar and here I stood watching him as he mingled among the crowd. The last months of residency had been taxing on both of us. It left little time for anything beyond rotations much less time to find our footing after Sam had come in and out of my life. The proposal had been a huge surprise to me. It came out of nowhere and was unlike anything we had planned. Grant and I had always agreed we would make no plans to marry or even get engaged until after we had completed our residencies. We both felt our education was the key focus in our lives. Or so I thought we did. Changes like these are what I noticed in him over the last several months. I suppose we all change a little when we grow. I know I had.

I looked down at the charm in the palm of my hand. A cicada. Nearly a year had slipped by since that night at the cabin. The night I answered my longing to feel Sam's kiss. Had we been lost in the song of the thirteen-year cicadas? The strength of the male's serenade drowned out nearly every other sound that night, including the sound of my fears and hesitations which screamed through me.

It wasn't until I felt my body give itself over to her that my fears returned. I couldn't unravel the depths of what it meant to be lost in the passion of her touch. She admitted to the same and actually stopped our passion from going any farther. My body and heart ached for her the weeks following our near night together. I tried my best to accept the boundaries of our relationship into one of a platonic friendship. Yet no matter what I did, the ache was there. Finally, one night alone in a hospital on-call room, I could no longer deny myself to feel her next to me again.

Memories of Sam's body against mine and of her kisses down my body caused tears to form in my eyes. I straightened my back and stiffened my body as I briskly wiped them away. No, I wouldn't let my thoughts travel any further down that road. That was then, this is now. Besides, she was the one who had cut off all contact with me. I turned from the window and prepared myself to join the party out on the lawn.

"Hi."

I stared at her, frozen. How is she here? How is Sam standing in my doorway?

"Hey," I squeaked out.

"Hey." Her voice was meek and her body's expression was drawn inwardly. She leaned against the doorjamb as if making a stand she would enter the room no further.

"I'm sorry." I rubbed the cicada I held in my palm but then tightened the grip around it when it nearly slipped from my hand due to my nervously sweating palm. The last thing I needed to add to our tension would be for it to fall onto the desk in between us. "I'm just really shocked to see you. I'm having trouble coming up with something to say."

"Don't worry about it." She turned from the doorway to take a step into the hallway.

"Wait!" I yelled as I rushed around the side of the desk. "Don't go. Please, Sam…don't go."

She slowly turned back toward me. "I really should go." She stared down the hallway and shook her head. "I mean, I don't know what I'm doing here."

"How are you here? At this time. On this day. Why now after all of this time?"

"Honestly," she said as she raised a small card in the air "by this." She tapped the card against her other hand. "Your mother actually sent me an invitation. To be fair, she sent me and my father an invitation."

"I'm so sorry. I didn't know she had done that."

"So, you didn't give her my mailing address?"

"No, not at all. I wouldn't do that."

"It doesn't matter anyway." Her voice cracked. "What does matter anymore? You know?" Again, she turned to step into the hallway.

In two quick steps I reached her and gently put my hand on her arm to stop her from leaving. That's all it was. Nothing sensual or passionate. Just a simple touch on the arm to stop her from leaving. Yet the mere sensation of her skin under my hand soared through my body as a current of energy. It took my breath. I felt her flinch underneath my touch.

"Come back in." Cautiously, I pulled at her arm as I urged her to come back into the room. "Please. Can't we please talk?"

"I don't know." She didn't move.

"I got the charm." I opened my hand to show her.

She looked down at it and sighed deeply. "I bought that for you so long ago." She reached out and rubbed it with a single finger. "Seems like a lifetime ago." Her eyes glistened with the dew of fresh tears. "I thought maybe one day you could use a happier memory to wear on your chain." Her eyes drifted to the gold cross around my neck. She briskly wiped the tears from her eyes before they were free to travel down her face. "Well, I don't suppose that will happen now. Not such a great memory after all." Her voice had grown cold.

"Says you," I mumbled.

She cocked her head to the side in the way that made butterflies flutter across my stomach. It was the one particular mannerism of hers that had haunted my visions over the last three months since I had seen or spoken to her.

I shrugged and looked up at the ceiling as I tried desperately not to cry. "Say what you want. Say it's not such a great memory for you but you won't take it from me. That night with you, that time with you, is one of the best memories I've made in my life. So, I love it."

"Shouldn't this be?" She raised her arms in the air. "Shouldn't all of this be your best memory? It's your engagement party after all."

I rolled my eyes and looked away from her. "Not exactly," I said as I ran my finger down the spine of a book in the bookcase next to me.

She took in a deep breath and slowly exhaled. "I certainly meant to give it to you under different circumstances."

"You surprised me with it." I walked to the desk and sat on its edge. I hoped the distance between us would encourage her to come into the room so we could finish talking.

"Yeah well." She followed but stood behind a high-back burgundy chair in front of the desk. "I was packing when I came across it. I didn't want to take it with me. You know I really wanted to throw it away." She didn't look me in the eyes but rather over my shoulder to stare out the picture window behind me. "But I couldn't. No matter how hard I tried, I couldn't."

"I'm glad." I sat the charm down on the desk. "Wait a second. Did you say packing?"

"Yes, Rayne, packing."

My heart plummeted to the pit of my stomach at the sound and tone of my name. The acid in her tone could not be denied. I missed Stormy. I missed the nickname she had given me and the way she used to say it. Hell, I missed the person who was Stormy. You don't realize how much something affects you until it is gone—the innocence of a nickname or the tenderness in the eyes of the person holding you as they say it. It's those things you miss the most when they are taken from you. I breathed in deeply to catch my breath.

"Hindsight, I should've found a way to throw the damn thing away." Sam shrugged. "Would've been smarter than this." She swept her hand across her forehead to brush away the fallen curls. Her cropped, blonde layers had grown out considerably since the last time I had seen her.

"Maybe for you but I'm glad you gave it to me. It means everything to me. That night means everything to me."

"Don't," she said through gritted teeth as she looked directly at me for the first time. "Don't you dare say something like that to me." Her tone was angry and bitter.

"Sam." I pushed myself off of the corner of the desk to take a step toward her.

"Don't, Rayne." She held up her hand. "I swear I'll walk out of the fucking door if you take another step."

I slumped back down onto the coolness of the wooden desk. I was shocked at how angry she spoke to me. I'm not sure what I expected when I saw her but I don't think I let myself imagine it would be this. "What do you want me to say? What can I say? You're really pissed at me so I'm thinking there's not too much I can say."

She was silent for several seconds. Her grip tightened and relaxed against the back of the chair several times before she spoke again. "I suppose I came for you to say goodbye to my face instead of your mother sending an engagement invitation. At least you mean more to me than to do something like that." She took in a deep breath, rolled her eyes toward the ceiling and exhaled. "You meant more to me than that."

"Past tense, huh?" I turned my eyes away from her and fixated them on a wedding photo of Jacques and Charlie Grace. "I told you I didn't know she had sent you an invitation."

"You don't get it, do you?" She shook her head. "You just don't get it. Whatever. All I did was come to say goodbye and have closure to this whole mess."

Mess. "What do you mean goodbye?" I asked flatly. "I thought we did that in December."

"I suppose so but I'm leaving Alabama and I won't be coming back. I gave up my fellowship."

I stood up off of the desk. "You did what? Why?"

"Again...you don't get it, Rayne."

My heart sank even further down the pit now swallowing it. Why? Why would she give up everything she ever wanted? I opened my mouth to say something but what felt like ten minutes passed before I could make a sound. "I guess I don't get it. I don't know why you would give up your whole life's plan."

"Doesn't make sense, does it? I was the strong one of us. The one who never got her feelings involved. Yet, it's me who was unable to pick things up where they left off and keep going on with my life's plan."

"That's not fair."

"Yeah, well, life's not fair."

"Where are you going?"

"It doesn't matter," She waved her hand in the air to dismiss the question of its importance.

"Yes, it does."

"Why?"

I walked around the desk and sat down in the chair as I feared my legs would no longer hold me up. Again, I looked at the bookshelf to take my eyes from her. This time they fell on Memaw's picture. In that instant, I felt the loss of her crushing down on me again. I had told her goodbye and now Sam was standing in front of me asking me to do the same to her. I felt the tears building inside of me. "Because how will I know where to find you? How will I gain any strength in knowing this life is worth something if I can't picture you in it? Picture your surroundings. Picture your life. I may not be in it but it doesn't mean I want to know a world without you in it."

Sam walked around the chair and sat down hard in it. She put her head in her hands and whispered. "I need to tell you goodbye."

"Why? Why does it have to be this way? Why do you have to give up your fellowship? It's not as if I saw you anyway. Ever since...since that night, I haven't seen or talked to you at all."

"Like I could see you? Like it would be possible for me to see you and not break down into a blubbering mess?" She again wiped harshly across her cheeks as if she hated the tears falling from her eyes. "You broke my fucking heart! Hell, up until you, the only commitment I ever made was to a night of sex. I was the one who never falls for anyone. Then I meet you and look at me now. I'm a crying idiot while you stand there perfectly fine."

Shocked at her words, I pushed the chair backward against the low-lying windowsill. The squeak of the ungreased wheels echoed. "You're not an idiot." I massaged my temples. "And I'm hardly fine, Sam."

"Oh, aren't you? Look behind you. Your engagement party is on the other side of that window."

"You think that makes me fine?"

"I sure as shit do. I'm not the one about to get married and spend the rest of my life with someone."

"No, you're about to take off to who knows where to live your life the way you want it. No excuses. No sacrifices. And with absolutely no consequences to your choices. That's what you're about to do."

"What are you talking about?"

I scooted the chair back up to the desk and leaned across it. "Now, who doesn't get it? Look at you. You come in here telling me how I don't get it. As if I don't have a clue to anything you feel. As if I wasn't a wreck…still a wreck. If you think for one damn minute I'm fine or that any of what is going on behind me is my heart's wish, then you don't have a fucking clue about me."

Sam sat back in her chair. She opened her mouth as if to speak but quickly closed it again.

"It's not so easy being on the other side of those kinds of words, is it?"

"If you were a wreck, if anything about what happened between us changed you or hurt you at all…then why did she send me an invitation? Her sending me an invitation showed me she didn't have a clue that anything had happened between us. You swept it neatly under the rug without anyone catching on to your dirty, little secret."

"Again, who doesn't get it?" I sat back in my chair and turned it side to side. "Did you hear anything I ever said about Charlie Grace? Did you listen to me at all? As if she would consider either of our feelings for one second with this engagement. Don't you think her knowing about my heartbreak would've encouraged her even more to send you an invitation? To gloat over her victory. To let you know she won."

"When is the wedding?"

"I don't know."

"You don't know?"

"Yes, I don't know. I only agreed to the engagement to have a little quiet in my life. After that night, everything was like noise in my head. You had left. All I wanted to do was curl up in a ball and shut the world out. When I couldn't do that, all I wanted to do was throw myself into school. But Grant and Charlie Grace were insistent to have an answer from me. The quickest way to feel some normalcy in my life again was to say yes." I turned the chair to look out onto the lawn. "And here I am." Instantly, I felt the weight of my words. Here I am. Exactly where they want me.

"Have you ever once thought about the timing of Grant's proposal?" Sam asked quietly.

It was the first time today her tone resembled how she had once spoken to me. I turned my chair back to look into her eyes.

She pushed one of the unwrapped presents to the side of the desk and leaned across it on her elbows. "Hadn't you both decided you were waiting until after medical school to get married? What happened? Why the sudden rush? Hasn't it even crossed your mind this is his way of holding onto you...of controlling you? Don't you think he saw the writing on the wall and took the most desperate time of your life as a way of sealing the deal?"

"I have."

"And?"

"You're probably right."

"So, it's okay for you to be manipulated your whole life? Whatever, Rayne. If you can't see the truth in front of you, then go get married. Ruin your life." She rubbed her temples with her fingers. "It's your life."

"As if you gave me the chance for anything else," I mumbled under my breath.

"What? What did you just say?"

I looked up into her eyes. The blueness of them sent a wave through my stomach that raced up my throat to form a knot of swallowed tears. "As if you gave me another option, Sam. I asked you to tell me how it would be between us—what we would have."

"No, you told me your well-thought-out plan of how it couldn't be. You had us all figured out before we even started. Where you wanted to live. Where I wanted to live. How we couldn't live."

"And you didn't argue. You didn't tell me differently. You walked away and cut me off. You wouldn't even speak to me after that night. I called. I left voicemails. Texts. Not once did you respond." I held up my finger. "Not once."

"I listened to them."

"But you never answered."

"You never said what I needed to hear."

"Which was what exactly?"

"That I was enough. That I was enough to try." She laid her palm flat against her chest. "Rayne, you wanted the guarantee. Your whole life has been about planning everything out to the letter. You asked me to tell you how our future would be before you even invested the time into us to give that future a chance. You wanted me to check off all of your perfectly squared boxes so you would have some type of reassurance before I was your choice."

"That's not how it was and you know that."

"Maybe not but that is how it felt. Your voicemails didn't say anything different. I'd save them to listen to at the end of the day. I hoped I would hear you tell me you wanted me—to choose me. That I was enough to risk the chance of an unknown future."

As I let her words soak in, I pictured her sitting in her apartment exhausted from the fatigue of the day as she sat slumped on her couch with her phone held up against her ear. I pictured a beam of moonlight flowing into her renovated, warehouse loft. The reality of the heart-break and pain we had both experienced played out in my vision as a trail of tears which flowed down her cheek were illuminated by the light of the phone. No, she was right. I never did say those things. Hadn't I planned my life out to the very last detail? Hadn't I let all of what I feared loving her would mean to my life's plan keep me from saying what she needed to hear or what I truly felt. Even in the times of begging to hear her voice, I didn't tell her the depth of my feelings for her.

"I'm sorry I hurt you. I'm sorry I didn't say what I truly felt. I was…I am broken without you. I didn't know how to put that into words."

Sam looked out the window behind me. I watched as she silently took in the scene. A single tear fell from her eye. She didn't wipe it away. "We are here now. None of that matters anymore."

"Everything about you matters."

"Don't say stuff like that to me. Especially now when it's too late."

"Why?" The weight of her once again walking out of my life caused a crushing pain in my chest. It began to smother me as it had over the last months. I tried to control my breath. "Why can't I tell you how I truly feel? Why does it have to be this way?"

"Because of that." She pointed out the window. "Because that is where you are. That is what you can handle."

"No. I can't handle you walking out that door." I pointed and shook my finger at it. "It'll break me again. I can't tell you goodbye." I didn't stop the tears. I never liked crying in front of anyone. It always seemed to be a private thing for me. Maybe it's because when I did cry, the tears came from my soul. But this time, I didn't stop them.

Sam's chin quivered when she held me in her eyes. She shook her head. "I can't. You'll break my heart again because you aren't ready. You'll want to be ready. You'll want to make me yours but you're not ready to stand up to all of that behind you. I'll be this little secret again. Each time you're confronted, you'll fold and tell me you'll be stronger the next time. I couldn't breathe after that night. I was shattered. Now, it's me who has a plan for where my life needs to go. I have to do it while I have the strength to go."

"Who's the one who has it all figured out now?" My crying had become forceful. It caused me to struggle through gasps of air to speak in broken words.

Sam stood up, walked around the desk, and knelt in front of me. "Oh Stormy." She reached up and lightly wiped away my tears with her thumb. "I'll always love you." She stood up and leaned over to place her lips against my forehead. "Always." She quickly walked to the door but stopped right before stepping through. "Goodbye," she said softly over her shoulder.

I laid my head on the desk and let my soul cry until it hadn't the strength to produce more tears. Any barriers I pretended to have were broken. I had cursed the numbness I felt after Sam left but now, I prayed for it. I couldn't feel all of this pain I was feeling. I wouldn't be able to breathe if I carried it with me. I yearned for numbness to overtake me. It would be my only freedom from the black hole that had started as a blemish on my soul when Memaw passed in my arms.

Watching Sam walk away from me again, I knew it would grow to become the nothingness I had in my life.

I looked down at the sparkle in the cicada's eyes. The rubies reminded me of a life I had once dreamt to be mine. I unclasped the chain from my neck and ran it through the loop found at the back of the locust's neck. I watched it fall against the gold cross before I put it back around my neck. The two women who have the most meaning in my life were now side by side. The only thing I knew for sure was that I didn't say goodbye. She said it to me, but I didn't say it back. Hope is both a curse and a blessing.

Chapter 2

*T*HE SKY WAS filled with a purplish hue from an early setting sun of a season where winter was slowly cascading into spring. Its light was held hostage to the hours that had not yet found daylight savings time. In the South, this was our season for outdoor events. The warmness of the day evolved into a crispness of night which made the temperature comfortably cool for an outside gathering. I strolled through the groups of guests as they mingled and stopped briefly at each to give my cordial greetings. Aw yes, Charlie Grace had trained me well.

Mother had planned the event down to the letter with the most picturesque part of the lawn designated as the primary party area. Large banquet tables adorned with white linen cloths and Aster pattern blue-and-white porcelain dishes sat under the majestic moss-covered branches of the oak trees that had lived on the plantation much longer than any of us. The centerpieces were my favorite of the decorations. They were made from wide-bottom matching porcelain bowls filled with artificial hydrangeas and Granny Smith apples. The contrast of green from the dark foliage of the hydrangeas and the brightness of the freshly plucked apples sat against gray moss as it spilled from the branches overhead. I say artificial. Surely, they had to be as the large flower had not yet bloomed here in the South. Knowing Charlie Grace, she could have very easily had the white and light green blooms shipped in for the event—easily, but expensive. I mean, what was a few thousand dollars when you were hoping the photographers would capture a shot worthy enough to submit for the cover of Southern Living Magazine?

I reached out to touch the petals of the arrangement. "I don't even want to know," I mumbled as I pulled back my hand.

The evening had lost its beauty to me long before Sam's visit but after seeing her, not even the setting sun could brighten my spirits. A gentle breeze swayed the flickering tea lights that hung over my head. Hundreds of them dangled from the trees. I watched their flames dance within the tiny bell bottom-shaped glass.

I began to think about Sam's question. Had I? Had I truly sat down and wondered about the change in the timing of Grant's proposal? She was right. Grant and I meshed well because we both had the same visions of our future. In fact, wasn't that the reason I had agreed to date him in the first place?

Grant was easy, never threatening or demanding. I could get lost in myself and not have to explain one thing to him. Yes, we had decided years earlier our goals were the same. Well, nearly the same, as I could've done without the necessities of marriage. Although I knew his and Charlie Grace's desires would have had to come to fruition at some point in my life. I always thought it would be much later after graduation.

Marriage to me was a stepping stone. One footstep of life that would eventually find its way into my future. I had never questioned this beyond those few thoughts until I met Sam. Sam had changed everything in me. It was as if she was a sky full of brilliant stars illuminating the footpath of life—a trail of roots and dirt in between a canopy of blooming trees. There was a time, before Memaw's passing, where my daydreams took me to that path and each time Sam walked along beside me. The darkness that filled me after Memaw's death took every star from me, took the blooms from the trees, and left a bare skeleton of what once was without the companion by my side. Memaw.

"Oh, how I miss you, Meems," I whispered as I looked up through the branches. So much of Charlie Grace's Southern Baptist teachings didn't sit well with me. Yet the thought of Memaw's soul somewhere in the skies above watching me throughout my day was a comfort. It was a comfort to feel her still with me in some way. Without it, I would be lost without the hope of recovery. Days were a passage of time after she left me. It was as if I could no longer feel anything without her in my world. Of course, I missed seeing her while I was away at school but there was this satisfying feeling of strength and security in the knowledge she was only a few hours or phone call away. Not feeling her presence, hearing her voice or laughter had left the blackest of holes in my soul.

"Have you ever once thought about the timing of Grant's proposal?"

No, actually. I don't think I have, not until now anyway. Had I been so numb with Memaw's death that I had not even thought of the meaning behind his untimely…or rather timely proposal?

"I didn't think you were ever going to get here," Grant said as he ducked under a low-lying branch. "Where ya' been?"

He rested his arm across my shoulder as he leaned in to kiss my cheek. His newly grown beard scratched against my face. It was worse when he kissed my lips. It matched the nauseous rumblings of my stomach as my thoughts traveled to the next step he wanted to follow our kisses. Before meeting Sam, I could turn my body off and let my brain take me somewhere else when our kisses flowed into the act of making love. Act. A good word for what I considered our love making to be. It was a necessity to our relationship. A necessity that had not found its way back into our relationship over the last several months. I knew this too shall pass as all things do.

"Sorry," I said and shrugged off his arm. "You know me."

He stepped back to look at me fully. "You okay, babe?"

Ugh! Babe! I couldn't stop the roll of my eyes. Not that I would've even if I could've stopped them. I hated when he called me a pet name, especially babe. Did an engagement ring really necessitate us starting silly habits such as pet names?

He chuckled as if he knew calling me that would get me riled up. "Okay…okay, I give." He waved his hands in surrender. "Are you okay, Rayne?"

"I'm fine." I waved my hand at the crowd around us. "Do you like all of this?"

Grant chuckled. I swear his voice continued to deepen over the years or maybe it was the beard aging his boyish looks that created the illusion of an older man in front of me. He brought the fluted glass to his lips and wiped away the trail of champagne from his whiskers. "It's not so bad."

"Isn't it though?"

"No, not really. These are our friends and family, Rayne. They want to celebrate with us. Besides, when we move back home and set up our practices, these types of events will be common for us."

"You've got to be kidding me right now."

"Come here." He grabbed my hand and pulled me behind one of the oak's massive trunks. He gently leaned my back against it. "Okay, now tell me. What's wrong?" He gave me a half-hearted smile. "You know this is really supposed to be a happy occasion. I mean, some would even say this is an event they look forward to. Don't girls usually live for this stuff?"

Live for this stuff? What the hell? I'm not some little sorority chick he picked up freshman year. I knew he was joking but I was too keyed up to let myself leave it there. I heard Sam's voice in my head again. Have you ever once thought about the timing of Grant's proposal? His joking and her question combined together pissed me off to high heaven. "Grant, there's something I've been meaning to ask you." Nothing like the present.

"There you two are," Charlie Grace said as she walked around the tree. Jacques followed in step behind her. She wrapped her arms around our waists. "The caterers are ready to begin serving the dishes. We should try to get everyone to take a seat." She brushed back the hair that had fallen onto her face. She looked radiant. The green of her dress lightened her gray eyes in such a way that they appeared to have a bluish hue. For a brief moment, they reminded me of Memaw's. I watched her eyes fall to my chest as the edge of her lips turned downward. "Must you? Must you always defy me in every single request I have?"

She lifted the locust pendant off of my chest and then quickly dropped it to let it fall back against my skin.

Jacques stepped in between us. "I'll round up the troops," he said as he leaned his six-foot-one-inch frame over to place a kiss on my temple. "Hey, pretty girl, glad you made it down."

My memories held only his image when I thought of the word *father*. The one who had been a part in creating my life had turned out to be nothing more than a donation. He wasn't the man who could settle for one woman in his life, much less one he created a daughter with. Although I had known Jacques as my only father figure for most of my life, I never called him Father or Dad. He was just Jacques, pronounced "Jack." But since Memaw's death, I had come to look at Jacques with different eyes. He was a comforting presence in my life. One who didn't change nor confirm to all of the desires of Charlie Grace and her social gatherings. He seemed to go along just as I did with one step at a time. His manner was stoic like mine when it came to such things. Sometimes when I caught him looking at me, I wondered what it was he was thinking. It was as if I saw an understanding in his eyes. An understanding that he knew I questioned the path before me. I didn't dare ask but I did often wonder if he knew I was a shell of the person I once had the opportunity to be?

It didn't take me long to find my assigned seat. Of course, I would be close to the head of the table and had no doubts I would be sitting in between Grant and Charlie Grace—Grant, as this was our engagement party, and Charlie Grace so she could keep a close eye on me. I knew she feared my tongue would embarrass her tonight. I decided as I watched her mingle from guest to guest that I would do my earnest attempt at curbing my comments for one night. After all, wasn't this really her party?

"Ooooh, Charlie Grace, this is all so perfect." Nadine fluttered her hands across her well-endowed chest. The material of her dress stretched across her shoulders to the point I feared I would hear a rip at any moment. Surely this was a figment of my imagination as Nadine had spent the days up to the party informing us of all the weight she was losing. In fact, to hear her tell it, she was a mere skeleton of her former self.

I shook my head as I tried to conceal the laugh that was building but then noticed the shift of a silhouette masked by Nadine's skeleton self. Sam was leaning against one of the porch columns. She stared directly at me. I held her eyes, vowing to myself I wouldn't break our stare until she did. I heard the sounds of chairs being slid back from the table and clinking of glasses against porcelain plates as people took their seats around us. Yet, I didn't move. Sam's body came fully into my view when Nadine took her seat in front of me. Sam's hands were clasped in front of her. I felt a tug on my arm as I was urged to take my seat. I didn't move. I wouldn't be the one to look away or take my eyes from her. Not this time.

Sam pushed herself off of the column and held her hand waist high. She held a tight-lipped smile as she gave me a small wave. I rubbed the cicada charm on my necklace instead of waving. Even in mannerism, I couldn't tell her goodbye. Nothing about me could say it to her. She came for closure. I understood that as her need but I didn't know how to say the words she came to hear. She dropped her hand and turned to walk away from the house. The air around me stopped circulating. A much-needed breath was smothered in the thickness of it. My chest tightened as it struggled to bring oxygen into my lungs. I couldn't breathe. Life. Conformity. Loss. They all began to suffocate me at once. Frantically, I reached my hand behind my back to steady myself with the chair behind me. Tiny white flashes of light danced across Nadine's face. Any moment now, I was going to fall flat out on the grassy lawn. I moved my hand back and forth but did not feel the back of the chair. Where the hell is the chair? Suddenly, my hand touched the warmth of flesh instead of metal. I looked over my shoulder to see Flossie standing behind me. She grabbed my hand with hers. She steadied the speeding rotation of the world.

"Here, baby girl. Let me help you." She placed her other hand on my arm above our joined hands. Gently, she pushed the chair underneath me as I sat down. She placed her hands on my shoulders, steadied the spinning world around me, and said, "There you go, sweetie. I've got you." She walked to her setting and winked as she sat down.

20

"I do declare I can't imagine what she's got in store for the wedding if this is what she's doing for the engagement." I heard Nadine's voice but was only partially aware of the actual words she had spoken.

"I'm sorry. What was that, Mrs. Thibodeaux?"

"Oh, honey, we're practically family now. You can call me Mom." In between her words, Nadine devoured a bacon-wrapped scallop broil in two bites. "I said I can't imagine what your momma's got in store for the wedding if this fancy shindig is what she does for the engagement." She placed her fingers around another scallop as she perched herself to engulf it in much the same way.

"Oh, right." I scooted the food around my plate with my fork.

I noticed Charlie Grace was glaring at Nadine. I wasn't sure if it was because of her delicate way of eating or her wishes for me to call her Mom. My guess was the former as I could hardly think of Mother having any jealousy over me.

"I think it will be a beautiful affair," Charlie Grace finally managed to say. She continued to stare at the jewelry around my neck. "All we have to do now is get these two to decide on a date. Of course, you know I will need a year to plan the whole thing."

"Mother, we've told you already. We don't plan on setting a date any time soon. This was just an engagement."

"I don't know, Rayne. Maybe we should go on and set one." Grant didn't bother cutting the scallop. He popped the whole thing in his mouth all at once.

Like mother like son. The thought caused a roll across my stomach.

"I mean, what's the point in waiting?" he said, trying to talk around his full mouth.

"What?" I knew the look I was giving him in front of everyone wasn't exactly one of endearing love but at that moment, I didn't care.

He looked at me as if he was surprised. "What?"

"What do you mean what?" I also didn't seem to care that my voice kept escalating. "First you spring the engagement on me in front of everyone and now you want to do the same damn thing with setting a date all of a sudden." I stopped myself before I let my anger and confusion of seeing Sam turn this into a scene. From the corner of my eye, I saw Flossie and Cora looking at us. "Actually, you know what?" I crumbled my cloth-napkin in a ball and tossed it onto the table. "I'm not doing this right now. I'm going to go say hi to Flossie and Cora. I'll be back in a few minutes."

No one said anything as I stood from the table. They waited until I had stepped a couple of feet away before they let their whispers run freely. I didn't care. Let them talk about the wedding. At least I didn't have to sit there and listen.

"Hey there, child. We were a'wonderin' if you were gonna come over." Cora dredged a forkful of shrimp through her fettuccine sauce before putting the bite into her mouth. "Lawd, child, this is some good vittles yo' Momma done did. Ain't you gonna eat?"

"Cora, leave the girl alone." Flossie pushed the noodles around on her plate before taking a bit of sun-dried tomato. Her tone was flat. Come to think of it, I hadn't noticed her voice having anything but a flat tone since we had lost Meems.

"I'll get something in a bit. I wanted to come over and speak to y'all first. Are you enjoying the party?" I knelt down in between their chairs.

"Are you?" Flossie squeezed a lemon wedge over her glass of ice tea.

"Aw hell, you know me, Flossie. I live for these things."

Flossie laughed. The sound of it caught me by surprise as I had missed it more than I realized. Her laughter eased some of my troubled feelings.

"Dat you do." She bit into the lemon wedge and puckered her face. "Damn, I've missed you, baby girl."

"Enough to let me steal one of these?" I grabbed a roasted asparagus spear from her plate.

"Hell yeah. Dem things make your pee stink."

I let my forehead rest against her temple. "Damn, I've missed you too."

A LIGHT RAIN had run most of the party guests under the protection of the large tents strategically placed around the grounds. Charlie Grace had prepared for the weatherman's report of ten percent chance of rainfall. Jacques fussed about the cost of the tents because a ten percent chance in Louisiana generally meant nothing but stifling humidity without a snowball's chance in hell for a drop of rain.

Under the largest tent was a dance floor and band, while the smaller tents had tables with dessert plates of strawberries with Chantilly cream and champagne. I could have been in any one of the tents pleasantly mingling as a proper hostess should be but instead I sat on the farthest corner of the back porch. It was my perfect escape. A dessert plate and half-empty bottle of champagne was my only company.

In the moonlight, the large tree branches swooped down over the lawn. They looked a bit eerie with their indistinctive clumps of leaves and long-hanging strands of moss. A small puddle of collected rainwater lay in front of me. I watched the ripples of the reflected porch light change with each vibration of the ground. If the beat of the music and tapping of feet on the wooden planks of the dance floor were any indication, this party wasn't going to end for quite some time.

"I'd figured as much you'd be out here. Mind if'n I join you?"

I looked over my shoulder to see Flossie standing behind me. She held an empty champagne glass in her hand.

"Not at all." I swung my legs off the side of the porch swing to make room for her to sit. I tilted my glass in her direction. "I heard Charlie Grace giving you hell because you wore denim."

"Yo' momma knows I don't be dressing up in dat fancy smancy stuff she do. Now Cora, dat woman goes all out. But she should a known better than to think I gone put on like I'm a highfalutin."

"Well, I love it. You look very nice." And she did. She wore a dark blue jean material pant suit with flare legs and a short-waisted jacket. Small flowers were embroidered on the lapels and around the large pearl buttons. The colors complemented her ivory shell shirt.

"How ya' holding up, baby girl?"

"I'm hanging in."

"I was sort of surprised when yo' momma told me you and your fella were gettin' married." She held her empty glass out to me.

I poured each of us a full glass of champagne. "Correction. We got engaged. Big difference." The freshly poured bubbles tickled my nose when I brought the glass up to my lips.

"Yeah, I'ma thinking they're pretty close. Y'all set a date yet?"

"Oh no, it's just an engagement."

"Aw." Flossie looked out at the lawn as she took a swallow from her glass. The bubbles must have affected her the same way because she rubbed her slender fingers across the tip of her nose. Several minutes went by. "Y'know that there Chantilly cream tweren't bad a'toll."

I looked up at her and noticed she was staring at the strawberry I held in front of my lips. I put it back on the plate in my lap and licked the thickened cream from my fingers. "I don't know, Flossie." I sighed deeply. "Things got so screwed up after…" I felt the lump form in my throat. The ripples in the puddle blurred.

Flossie put her hand on top of mine. "Dat it did." She patted my hand. "But don't got to stay dat way. She wouldn't want dat for neither one of us."

"Seems like I can't find anything but screwed up these days." I swirled the strawberry around in the cream and popped it into my mouth. The juice of the strawberry dripped from my chin.

"It won't feel like dat forever. I promise you dat." She handed me a napkin. "It won't."

The chains of the swing squeaked as we gently swayed the bench back and forth. Even through the beat of the music, I could hear a few cicadas singing in the night. I found the coolness of the golden cicada between my fingers again. Oh Sam, why did I let it get so screwed up?

"I'm afraid I'll feel this way forever, Flossie."

"Then maybe some of dem choices you done made ain't the best for ya'."

"No, they aren't, but they're the only ones I had."

"Sis, there always more than one choice if'n you want it to be."

I gave her a half smile. "Not this time, Flossie." A gentle wind blew in the scent of the climbing jasmine. I breathed in its aroma deeply as I looked out across the lawn. At the moment, I was thankful the frogs were starting to drown out the cicadas. I didn't think I could handle hearing them sing another chorus. I remembered the forgotten champagne glass in my hand and took a generous swallow. "I love it here. All I ever wanted to do was to come back. I had it all planned out. I would go off to school. Come back. Set up my practice and just be home."

"It is yo' home. It's who you are. Just like Addie. But what dat got to do with what we talkin' about?"

"Because see, Flossie, to have that, I had only one choice to make. I couldn't have both. It would've never worked. I made my choice so I could come back."

"Ain't no choice ever takin' away yo' home. Not ever."

"This one would've," I said as I brought the glass back to my lips. "Trust me."

Flossie shifted in the seat of the swing to face me full on. "You listen to me, Sis. Ain't nothing you ever gone do or say gone change who you are or where you from. This yo' home and always gone be."

I emptied the champagne bottle evenly into our glasses and handed one of the two remaining strawberries to her. "I don't want to go back to school."

"What? That crazy talk."

"It won't be the same when I do." It wouldn't be either. Without the chance of seeing Sam walk down the hallway. Without the opportunity to breathe in her scent of eucalyptus mint when she passed by me. The remembrance of her scent remained with me no matter where I went. The breeze caught in an opening door seemed to carry it to me. The pillowcase of my bed seemed to hold the fragrance in their fibers even though her body had never rested on its sheets. Nor would I see the smile that had taken the strength from my legs cross her face again. At least, knowing she was in Birmingham had given me some hope I would see it again. We hadn't spoken and I hadn't seen her but the possibility had always been there. Many days, it had been the sheer possibility of seeing her that held the power I needed to make it another day at the hospital. The possibility was my oxygen. Now that chance was gone. Sam had left Birmingham and she was not coming back. The heaviness of her absence was a weight I could hardly bear.

"I just can't imagine going back there, Flossie."

"Sure you can. You got lots more learning and you love doctoring. It's who you are. Who'd you always wanted to be." Flossie pushed her foot against the porch to give the swing motion. "And once you done soaked up all dat learning, you gone come back here to yo' home to bring what you done learnt to us."

I looked out at the remaining flickering tea light candles. Some had managed to stay lit through the light rain while others had grown dark. I let my ears open up to the laughter behind the dancing footsteps. I let my mind look beyond the sadness of Sam's moving away and let it drift to the people behind the laughter. They were my family. They were the reasons why I called this place home. In some moments, there were flickers of light in the darkness. Flickers which held enough of a flame to brighten the darkness. This was one of those moments.

I clinked my glass against hers. "And thus, another reason for the decisions I made."

Chapter 3

"HELLO, MRS. LAMBERT. I'm Dr. Storm. Your OB doctor requested a surgical consult about your gallbladder results."

"Yes, come in." The young woman positioned herself to sit up straighter in the bed. Her very pregnant belly made even this simple task difficult.

"Here, let me help you." I set the chart down on the bedside tray table to help her adjust the pillows.

She panted breathlessly as if she had just run a three-mile marathon. "Thank you. To remember the day an entire hour-long aerobics class didn't make me this out of breath."

I smiled at her. "It's not entirely your fault, you know? The pregnancy is causing pressure against your diaphragm which makes it difficult for you to expand your lungs fully."

"You're sweet not to mention my fat ass when I tell you about my old aerobic days."

"You'll be back to class in no time." I flipped the chart open to review her results once more. Not that I needed the reminder. I had noticed over the years of rounding at UAB that patients seemed to be more comfortable when you opened their chart in front of them. I'm not exactly sure why but always guessed there was a hint of worry when a new doctor came into the room that they didn't know everything about their history or because we see a large number of patients in a day that we will somehow get them confused with another if we didn't have their information right in front of us. I have even caught some of them turning their heads to try to read the name on the side of the chart.

I tried my best to stifle back the developing yawn but failed miserably. "I'm so sorry," I said as I closed the chart. In less than an hour, I would be getting off after a solid twenty-four-hour work day. I had managed to snag a couple of hours sleep in the on-call room. Beyond those, these eyes had not seen sleep. Maybe the patients were onto something after all. I was so tired I could easily forget my own name.

I rubbed my eyes and started again. "Your doctor consulted us due to your abdominal pain with nausea and vomiting. She was concerned for gallbladder disease as a cause of your symptoms. Your blood work was fairly normal except for a mildly elevated white count and amylase. Both of which can be increased with gallbladder problems. The ultrasound didn't show any signs of gallstones which is a good sign. Considering your pregnancy and the associated risk of further testing or surgery, we have decided—"

"Hey, Beth, how're you feeling today?"

The door flew open so much that I fumbled the chart in my hands and nearly let it fall onto the patient's feet. Dr. Breaker seemed to notice because her eyes darted to the chart and a smile crossed her face at my recovery.

"Aunt Violet, I wasn't expecting you until later."

I looked between the two women. Violet? Aunt Violet? I can't say I saw a family resemblance.

"Hey, kiddo. I got out of my last meeting early and thought I would swing by." Dr. Breaker winked at Mrs. Lambert before walking toward me with an extended hand. "Good evening, I'm Dr. Breaker." Her grip was strong as she gave me one brisk shake of her hand and then released it quickly.

"Good evening. I'm Dr. Storm from surgery."

"And your findings?" Her expression suggested she was already bored with my presence.

"Oh…er…sorry. Yes…I was just telling Mrs. Lambert that her WBC count was mildly elevated, as was her amylase."

"And her liver function tests?"

"Both the AST and ALT were within normal limits."

"Which leads you to?" *She is pimping me. Aunt Violet is pimping me.* I suppose now would not be the time to make a mistake and accidentally call her Aunt Violet.

"With both normal liver function tests and a normal lipase with only a mildly elevated amylase, we aren't concerned for a stone obstructing ducts to the liver or pancreas." I decided to speak quickly to try to avoid any further questioning by her. "Plus, the ultrasound didn't show any signs of a cholelithiasis. Given her timing in her pregnancy, we are recommending to postpone any further testing or surgical intervention at this time." I directed my attention to Mrs. Lambert who had a wide grin. "There would be an increased risk to the baby to do a Hida scan to determine the function of the gallbladder secondary to radiation of the injected radioactive tracer. Any surgical intervention at this stage in your pregnancy would also be a risk and would have to be an open procedure versus laparoscopic. Therefore, I'm going to recommend to your admitting physician bowel rest, intravenous fluids, and antibiotics if your white count does not start to normalize on its own. Upon discharge, I would recommend you avoid high fatty foods to prevent another event." I realized I may not have taken a breath with my hurried speech.

Mrs. Lambert laughed and looked at Dr. Breaker. "You should be ashamed."

"What? What'd I do?" Dr. Breaker pointed to her chest and stepped in between us to sit down on the edge of the bed.

Mrs. Lambert rolled her eyes and looked up at me. "She wouldn't want you to know she is a big ole teddy bear once you get to know her."

Dr. Ball Breaker a big ole teddy bear? Somehow, I seriously doubted it.

"Is that all, Dr. Storm?" Dr. Breaker asked with a side glance in my direction.

Yep one big ole teddy bear. "Yes, ma'am." I looked back at Mrs. Lambert. "Do you have any questions?"

She smiled and shook her head. "No, Dr. Storm, you explained everything perfectly. Thank you."

"Okay, then. I'm going to go write some orders. It was nice meeting you, Mrs. Lambert. I'll check on you tomorrow." I tucked her chart under my arm. "Dr. Breaker."

"Dr. Storm."

As I walked out of the room, I heard Mrs. Lambert saying, "You're such a bad ass."

"They don't call me ball breaker for nothing."

I swear I heard her laughing before the door closed behind me.

"Hey. Sorry I'm late." I plopped down hard in the booth seat across from Grant. "I got a last-minute consult up on OB."

"Oh yeah? Anything good?" He didn't look up from flipping through his *Journal of Vascular Surgery.*

"Nah, not really. A non-operable gallbladder on a seven-month pregnant female."

He looked over the edge of the magazine. "See. Why do they do that shit? That is a bullshit consult and they know it. They shouldn't consult us on crap that isn't going to the OR."

"I didn't mind. She was really nice and I think the reassurance helped her."

"Yeah, well, glad they sent you. I've got better things to do than see bogus consults."

"Seriously? You're going to be that guy?"

"No." He shook his head and closed his journal. "No, I'm not. Sorry. I had a case go bad today. I can't shake it."

"Do you want to talk about it?"

"Not really. If that's okay. I've gotta step up my game is all."

I reached across the table to place my hand on his. I hadn't noticed the stress in his eyes until now. He was one of the best residents in our class, yet he never gave himself credit. I had watched him put more and more pressure on himself over the years. To be honest, it was hard for me to see sometimes. "Grant, you're one of the best residents we have. Your skills are insane. You're too hard on yourself."

"It's down to the wire here. This isn't the time for me to make stupid mistakes. I've lost some of my focus."

I didn't want to bring up the engagement stuff, but this seemed like the perfect time to remind him as to why we had always decided to wait on getting married. This was our one shot in school. Now wasn't the time to lose sight of that. "Remember, that's why we always said no big plans until after school. We can slow all of this down. Don't let Charlie Grace change what we have always planned."

"It's not just her, Rayne." He turned his hand over to hold mine. "I'm ready to be your husband. I'm ready to come home to you every night. I miss you when I stay at my place. I'm lonely without you. You're not only my fiancée, you know? You're my best friend."

"Can I get you anything else?" The waitress stopped by our booth as she passed by. "Ma'am, would you like to order something."

I looked at Grant. "Have you already eaten?"

"Yeah, I'm sorry. I got here earlier and was starving. Go ahead and order something. I'll sit with you while you wait."

I looked up at the waitress. "No, thank you. I'm fine." But I wasn't. My stomach had growled the moment I opened the door to the Corner Café. Yet after Grant's words, the guilt had trickled in and I was really ready to leave. He was a good guy who had always treated me better than I sometimes deserved. The feelings I had for Sam slipped up on me. I couldn't blame him for the jealousy he had felt. Hell, if the marriage proposal was planned, if he had jumped up the timeline because of her, could I really blame him? He had known me nearly my whole life. Did I honestly expect he wouldn't see the difference in me after she came into my life? Did I truly believe he hadn't seen all of the confusion in me?

"Why don't you go ahead and go? I think I'm too exhausted to eat anyway. I'm going to go home and crash."

"Oh, okay. Are you sure?"

"Yeah, I'm sure. I'm going to run to the restroom before I go. I'll see you tomorrow."

He looked around the restaurant. "So, you don't want me coming over tonight?"

"Not tonight if it's alright." I leaned over the table and kissed him softly on the lips. "I'll see you first thing tomorrow. Good night."

He laughed when I rubbed at my lips. "They still tickle, don't they?" He ran his hand over his beard. "I can shave it off if you want."

"Nah…I'll get used to it." I winked and slid out of the booth.

Right on cue, my stomach growled again as I walked out of the bathroom. Maybe I should eat after all. The booth Grant and I had been sitting in was now occupied by Kylie and three other girls. I sat on a barstool next to their table and ordered a basket of fries. Thank the Lord for comfort food.

The guilt I started to feel was beginning to expand into self-loathing. I felt pulled in so many different directions. Even with Sam gone, the feelings she had stirred remained. She had opened Pandora's box. I knew I had been less than receptive to Grant since the engagement party. I was distracted, preoccupied and well, quite frankly, uninterested in anything he had to say. I was angry and there was no way to pretend otherwise. A part of me knew I found it easier to be angry at him than to let what I know to be true of how my life had changed stream into my consciousness. I wasn't ready for that conversation with myself or anyone else. I knew I needed to treat him better. It wasn't his fault at all. I also knew just as strongly that Pandora's box waited for me.

"Are we hitting Pineapple Post this weekend or what?" It was Kylie's voice. That woman had no decorum. Her loud voice was obscured as she tried to talk around a large bite of food in her mouth. In fact, I pictured tiny morsels flying out of her mouth to land on the table between the group of girls. "Come on! It's ladies' night."

"Ky, it's the hottest new lesbian bar. It's always ladies' night." I didn't recognize the girl's voice but she sure had my attention.

Kylie's laugh was piercing. "Exactly! And besides that, the deejay that's playing is fucking hot. H-O-T. Hot. I'd do her in a New York second."

The group of girls carried on about the deejay and made plans not to miss her on Saturday night. In fact, a round of drinks was on Kylie if she wasn't successful in convincing the deejay to dance with her before the night was over. I played with the leftover french fries in my basket while I listened to them. Pineapple Post had only recently opened a couple of months ago but it had quickly developed the reputation as the place to be if you were a lesbian or at least that was the talk I had heard around the hospital. If there was any way Sam was still in Birmingham, I bet she would go to the new bar. In the deepest recess of my mind, I knew she had left just as she had said she would, but I couldn't deny there was a small piece of me—okay, a rather large piece of me—that wondered if she had transferred her residency to one of the other affiliated hospitals and not actually moved away.

Chapter 4

MEMAW USED TO say if it rained the first day of the month, then more than half the days of the month would see rain. So far, her prediction was spot on for this April. I had only walked a couple of blocks before the first drops fell. I tried to protect myself from the falling rain by standing under a canopy attached to the wall of a building in the seventeen-hundred block of downtown. I knew the location because I had to search for a physical address when I called for a cab.

The tree-lined streets of this block were one of my favorites in the downtown Birmingham area. The trees were dwarfed in comparison to those back home, but if I positioned myself just right under their branches, they were tall enough to block out some of the city's lights.

I inhaled deeply to take in the smell of the freshly falling rain but was choked with disappointment at the sickening mixture of exhaust fumes and people's waste. The voices of those walking along the crowded streets permeated the air around me. They rose above the sound of rain dropping on the cloth canopy to be all I could hear. I strained to listen beyond their chatter. That was it really, the reason why I hated the city. Back home, this night would bring me peace. It would bring me smells and sounds of an entirely different night life. Back home, I would smell rain falling on a field of new spring grass and hear the sound of raindrop patters on the tree leaves above me.

A car horn blared as it pulled up quickly to the curb. "Hey, you the lady calling for a cab?"

I tried to compose myself after he scared me right out of my skin.

"Well, are you?"

"Uh…yeah, that was me."

"Get to it, lady. I ain't got all night."

The stench of the cab overcame me as I opened the back door and climbed in. So, this was what a boy's locker room smelled like. Lovely.

"Where to?"

I stared out the window. Even with a complete stranger, I found myself intimidated, afraid to tell him where it was I wanted to go.

"Come on, lady. Out with it. Where to?"

"Ummmm…The Pineapple Post."

The man turned in his seat to look at me. "You know it's only about three blocks in that direction." He pointed out the front windshield.

"Yes, I know."

"Sure thing, toots. It's your dough not mine." He flipped the meter on and pulled out into the street.

What he didn't know was the fact I had tried to make the short walk a few times before this night. The closest I ever got was looking around the corner of a building to see the bright yellow entrance door. Tonight, a cab driver would stop me right in front of the door with only a few steps needed on my part. Surely, I wouldn't back out if I got that close to the door.

He sped quickly past the door before taking a serious U-turn in the road and braking hard in front of the entrance. "That'll be fifteen bucks."

I gave him a twenty and got out quickly. The aroma was a good deterrent to me chickening out. There was no way I wanted to be a minute longer with that odor absorbing into my skin.

I had not been to many bars in my life. A few scattered here and there when I was in college but they were nothing like this place. I only remember them to be not much more than a place to order a drink, a couple of pool tables, and a small dance floor. This place was a nightclub. The long bar off to the right was, in the simplest term, gorgeous. It was designed of different stained wood colors and had lights underneath it which shined onto the matching wooden bar stools. The overhanging lights were varied colors of reds and oranges. Beyond that, I would have to say it was also empty—very empty.

The sound of glass bottles clanking against one another came from around the corner of the bar. A woman stepped into view. She hoisted the large box onto the top of the bar and stopped to look at me. She rested her elbow over the top of the box but didn't say a word.

Suddenly, I was nervously aware she was staring right at me. She didn't say a word. She just stared right at me. I looked over each of my shoulders as I hoped someone had walked up behind me and caught her attention.

"Oh, honey, please tell me you're meeting someone here."

"Um, no…I'm not."

She looked up at the ceiling. "Gonna be one of those nights."

"I'm sorry."

"You're fresh meat in the meat market." She started unpacking the box of beer bottles.

"Are y'all open?" I looked around again but saw no one else.

The girl behind the counter looked at her watch. "You do realize it's only eight o'clock, right?"

"Yes, I do. The phone recording said you opened at seven-thirty."

She laughed a deep, throaty laugh. Not that I expected it to sound differently as her voice matched its depth. "Yep, gonna be one of those nights." She motioned to the barstool in front of her. "What can I get you to drink?"

I don't deny I was more than a little confused as to her meaning but a drink sounded much needed at the moment. "I'll take one of those beers." I used the step bar to take a seat onto the barstool. The woman looked like she was a good six inches taller than my five-foot-four-inches.

"One of these hot beers?" She held up a bottle from the box. "Or one of these?" She reached behind her into the icy tray of beers. A piece of crushed ice fell from the bottom of the bottle.

"One of those iced-down ones looks pretty darn good."

She popped the top and slid the bottle toward me. She folded her arms as she leaned against the metal bin behind her. "Look at you. I haven't seen a fresh Bambi face like this in a really long time." She reached back into the ice bin and pulled out another beer, popped the top, and took a long swig. "The girls are going to eat you up." She pointed the neck of the bottle at me and grinned. "And I do mean that literally."

What? Wait…eeeeww. No, no. I'm not here for that.

All of her features were highlighted directly under the recessed lighting and she was beautiful. Like model beautiful. Even down to being a touch too much on the skinny side. Her height probably didn't help with that. Her shoulders and neck were accentuated by the spaghetti strap shirt she wore. Its material hugged her lean frame closely from her chest down to her torso. The neck of the shirt formed a scoop underneath her collarbones which left her olive-toned shoulders completely bare.

She cleared her throat and broke me from my stare. She shook her head. "What's your name?"

"Rayne."

She smirked and took a swallow of her beer. "Cool name."

"Thanks."

She smiled broadly, showing off the two dimples in her cheeks. "It's unique. One you don't forget when you've heard it."

"It is."

She took another swallow of her beer. "I'm Jazlyn." She spoke over the neck of the bottle. "Not that you asked or anything."

"I'm sorry. I'm—"

"Nervous?"

"Uh…er…"

Jazlyn stepped closer to me and rested her elbows on the bar. "You'll be safe for a couple of hours. The place doesn't start jumping until well after ten."

"Oh." Memaw had a saying about dimples. She said they were the marks left from an angel's kiss. The angel must have loved giving Jazlyn kisses because she had a cleft in her chin too. Her dimples kept shining as she had yet to stop smiling at me.

She slapped her hand down on the bar. "How about a tour?"

"Sure." I jumped down from the stool to meet her at the end of the bar.

The rich red-and-gold color scheme followed us as we stepped down two small stairs leading from the bar area onto the dance floor. Gold track lighting illuminated the stairs while strands of red hung tightly against the ceiling.

"What kind of music do you listen to?" Jazlyn asked over her shoulder as she walked across the dance floor to the deejay booth in the back corner.

"Anything but country really."

"Alright. Then you get to hear the mix I listen to while I get the place ready for the night," she said as she stepped up into the booth. "But don't you dare tell my deejay I was messing with her board. She'd have my ass."

"Done."

Within a couple of minutes, the dance floor exploded in lights. Large circles of gold-and-red designs moved in rhythm with the music now playing through the elaborate speaker system. Exposed metal beams attached to the ceiling hung a good twenty feet above me. Across the beams was a mix of speakers, lights, and two large-screen televisions.

"I love this song."

"Me too. I have to pamper my ear drums a little before a night of bass pounding techno." Jazlyn walked under a monitor of Tracy Chapman singing "Fast Car" as she came back toward me. She swung her arms out to the side. "So, this is this dance floor. Look at it now because in a couple of hours you won't see anything but women packed in here like sardines in a can."

A flash of Memaw's face smiling at me as she let a sardine dangle over her open mouth popped into my head. I'd get those time and time again. Flashes of her. I had yet to let them give me anything but sadness. This time, I looked up into the disco ball hanging over me and let its light give me the illusion of spinning slowly in a circle.

"I've never seen a place like this before."

"What? You've never been in a bar before? Oh, you are a Bambi."

"No, I've been in a bar before but not a bar like this. Not a club. The bars I've been in are just that…bars."

Jazlyn laughed. "Well, then follow me." She pointed down a hallway in between a wall with another large-screen television hanging on it. "Back that way are the bathrooms. And then up this way." She stepped up another set of two stairs to a smaller bar area like the one in the main entrance. There were no tables in this narrowed space but rather waist-high leather booths along the left side of the wall. Small, circular, pub-like tables were in front of them.

"This is a small overflow bar." She pointed to the bar on the opposite wall. Shelves with glass bulb lights in their centers hung above the liquor bottles. "Back here is what we call our sit and chat area." She stepped into an expanded doorway and sat on one of the big circular ottomans in the center of the space. It was large enough to sit another three people comfortably. "Have a seat." She pointed to the booth seating attached to the wall across from her.

I ran my fingers along the velvety drapes hanging along the wall. Imbedded lighting in the vaulted ceiling and columns along the walls kept the room bright enough to see Jazlyn sitting across from me but not so overpowering to feel as if I was under a spotlight. I sat on the leather bench and let my hand brush along the coolness of it.

"What brings you out tonight?"

Tipping the bottle up for another drink, I realized I had consumed its contents rather quickly as I only had one good swallow remaining. "I heard a girl talking about it the other night at the Corner Café."

"And you thought, 'Hey, a lesbian bar. Think I'll check it out.'"

"No, not exactly."

Jazlyn stood, walked to the overflow bar, stepped on the lower rail, and bent over the counter to pull out two more beers. She flipped both tops into the trash on the other end of the bar—no doubt a regular nightly occurrence. "It's okay. We don't have to talk about it." She handed me one of the bottles and sat facing me with her back against the wall. She bent her leg to rest it on the seat between us. "What do you think of the place now that you're seeing your first club?"

"It's very nice. Not at all what I expected."

"Oh, what? You thought I'd run some hole in the wall dump?" She laughed and tapped the neck of her bottle against mine.

I laughed which made her smile stretch even further. "No, I didn't mean that. Although, I've pretty much only seen those. Some smoke-filled space with a few pool tables, lots of beer, and chairs you're almost too nervous to sit in because they look like they may break at any minute. This is very nice."

"Thank you. I had trouble designing the color scheme. I really wanted purple but with this being Alabama and LSU such a rival, I thought I'd better be safe."

"You designed this place?"

"Yep, from the ground up. Or should I say from the start of renovating this old building."

"So, you're the—"

"Owner."

"Wow, very cool." I looked at my watch. Surely the place was bound to start hopping any minute now and I wasn't overly sure I was ready for the description she had given earlier. "It's been very nice meeting you."

She showed her dimples to me again. "But you have to be going?"

"Yeah, I think I do. How much do I owe you?" I reached into my pocket for money.

"It's my treat." She placed her hand on my forearm and squeezed. "I enjoyed the company."

Jazlyn walked me back toward the front of the club but stopped at the main bar. "Hope to see you again, Bambi."

Chapter 5

M Y RESIDENCY WAS never the wiser to the internal struggles imprisoning my mind. I'd come to face them as more than mere thoughts of Sam lingered there. Buried in the center of me, I knew the development and awareness of them was something to become more permanent in my life. How permanent was the question I asked myself repeatedly. I let my dreams envision Jazlyn's club filled with a Saturday night myriad of women enjoying one another's company in conversation and dance.

"Hiya, Doc Storm."

I hadn't seen Angie sitting behind the nurse's desk as I walked passed it on my nightly traipse through the emergency room. "How goes it tonight?" She peered up over it at me. Tonight, her ever-changing hairstyle was short with blonde spikes and a line of jet black at the base behind her neck.

"It goes good, Angie. Finishing up the night. Thought I would ward off evil spirits and take a walk through the ER before heading home. Got anything brewing for me yet?" It had been a busy day. In fact, I hadn't even found the time or the energy to change out of my scrubs. Dried betadine solution splatters decorated the royal blue material. I had spent the majority of my day in the free clinic treating wounds of all varieties. Truly, I dreamed of the only thing brewing to be my coffee pot at home and a nice long shower.

"Can't say that I have anything for you, Doc. But what I will say is we don't get to see enough of you down here since you changed to plastics."

"Says who?" I snickered. I can't say I missed the near nightly two a.m. calls to the ER.

She snapped her head up. "Most everyone here who has to put up with Dr. Dick. The jerkwad that took your place. That's who." She looked back down at the chart but then raised her head again. "But I think I've missed you the most." She slowly winked at me which exposed the thickly covered blue eyeshadow she wore.

"Oh? Who is it that took my place?" I said hurriedly in an attempt to speed along the conversation. "I don't think I recognize a Dr. Dick in our program. Unless perhaps he is a urology transfer."

I flinched at the shrillness of her loud laugh. "Damn, I miss your humor. Almost as bad as I miss that beautiful smile of yours."

There it is again. The wink and the compliment. *Is she flirting with me?* No matter what its intention, it was making me extremely nervous. "Oh…ummm…thank you. So…what's his real name?"

"Dr. Reed," she said absentmindedly. She then stood from her chair and motioned me toward the medical supply room down the hallway. When we were alone, she turned to me and asked, "Can I ask you something, Doc?"

"Sure. Although I must tell you my brain is fried. If it's something requiring medical deduction, I may need to catch you after a good night of sleep."

"Oh, I think you can handle it." She pushed open the door to the small room. We had only a small amount of space to stand as we were surrounded by shelves filled with every kind of casting material, braces, and crutches imaginable. "You know, Doc, I've wanted to talk to you for some time now, but damn we're always slammed when you're here."

"You can always call me when you need something. You know that."

"What I need…or well…rather want is for you to go to dinner with me. I can't seem to get enough of you in the ER."

"Oh. Ummm…well…" I took a deep breath. "Angie, I'm flattered but I don't know if that's such a great idea."

"Why? Because you don't date coworkers?"

Date? "Uh…well for starters, I'm engaged." *Did I just do that? Did I really just play that card?* "But more importantly—"

"GONORRHEA!!! You gave me that bitch's fucking nasty-ass disease! I'll kill you, motherfucker!"

Angie and I jumped. We began running toward the sounds when we heard yet another scream. This one was deeper than the first and was followed by a loud clanging of a metal bedside table falling to the floor.

As we rounded the nurse's desk, Angie's expression changed. I looked around her to see a man staggering backward toward us. When he turned, I could see his eyes were filled with terror. He was desperately grabbing at the side of his neck with his hand. Bright red blood flowed between his fingers and soaked the collar of his shirt. The blood pulsed as it continued to pour through the fingers of his hand. The fear in his eyes turned to black as his pupils dilated before rolling backward under his eyelids.

"Holy shit!" I yelled as we quickly stepped toward him. I grabbed behind him and felt the weight of his body against me as his knees buckled. Angie and I maneuvered him gently to the ground. Crimson blood poured freely through my fingers as I now tried to hold pressure upon the force of blood escaping from his wound.

"Security! Security!" Angie screamed when a woman came into view at the doorway. She held the black grip of a knife as she walked toward us. Drops of blood trickled from its blade to collect on the freshly polished linoleum floor.

"Get away from his sorry ass! I'm going to kill this motherfucker and his nasty ass ho," she yelled as she raised the blade high in the air.

The force of the two security men slammed into her and knocked her against the side railing of the wall behind us.

"We've got her, Doctor," the bigger of the two guys called over his shoulder as he secured her against the wall with his arm across her neck.

The other guard had a hold of her hand and peeled the knife from her grasp. Once the knife was secure, the guards swung her around and pressed her face against the wall.

"Hold still, lady," the first guard said. "Ain't nobody killing nobody on my watch." He kept his arm pressed firmly against her back.

"Let's hope that's true," I muttered under my breath.

The bleeding was not slowing to pressure as I kneeled in a growing pool of warm red. I could feel it against my skin as the scrubs were not much of a barrier to the large quantity this man was rapidly losing.

"Call the surgery team, STAT!" Angie bellowed to the nurses and doctors who were now running down the hall to our aid. "And get us a gurney."

"Angie, this bleeding isn't slowing down. He's going to bleed out before that call is even made." Looking over my shoulder, I tried to see what supplies were readily available to me. *Cast material, gauze, tape, splints, suturing kits, Foley catheter, scissors. Wait, Foley catheter.* "Grab me that Foley. Get the largest diameter you have."

"Here ya' go. Surgery will be here in two minutes," Angie said as she handed me the sterile pack.

"Get it open. Give me the catheter and fill the syringe with saline." I quickly grabbed the catheter tip from her hands and passed it into the one-inch wound that ran along the side of his neck. "Let's pray this works." I pushed the fluid from the syringe into the end of the catheter to fill it to its full size. The filled bulb caused pressure inside of the wound and squeezed off whatever vessels had been incised with the passage of the blade. I slowly released my hand off of his neck and silently prayed the pulsating blood would not follow. Nothing. The catheter tip moved in rhythm with his pulse.

"Hot damn, Doc. Would you look at that."

"This only buys us a little time, Angie. He's lost a lot of blood. Where the hell is surgery?"

"Right here, Dr. Storm."

I looked up and saw a mass of green scrubs with gurney in tow sprinting their way down the hall. Their precision was synchronous as they moved the man from the floor to the stretcher.

"I don't know what vessels were cut. But the way that son-of-a-bitch was pumping, my money is on the carotid," I called to the team as they hurried the gurney down the hall to the operating room.

"Thanks, Dr. Storm," the anesthesiologist yelled over his shoulder as the gurney turned the corner and went out of sight.

"I guess I better find you a clean pair of scrubs," Angie said as she looked down at my pants.

My once blue scrubs were now covered in blood. The pants were soaked while my shirt had swipes of blood across the front where I had attempted to wipe the blood from my hands. "Yeah, I think I better get this washed off my hands too."

"There's a wash area in the women's locker room behind the lounge. I'll meet you in there as soon as I get the scrubs from central supply."

When a patient's health is in danger, their care and life-saving measures are top priority. Generally, their modesty or privacy is of little concern at times of trauma or surgical needs. Over time, healthcare workers have been known to become immune to their own personal shyness once the numbness to nudity has been experienced. I was no exception to this long-lived urban legend of the OR. My main concern was to remove my clothing soiled in a stranger's blood. There was no time or even an inkling of a need for modesty.

"Engaged, huh?" Angie asked as she entered the bathroom to find me bent over the sink clad only in bra and panties.

One eyebrow was arched higher than the other as she took in the full view of the pink satin material. This is when I became the exception to the rule. I felt my face flush as she stared at me. A numbness to nudity and seeing a woman visually appreciate your body were two entirely different things. Yet this wasn't a flush of embarrassment or uneasiness, this was a flush of something else—something exciting. My body was reacting to the way her eyes were drinking me in. The hunger she left so blatant upon them was stirring my every reaction to her.

"Uh yeah, about that."

"No explanation needed." She held up a hand. "But it's a damn fine shame, Doc." She placed the crisp new scrubs next to me on the counter before turning to leave. She tilted her head to the side. "A damn fine shame."

I splashed a handful of cold water on my face. The water ran down my neck and over the gold chain that carried a cicada and cross. "Hey, Angie, can I ask you something?" I patted my face with a towel and turned to her.

"Sure."

"Why did you ask me out? Was it because you thought I was gay? Something I did or do that makes you think I'm gay? Is that why?"

"Nah." She let her eyes unequivocally roam my skin again before shrugging lightly. "I think you're hot as hell. That's why I asked. I'm not one to horn in on someone else's territory, but for you I'd make an exception. If you ever change your mind, you know where to find me."

I splashed another handful of water on my face and studied its reflection in the mirror. The redness of my neck was the perfect defense to the constant argument I had of late been having with my body's unfaltering yearnings.

"Hi. This is Dr. LeJeune. I'm sorry I missed your call but if you will leave your number, I'll call you back as soon as I can. Thanks."

I wasn't sure why I had dialed Sam's number again, yet here I was listening to the same recording for the fifth time in the last thirty minutes. I had stopped leaving voicemails at this point because I accepted a while back that she wasn't going to call me back. It's not like she wasn't seeing my number in her missed call list. Sometimes when I thought of how many times she saw I called, I would get embarrassed or even feel weak. But the other times, all I wanted to do was to hear her voice again. This was one sure fire way I could. The times I felt most pathetic were when the call went to voicemail after only two to three rings. It was then I knew wherever she was or whatever she was doing, we were connected. If only for a brief moment, I was calling while she was holding her phone. Yes, she quickly ignored the call. But, in that moment, we shared the same space and time. Pretty pathetic.

I stared at the piece of paper announcing it was deejay night at Pineapple Post. "Doors Open at 10pm." I looked down at my watch which sadly told me I was two hours early.

"You know, hovering outside of someone's residence while trying to peek into the window is actually a crime and could get you arrested. I bet you look good in all kinds of colors, but I'm not sure orange is one of them."

I laughed as I turned to Jazlyn. She must have walked up from the side of the building without my noticing. Geez, I have got to start paying more attention. "Somehow I was thinking this was a place of business and not someone's home."

She closed the distance between us with her long strides. "It's technically both as I live just up there." She stretched her long arm up to point over my shoulder. I could see light filtering through drawn curtains in an expansive display of windows. "My guess is you aren't planning on staying yet again tonight but I'm not opening until later."

"Yeah, I just read that," I said as I looked back at the sign on the door. "Hey, wait a minute, how do you know if I wasn't planning on staying tonight?"

She laughed a deep throaty laugh. "Um, because you're in scrubs and a T-shirt." I followed her finger as she motioned down at my betadine-covered clogs. "And not in your dancing shoes."

"Very observant."

She shrugged. "I'm a bartender. Comes with the territory." She turned her head toward the street when a car drove past. Its headlights reflected off of the freshly dampened asphalt. Moments earlier, a light rain had come and gone. "When did it rain?"

"Oh yeah, very observant."

"Ha." She chuckled. "You've got some smartass in you." She smiled broadly. "I like it."

"Thanks. It's genetic. You didn't miss much. It was only a sprinkle.

Just enough to wet the ground and smell the air." This was the only smell that reminded me of home. The one when an asphalt road is dampened with rain. I inhaled lightly so as not to be noticed.

Jazlyn turned back at me. "I can offer you a drink but first you have to keep me company." She pointed down the street. "Care to take a walk with me?"

"Sure." I stepped quickly alongside her to prevent being lost once her long legs began their walk. "Where are we headed?"

"To get my Thai take-out. I'm starving."

The leaves of the small Bradford pear tree stirred against the light breeze that followed us as we stepped off the curb into the street. I let my hand trace down its rough bark as we passed by it. It stood alone among lines of parallel-parked cars.

"But wait, isn't the Thai place on this side of the street?"

Jazlyn, already a good two to three steps ahead of me, turned around and walked backward. "Well, yeah, but then we couldn't walk under the Alabama sign."

Above Jazlyn's head was the sign proclaiming the site of the old movie theater.

"Ummm…okay."

She held her hands out for me as we reached the sidewalk under the sign. She moved me to stand directly under the vertical sign composed of bright red-light bulb lettering with a blue tile backdrop.

"Now, look up," she instructed before standing next to me and doing the same.

The brightness of the bulbs burned my eyes but I refused to close them. They stretched into the sky nearly as far as I could see. They seemed as brilliant as the stars beyond them.

"This place was built in 1927. It opened the day after Christmas." Her voice was strained as she kept her neck stretched up. A smile crept across her face. "It's one of the few remaining theaters from that era with seating up to twenty-five hundred people. Look at those windows."

The glass had a bluish tint as it contrasted against the rustic brick. The panes were separated by thin pieces of wood.

"Do you know it was the first public building in Alabama to have air conditioning?" She looked down at me with a child-like innocence of excitement.

Her happiness in describing the building was contagious as I felt the confusing dread of the day disappear. "I did not know that."

"Come here." She took my hand again to pull me to the large window next to the entrance. "Look...look in here. See that?" She tapped the glass.

Sitting in front of a long golden drape was an expansive red and golden ornate organ. It was an elaborate instrument with four rows of ebony and ivory keys in front of a rather odd-shaped seat.

"This little baby saved the place. You're looking at a Crawford Special-Publix One-Might Wurlitzer organ." She stepped back and looked across the front of the building. "Originally, they played silent films here. The American Theater Organ Society stepped in when they were set to plow this place down to make a parking lot. Can you believe that? A parking lot."

"How do you know all of this?"

Jazlyn looked directly at me and shrugged. "It's my thing." She stepped away from the building to walk down the sidewalk.

"Your thing?" I sprinted to catch up with her. "What do you mean?"

"My thing. You know the thing that calms you when you're stressed, makes you happy when you're sad, comforts you when you're lost. My go-to—my thing. What's yours?"

I stopped momentarily and tried to think of what it was that calmed me when nothing else could. Unfortunately, I had felt anything but calmness in a very long time.

"I don't think I have a go-to."

"Sure you do," she said as she shrugged. "You just haven't figured out what it is yet."

WHEN WE WALKED into Jazlyn's apartment, I was reminded how quickly sadness could overpower happiness. I had felt lighter and happier while walking with her but those feelings were threatened the moment we walked into her loft. It reminded me so much of Sam's. In fact, their similarities made me question if the developer was the same.

The same but different. Find the difference, Rayne.

Jazlyn's apartment was a narrower space than Sam's. It reminded me of the shotgun homes of Louisiana. The walls were stark white with accents of natural pinewood, chrome metal, and black. *Different but the same.* I steadied my breath and stopped the tears before they could form. Flashes of memories of her did that to me no matter where or who I was with.

"Make yourself at home," Jazlyn said as she walked in behind me. "I'll put some music on and set the table."

"Oh no. I can't eat your food. You weren't planning on company tonight."

"Honey, I was starving when I ordered so I can assure you there is enough here to feed you, me, and a small army."

The sofa and loveseat were eclectic pieces of furniture in the center of the living area. As focal points, they brought the architectural design of the room together with their oil bronzed metal bases and thick black cushions. I ran my fingertips along the cold metal of the back of the loveseat as I followed Jazlyn into the space. She walked to a stereo system that rested on top of pinewood shelving hung in symmetrical lines across an exposed brick wall. Soon the slow sounds of a trumpet followed by a violin's strings bellowed through the speakers. The sultry, smooth voice of a woman began to sing.

"Ah, yes," Jazlyn murmured and began to sway to the music. She lifted her head as if she was trying to drift into the air to be as light as the music floating up into the piping that hung from the ceiling.

"Who is this?"

"This is the First Lady of Song, Ella Fitzgerald. I hear her voice and I can't help but to want Lady Ella to sing to me all night long."

"Wouldn't she get drowned out by the club noise at night?"

"Not that Lady Ella couldn't be heard over any noise but I help her a little. The walls are soundproof. I hear nothing but her." She let her hips sway to a snare drum's beat as she set places for us to eat. "My friend, Mo, introduced me to jazz several years ago. She's one of those that listens to anything and everything. Music is her thing."

The table's modern feel matched the rest of the loft. The bright white chairs and table reminded me of elementary school days with its simple plastic design. The wall-to-wall windows were separated by a large white beam but instead of downtown city lights shining through, I saw only white-washed reddened brick. *Different*.

She wore her long, black hair down tonight. I watched the length fall across her face as she leaned over to set the table. "What do you want to drink? I have beer, wine, or I could make you a mixed drink. Oh and of course, water. But who wants that with Thai?" She tucked the fallen strands of hair behind her ear as she looked back at me.

"A beer would be great."

"Thought you might say that. No problem, but will you at least taste this wine I'm going to open? I'll feel foolish opening a bottle to drink all by my lonesome."

"Sure, but I gotta tell you, I never really developed a taste for it."

"But see. You're open to it. You said you haven't yet, not I don't like it. It's all about pairing the right wine with the right setting and the right palate. And of course, the right person," she said as she smiled broadly.

"Club owner. Jazz. Wine. You keep surprising me." I pulled the plastic chair away from the table to take a seat.

"It's all about the company you keep. I learn a lot from my friends." She filled two stemless wine glasses with wine and sat one in front of me. "This is a riesling. It has a kiss of sweetness which mixes well with the spices of Thai food. Taste it for now but hold your reservations until after we start to eat. Which is in two seconds. I'm starving." She laughed and sat down behind a row of take-out containers. "See I told you there would be enough. Hope you like spicy."

"I'm from Louisiana. Spicy is all we know."

"Then let's start with this." She handed me a bowl filled with a greenish liquid topped with fresh basil and sliced red pepper. "This is green curry chicken. The green curry paste is one of the spiciest of the curries."

I filled my spoon with basil, chicken, and red pepper. The spicy flavor was delicious but she was right. The sweetness of the riesling softened the bite of the spice in a way that really added to its flavor. It was a very good combination.

Her dimples gave the telltale sign of a beginning smile as if she knew the swirling tastes were having a party in my mouth. "Good, right? Or should I still get you that beer?"

"No, you're right." I took another bite of food and sip of wine. "This is excellent."

"Wonderful. I was hoping you'd like it." She pointed her spoon in my direction. "Not that I don't enjoy your unexpected company tonight but what brings you to the club? I mean, scrubs are hot alright but not the typical attire for a night out."

She had Sam's ability to make me smile. *Different but the same.* "I don't know. I had a pretty big day and thought I could use a drink before going home."

"Simple enough. Yet you passed at least a dozen bars to come to a lesbian one to get that said drink."

"Well, it just happens to have the coolest bar owner I know running it."

She laughed and pointed her spoon at me. "Which is the *only* bar owner you happen to know."

"Well, if we're being technical about things." I returned her laugh and stirred my spoon around the bowl before taking another bite.

"Forgive me for asking the obvious." She let her spoon rest against the bowl and focused her attention on me. Her cheekbones seemed to stretch up to the corner of her eyes. Eyes of dark chocolate stared directly at me. "Are you a lesbian?"

And there it is…lesbian. The word that strangled in my throat and cut off my speech. *Lesbian.* Hadn't it scrambled my insides each time

I heard it pass from Sam's lips? Wasn't it again burning within me? Truthfully, had it ever stopped?

Jazlyn wrapped her long fingers around my hand as it lay frozen on the table. "You're safe here. Safe to express what you feel. Safe to express what you know and even what you don't know." Her fingers tightened around mine. "There's no judgment or pressure. No family. No woman sitting across from you, holding onto your every word hoping to hear what she's been waiting for you to say." She rubbed her thumb tenderly across the back of my hand. "It's just a friend."

"Baby, I'm home."

The front door opened widely and made me jump in my seat. Jazlyn must have been startled as well because she released my hand quickly. There in the doorway stood Dr. Breaker dressed in her salmon-colored obstetrics scrubs. Her usually spiked hair was flattened on her head, no doubt from wearing a scrub cap most of the day.

She stopped abruptly in the doorway. "What is *she* doing here?" Her tone was sharp, if not angry.

Jazlyn slid her chair back and walked to her with her hands out. "Baby, wait one second. Just listen. I saw her outside the club when I was leaving to grab dinner. We've been talking, that's all."

"I'm sorry, but how does her being outside your club end up with her in my house having dinner and wine with my wife?"

Wife?

Dr. Beaker slammed the door. The chain lock banged against the metal door repeatedly until it slowed to silence. She lifted her head. "I'm sorry, but is that jazz I hear? What the fuck is going on?"

"Vi, come on. I'm just having company for dinner on a night you're on call." Jazlyn ran her hands down Dr. Breaker's creamed-coffee colored arms before taking her hands within hers. "You called earlier and said you were stuck at the hospital. I was starving so I called and got take-out. I ran into her on my way to get it. I wasn't expecting you home, so I invited her up. That's it. That's all."

"And what? That makes it alright? If it had been anyone but her, maybe it would've been. But her?" She shook her head and looked directly at me with very near the same color of brown eyes as Jazlyn. Yet, these didn't seem to harbor the same tenderness as hers. "Whatever." She stomped on the metal stairs as she ascended the staircase toward the clear glass wall that lined the upper loft area. She quickly disappeared from sight.

I stood from my seat with only a quick exit on my mind.

Jazlyn turned around. "No. Please. Sit." She held up her hand. "Don't go."

"Jazlyn, I really don't think it's a good idea for me to stay." I wanted to get the hell out of there before Dr. Breaker came barreling back down the stairs.

"Please, Rayne. I'm asking you to stay. Please. Just give me a minute to go talk to her. I promise this is a misunderstanding and will all be okay."

I sat back down and watched her follow Dr. Breaker up the stairs.

The acoustics in the apartment that had complemented the music so well became a megaphone to their upstairs argument.

"Baby, why are you so upset? I've had friends over before."

"Friends?"

"Yes, friends. I know this isn't some sort of jealousy. We don't do that…you don't do that. So, what is it?"

"Don't play coy with me." Dr. Breaker's voice was so loud I had to look around to ensure she wasn't standing right beside me. "That woman is *not* a friend and she never will be. You got it? She *never* will be."

"Ah, I see. So, this is the phase of our marriage where you'll dictate who or whom isn't my friend? I'm sorry, I didn't realize we had grown to be this couple where I had to ask your permission before I made a new friend."

"What about *our* friend?"

"You mean *your* friend."

"No, I mean our friend," Dr. Breaker said as if through gritted teeth. "Do you not remember what she did to Sam?"

Sam! Did she say Sam?

"Do you not remember her crying night after night after night over what that girl down there did to her? Because I remember it very well!" She was yelling at this point. "I also remember the fact that she was so destroyed she threw her whole fucking career away. Where is she now? Oh, that's right. No one knows because she left. I don't get to have take-out with her."

"I know, Vi. But you know as much as I that Sam had a very skewed idea of relationships. She wasn't really one to invest in anything long term. She was always more of a player."

"A player?" Dr. Breaker screamed. "You want to talk about a player? Why don't we talk about your friend Mo then? At least, Sam didn't lie and manipulate her girlfriends to get them into bed."

"Okay. Let's calm down a little. We are starting to go down a road that really has nothing to do with tonight. All I'm saying is we only heard one side of the story. Don't you think there may be two sides to everything that happened?"

There was a brief silence followed by the sound of footsteps.

"Is this about her or about you?" Dr. Breaker asked as she appeared at the top of the stairs. "All of that is in the past and there it will stay." She stopped on the bottom step, looked directly at me and snarled, "I'm going back to the hospital. Enjoy my dinner." She slammed the door behind her.

"Sam? Did she say Sam?" I couldn't stand from the table. My legs wouldn't allow it.

Jazlyn rested her forehead against the door that had been slammed twice this evening. She didn't turn back to me as she sighed and said, "Yes, Rayne. She said Sam."

"So, you know who I am? You know about Sam? You know about me and Sam?"

"Yes." Her voice was nearly a whisper. "Yes, I do."

"Then why? Why bring me here? Why pretend to be my friend?"

"I wasn't pretending. I'm not pretending. I want us to be friends."

"Then why?"

She turned around and leaned against the door. "Because I remember."

"Remember what?" None of this was making any sense. Sam had been here. Sam knew them. I rubbed the charm at the base of my neck.

"What it was like when I met Violet. How hard it all seemed. We aren't so different you and I." She returned to her chair. "Except I wasn't engaged." She paused as she tapped her finger against her chin. "I was married."

"Married?"

"Yes. He and I had been married only a few years when I met Violet. I fell in love with her instantly. Everything in my life seemed to make perfect sense, yet at the same time be the most confusing of my entire life. I think we both may need more of this." She topped off our wine glasses and shook the empty bottle. "And if we have more of this, I know we need more of this." She filled the bottom of our empty bowls with rice and covered it with a shrimp sauce. "I'm sorry, but I have got to eat more or I'll never make the night. This is tom yam goong." Her voice didn't hold the same excitement as she described the dish.

I passed my spoon through the food which released the aroma of lemongrass, lime, and shallots. The kick of the chilies and fish sauce was chased with perhaps too large of a swallow of the riesling.

"Let's go back to the question at hand and you answer with all honesty. Remember, I have sat where you are. I have felt the tornado of feelings inside of you. Lived through the not knowing of what was next. The dread and fear of what could possibly be next." She slowly chewed a bite of her shrimp dish as if giving me time to process what she had said. "Are you a lesbian?"

I took another swallow of wine. This time, I was certain it was too large of a swallow as I didn't taste the flavors on my palate but rather felt the burn of the alcohol in the pit of my stomach. "I don't have an answer or even know how to begin to answer that question." I shook my head. "I don't know is the best one I can give."

She tipped her wine glass to me. "Now there's an honest answer."

"But shouldn't I? Shouldn't I know if I'm gay or not? I mean hell, who else is going to know if I don't?"

"Then shouldn't you give yourself time to answer the question before you answer it for someone else?"

I bit my lip as I stared up into the pendant light shaped like a globe that hung above the table.

"Ask."

I looked at her.

"Ask me what you're thinking."

I bit my lip again for fear of invading a personal memory for her, but who else could answer better than her? "What was it like with your husband?"

"He was my best friend. I loved him for all that he was and all that we had in common. I loved him for the strength of his love for me. But I was never in love with him the way I was instantly drawn to Violet."

"Did you know you had feelings for women before her?"

"Not really. I knew something was different but I had never pegged it."

"When did you know?"

Jazlyn let a smile sweep across her lips. "When she kissed me. I don't think I'd ever been kissed before that kiss. I'd never been kissed to where I felt everything someone had left out in words to tell me. Okay, wait. That made no sense whatsoever." She took a sip of wine and held it in her mouth before swallowing. "Let me try again. Before Vi kissed me, a kiss was just a kiss. It was nice. But when she kissed me for the first time, I felt it everywhere. I don't mean in a sexual way. I mean I felt everything she thought and felt about me in that kiss. I wouldn't have felt or believed it more if she had used words to tell me. I was hers from that moment on."

I felt the tears wet my eyes. Sam's kiss still burned my lips in my dreams. I felt the tingle in them with the thought of her lips against mine. I shook my head against the painful memory of it.

"It was the same for me," I whispered.

She seemed to sense the pain building up inside of me. She stood from her chair and walked over to sit next to me. She took my hand and turned me in my chair to face her. Her eyes were soft, yet strong. The way she looked at me kept the pain from toppling any strength I had tried to convince myself I had. She let out a deep breath.

"Aw hell, honey, do I remember what you're feeling. That feeling of brokenness and confusion with no right answer in front of you." She wiped a fallen tear with her thumb. "Believe me when I say this." She cupped my face in her hands. "It will get better. I promise you won't always feel this. You'll find your answer for yourself and then you'll forge ahead. There will be a day when all of this shit you are feeling now won't be much more than a blink of a memory." She pulled me against her chest and held me.

I dampened her shirt with thoughts of the tears falling from Sam's eyes as she said her goodbye. "But I've lost her."

I wasn't sure if I had spoken the words out loud or left them to be mumbled against the cloth of her shirt. Either which way, she didn't answer.

Chapter 6

"Hey!" Grant jumped over the arm of my sofa and ran to me as I walked in through the front door. "Where have you been?"

"What are you doing here?" For a brief moment, I wondered if my tone was as abrasive as I felt it to be.

The look on Grant's face took every bit of the questioning away. He stopped short. "I've been waiting for you," he said with less excitement than before. "I wanted to see you."

"I'm sorry." I walked over to him and took his hands in mine. "Really, I'm very sorry. I didn't mean to snap at you. I was caught off guard when I opened the door but I still shouldn't have talked to you like that."

The enthusiasm returned to his face. "It's okay. I'm sure you're tired."

"Yes. It's been one helluva day."

"I know. I heard." He squeezed my hand and shook it a little. "It's all over the hospital." He turned to walk back to the couch and pulled my arm to follow him. "I bought us some beer and pizza to celebrate. I've sort of already started eating and well…drinking, but I saved you some."

"Celebrate? What on earth is there to celebrate?"

"Your ER trauma today. It's all over the hospital."

"People are talking about it, huh?"

"Not just some people. I mean everyone is talking about it. Damn girl…a Foley catheter? How in the hell did you pull that one off?"

I shrugged and collapsed on the couch. "I don't know. It just came to me. I'd read about something like that a while back in a trauma journal but thought there was no way it would work. Damn if it didn't. Did you hear how he did?"

"Hear? I was in the case. His carotid was toast but we were able to repair it with a nice-size graft. He'll be fine," he said, talking around a bite of pizza. "Until he goes home that is." He laughed and handed me a slice of pizza.

"I'm not hungry but thanks."

He held up a beer. "How about one of these?"

"One of those I can do."

"So, where you been? I got here like an hour ago." He started eating the piece of pizza I had rejected. "I was afraid there wasn't going to be any pizza left for you." He smiled as he pointed the last piece to me.

"I was pretty wound up after leaving the hospital so I stopped off for a drink."

He looked at me with surprise. "By yourself?"

I nodded.

"But that doesn't sound like you. You don't really like bars much less want to go to one by yourself."

"I know. I just couldn't come home right after."

He tossed the unfinished slice back into the box and turned to me. "Shit. I'm sorry. I didn't even think of it upsetting you." He scooted closer to me on the couch as he raised my hand from my lap to rest it on his. "Sometimes I get so wrapped up in cases and stuff that I forget about emotions. I'm sorry."

"It's okay." I squeezed his hand all the while feeling like a complete ass because it wasn't truly the traumatic event in the ER that kept me from coming home tonight. It was then I recognized my own disconnection. A man's life was held within my hands. His blood had soaked my scrubs. It was a haunting realization to know it was the Pineapple Post and Jazlyn to where I ran instead of Grant.

"No, it's really not." His whiskers scratched my forehead as he laid a gentle kiss there. He pulled away and looked me in the eyes. "I was so proud of you, Rayne. When the whole OR was talking about what you did, how you did it, and how composed you were." He shook his head a little. "I was just so damn proud of you. I sat there in the case thinking, 'My fiancée did this. My fiancée saved this man's life.' I've never been prouder of us."

He leaned in and kissed me. A soft kiss. I felt guilty and ashamed of my selfish behavior where he was concerned. Yes, I had become disconnected in so many ways. I suppose that's why I didn't dodge the deepening of the kiss as I had done many times before. He seemed to notice as he pulled me in closer.

"I've missed you…missed this so much," he moaned against my lips as he let his hand travel down the front of my T-shirt. I tried desperately not to flinch when he squeezed my breast. At first, I feared he had noticed when he pulled away from me but then I quickly realized he was standing for other reasons as he reached down for my hand. I searched his face until I saw the small scar in his left eyebrow. It reminded me of the little boy I had grown up with. The little boy that was now a man. I saw the freckle on his bottom lip. When we had first started dating, I used to focus on it before each kiss. Those things helped me to see the man who stood behind my questions of my sexuality. They helped me to see Grant. I did love him for who he was and who he had always been to me. He was a man who had the same drive and ambition as I did. We both wanted to return back home to care for the family and friends of the town that raised us. Our future was our goal which made it so incredibly easy to be with him. I didn't have to concentrate on our relationship nor give it quality time as Grant and I just were. We moved in the ebb and flow of us with ease. Somewhere deep in the recesses of my mind, I knew the ease and comfort of us was my only attraction to being engaged to him. He was my friend and my companion. Now, he needed me to give to him the things he needed to stay in the comfort of us. He needed to feel we were okay. Caught in the tangled mix of those feelings, I stood and took his hand.

THE TEARS WERE silent as they fell on my pillow. Grant's slumbering breath was against my ear. He had been soft and tender during our love making. *Love making.* There's a fitting description, although the full meaning of the description to me is probably far different from those when they describe the act he and I had shared. For most, I would think it to be a connection filled with expressions of being in love with one another. For me, it was a way for me to show how much I truly did love the man lying behind me. It was no longer a feeling of being in love with him but more a feeling of not wanting to see hurt or rejection in the eyes of a man who had always treated me well. A man who had his whole future planned around sharing a life with the woman he loved. The tears began to fall readily as my heart screamed at the pain of knowing this was a future I no longer thought I could live. I loved him but even in the height of feeling this emotion with him, the act of expressing that love left me crying silently against my pillow. These were nights I knew I could not live for the rest of my life.

Perhaps the questioning of my sexuality had actually led me here. I pulled his hand away from my chest and studied it. Wasn't there a part of me that needed to feel him against me again to help know the answers? It had been so long since I had given myself to him. It had been since Sam. The mere mention of her name in my thoughts crushed me as I lay next to him with nothing between our bodies. I interlocked my fingers with his and sighed at the difference of the two. When I held Sam's hand, we fit. We just fit. Our fingers. The softness of them against one another. I started to feel as if it were Sam I had just cheated on. As if I had been unfaithful to her. But then it hit me. I had been unfaithful to myself. I had cheated on my true feelings. I let his hand fall back against my chest, listened to his gentle snore, and wondered if this would be where I would ever let myself be again.

Chapter 7

"*I* WASN'T SURE YOU'D be back."

"You asked me what brought me out the other night," I said quickly so as to get the words out before they became lodged within me.

Jazlyn paused in mid-circular swipe of the bar. She tossed the rag to hang over her shoulder, rubbed her fingers in its end, and motioned for me to continue. I think she knew my strength dangled from a delicate thread. I walked slowly to the bar. My hands were buried deep into the front pockets of my jeans. I had practiced what I wanted to say in my head but it was still a jumbled mess as I approached her. She stood behind the bar, frozen and waiting on my next words. I pulled the heavy barstool away from the bar and climbed up to sit. I let out a deep sigh and pinched the bridge of my nose.

Jazlyn took two beers from the ice-filled tray. She clasped her hand over mine as she handed me the bottle. "On the house. Looks like you may need one."

"Or a hundred but who's counting?" I took a long swallow of beer. "I think you're my only friend. How pathetic is that?"

"Hey now. I may take offense to that."

I snapped my head up to look at her. "No, I didn't mean it like that. I…I meant…"

She tapped my hand with hers. "Sister, I'm only joking. Now spill."

"You asked me why I had come in that night."

"Mmm hmmm." She hummed over the neck of her bottle as she took her first sip.

"It wasn't the absolutely crazy trauma I had earlier in the evening but the conversation I had around it." I picked at a knot left rough in the otherwise smooth bar. "I was asked out. A nurse…a female nurse asked me out to dinner."

"Ah." She took another sip as if to give me the pacing I needed.

"She had pulled me into a supply closet to talk to me. That's when she did it. When she asked me out on a date."

"And? How did you feel about it?"

"It scared the hell outta me at first. Inside, I was freaking out because I wondered what she saw. What was I doing to make her think I was that way? It scared me on so many levels." I remembered the sickening swirl I had felt in the pit of my stomach when Angie had asked me out. "But then I got this other feeling."

I looked at her and hoped she would fill in the blanks for me or that she would ask more questions so I could answer those instead of continuing to pour my thoughts out across the bar.

She stood motionless except for two quick blinks of her eyes as she said, "Please continue."

"Afterward, I felt exhilarated. It was exciting to have her ask me out."

She took a swallow of beer. I had very nearly forgotten about my own and took a large swig.

"Did you accept her invitation?"

"No."

"Did you want to?"

"No. I didn't want to accept. I don't want to accept." I put my face in my hands and grunted, "Ugh. I don't know what I'm saying."

"I'm not sure you've said much of what you really want to say."

"I guess mainly I'm trying to say, I don't look at her in that way. I'm not attracted to her physically." I lifted the bottle and drained the last of the beer. Apparently, I had made up for lost time. "So, when you asked me if I was a lesbian—if I'm a lesbian—I don't know how to answer. Wouldn't I have been attracted to her and wanting to go out with her if I was?"

Jazlyn gave me a low chuckle as if it had started deep in her chest. "Oh, honey, no, not at all. You don't have to be attracted to every woman to be a lesbian."

"And if I've only ever been attracted to one?"

"Well, my friend, that just means you've got a hurting lesbian heart."

"I've tried to call her. I've text her."

"But she's not answering?" Her voice was soft.

I sucked in a breath and tried to force back the lump in my throat. "No, she's not." I couldn't hide the sadness in my voice. I looked up at the ceiling to try to stop the trail of tears that seemed to believe they belonged upon my cheeks. "I've lost her. She doesn't ever want to hear from me again. She doesn't even want to know I exist in this world."

"I can't say necessarily if that is true or not. I think time is what's needed here." She reached across the counter, squeezed my hand, and took the empty bottle from me. "Time for both of you. You both need to figure out what your experience together meant to you. Why it happened. Rayne, some people come into our life to change it. Maybe they stay. Maybe they don't. But their reason for coming into it is still met."

"I guess she was meant to come into and then go out of my life?"

"I don't honestly know. But think about this. Are you really ready for her to be in it now? Don't you have some things you need to work out for yourself before you try to save or salvage a relationship with Sam?"

I nodded my head because I knew she was right.

She handed me a fresh beer. "Then hold the worry for what will or won't be until you get those things worked out. Okay?"

I felt like a bobble head doll as I sat on the stool constantly nodding my head up and down in agreement with her. I knew she was right. I did. Yet all of the things she talked about seemed so very hard to do.

I wanted to be with Sam again. In her arms, I felt a happiness in life I had not known before. I ached to feel it again but there were so many obstacles between me and that dream. Two of them had little to do with Sam. One was centered around a man who had held me in his arms the night before and the other around a town that had held me in their arms my whole life. Letting go of both of them pained my heart. I didn't want a life where I didn't know Grant. It hurt to think of living special events in my life and not being able to share them with my friend. It hurt me to think of how badly all of this would hurt him. We had been taking the biggest step of our lives together. What would happen to our dreams if I changed our course? The town was something else altogether. I couldn't even begin to think of what all of this could mean to my core foundation.

"Hey, Jazlyn?" I looked up from staring at the wooden bar to see she was already looking at me. My guess is she had watched me the whole time I had been sitting silently.

"Yes," she said soothingly.

"You left home, didn't you?"

"I did."

"Why? Did you have to? Were you not welcome any longer when you came out?"

"No, not exactly." She leaned back against the opposite bar and tossed the rag behind her shoulder. "Of course, it was hard with Zach and his family after I filed for divorce. It was hard on all of us. I missed them. I missed him."

"Is that why you moved away?"

"Maybe a part of why but not all of it. There wasn't really anything there for me any longer. Not anything that brought me happiness. Vi was what made me happy. Shortly after the divorce she got this great opportunity with a large OB group. I moved with her and the rest, as they say, is history."

"You never went back?"

"No. I never did. I was only two hours away when we first moved away together. There were a few times when I got in my car to go back home. But each time I realized my home was with Vi and I turned around before I ever got there. There was nothing there for me anymore." She took a swallow of beer. "I had found my life. There was no going back after that."

I felt the sadness build in me as if it was an erupting volcano about to spill over. The heat of its lava burned my stomach. I couldn't imagine ever being fully happy without the people of Brennin in my life.

"Hey?"

I swallowed hard in an attempt to keep the tears down.

She put her hand over the top of mine. "Just because that is how it worked out for me...just because that is what was best for my life doesn't in any way mean it's what will happen in yours. You know that, right? Accepting who we fundamentally are doesn't mean the same future for everyone. Nothing says you can't go home. Nothing says you can't be exactly who you want to be and still be true to yourself." She squeezed my hand. "You get that, right?"

"Yeah, I guess a part of me knows that but the hard truth is it's a really small town with even smaller values. As you said, fundamentally we are who we are. In this town, there's a rhythm. Even if you overlook the religious stuff, there's still this expectation the town has for its kids. They grow up, get married, and have kids of their own. It's a cycle of everyone doing and being the same. I won't fit into that anymore."

"And why is that?"

"What do you mean why?" I said with confusion.

"Just that. Why won't you fit in anymore? Why can't you have exactly what you just said?"

"Because...well...because I would be different."

"We are all different, love. All of us. It's what makes this world grand. Home is where your heart takes you. If you search past your fears to remember the hearts of the people you want to go back home to, do you really think they'll not want you back if you're a lesbian?"

Faces of those back home flashed across my mind—Flossie, Cora, Mrs. Bell. They were all smiling at me as they came into my mind.

Then Charlie Grace's face came into view. Hers held a much different expression.

She patted my hand. "Don't answer now. Just think about it." All of a sudden, she slammed the palm of her hand down on the bar. The sound almost caused me to fall from the stool. "What are you doing this weekend?"

This weekend. Maybe that was it? Maybe that was why I kept breaking down in tears. This weekend is Memorial Day weekend. The weekend I danced with Sam to the music of Memaw's laugh and country tunes under a blanket of stars. The weekend Sam stole my breath, captured my heart, and overpowered my every thought with her lips and tongue soft against my own. The weekend I first felt my body begin to lose control within the arms of another. *Sam.*

"Are you working or off?"

"I'm off."

"Do you have plans?"

Plans? Yes, to stay as far away from Louisiana as possible. "No, no plans."

Jazlyn burst into a beaming smile. "Then come with us." She grabbed both of my hands across the bar. "Come with us to the beach. We're going down to our condo in Seaside. One of my very best friends is meeting us there. It's the neatest little beach. We're going to have a blast."

I leaned away from the bar, shaking my head. "Are you insane?"

"Possibly. The verdict is still out on that." She laughed. "But really, you should come. It's perfect timing and just what you need. A relaxing getaway of sun, surf, and friends."

"You mean friend as in singular. I highly doubt Dr. Breaker would consider me that. And there's a snowball's chance in hell she wants me coming along."

Jazlyn swooped both of our empty beer bottles off of the bar in one motion and tossed them in the plastic trash can behind her. "She's a pussycat outside of the hospital." She reached into the ice to steal two more beers. She popped the tops, twirled the bottle opener around her finger, and tucked it into her back pocket. "You let me worry about her."

"I seriously doubt she is." I pulled the beer close to me. "And you can have every bit of that worry because that pussycat scares the shit out of me."

"So, is that a yes?"

Sam. Meems. A bayou without either. "I want to tell you yes more than I can admit but I'm really afraid you are misjudging her. She was not too happy when I saw her last. I think she will be super pissed at you for inviting me."

"I don't doubt that at all. But trust me. I know Vi. I'm one hundred percent sure I can make this okay and she'll go along with it."

I picked at the label on the bottle and considered her invitation. I really didn't want to be alone this weekend. Nor did I want to be with Grant or go home. Everything and everyone excluding the setting she was offering would be a reminder of Sam on the dock with me. "Are you really sure?"

"Oh, I'm sure. Is that a yes?"

"Yeah, it's a yes."

She tapped the neck of her beer against mine. "Hot damn."

Chapter 8

WE ARRIVED IN Seaside much later than we had planned because neither Dr. Breaker nor I could leave the hospital until early evening. I would have found the silence of the backseat awkward had I not realized early into the trip that Dr. Breaker had fallen asleep. Occasionally, I would look away from the passenger window to see Jazlyn's eyes watching me in the rearview mirror.

Because of our late arrival, I had missed the sunset the night before but tonight I had a front row seat as I sat quietly on the condo's fifth-floor balcony to watch the sky be painted by the lowering sun. It was filled with the most glorious purples, oranges, and yellows. Below it, emerald crystal blue waters stretched as far as I could see. The silhouette of seagulls perched atop their twig-like legs scurried along the shoreline as they hunted for crumbs left behind from those who had occupied the beach in the prime of day. I couldn't hear the ones found closest to the shore but the grunting squawk seemed to be all around the balcony as they flew about from one group to the next. I watched the last few beachgoers pack up their day's essentials as they darted in and out from under the condominium's royal blue umbrellas. The sun was all but tiny streams of bright light bursting from around thickened clouds. The low-lying purple masses with their outline of colored rose rested just above the surface of the water.

"Mind some company?"

I hadn't heard or noticed Jazlyn come up behind me. "No, not at all." I turned in my chair to look at her. She looked fresh out of the shower with damp hair and minimal make-up. "I'd like it."

"Vi's getting dressed. Thought I'd come out and sit with you before starting dinner."

"I didn't know you were cooking."

"I'm making Mo's favorite. She should be here in an hour or so." She walked to the chair next to me and patted my leg as she sat down. "So, tell me, did you have a good day?"

"Most definitely. You were so right. This place is beautiful." It had been hard for me to imagine the clearness of the water when she had described it to me. I had never seen water this clear. Even while standing in chest-deep water, I could see my feet on the sandy bottom. "The water was amazing. I've never been to an ocean like this before. All we ever did growing up was go with Jacques to Grand Isle to go deep sea fishing. I can assure you that water was anything but clear."

She scooted her patio chair close to the edge of the balcony and stretched her legs out to rest her feet on the railing. Her shorts made her legs appear even longer. "You and Vi seemed to be getting along okay. I told you she'd be fine once she was around you."

"She's been nice."

Dr. Breaker had been reserved but cordial. I could sense she was putting on her best behavior for the weekend. She was nice but not what I would term pleasant. She was tolerating me for Jazlyn's sake. The tone of her voice when she spoke to me was different when we were alone versus around Jazlyn. It was obvious her impression of me had not changed and all of her actions were simply for Jazlyn's happiness. It was yet another reason I was envious of them. The second-nature affection shared between them when their bodies came in close contact, the side glances when a smile was shared, and the sacrifices made to ensure the other's ease or happiness, all of these things I watched in longing. All of these things I knew I did not have with Grant. And all of these things I knew I could have had if only I would've had the strength to make different choices not so long ago.

"What's going on in that head of yours?" She put her hand softly on my arm.

"About?"

"You looked deep in thought just now."

I turned in my chair to face her as I covered her hand with mine. "Thank you for bringing me here." I squeezed her hand before releasing it.

"You're very welcome." She smiled broadly, stretched her long arms over her head and arched her back. "Care to elaborate on your thoughts, though?"

"The last place I wanted to be this weekend was back home."

The tightness in my chest blocked any answer I could have given Grant when he mentioned us going home for the long weekend. Before the engagement, I could hardly get him to go but now it seemed as if that was all he wanted to do. I swear he and Charlie Grace were looking at real estate property for our offices. But if it kept them occupied with each other, who was I to argue? Besides, Grant was on a mission of looking solely at commercial property instead of considering any residential listings. This sat well with me. Viewing homes or offices for the purpose of establishing my dream of practicing back home was much easier to handle than a home with the hopes of filling extra bedrooms with the sound of children.

"One year ago, I felt like my world was turned upside down. I felt scared and different and confused. So very confused," I said as I stared out at the ocean. "I can't say that has changed too much but being here away from it all has been a welcome change of scenery. It's made me feel like maybe I'm not completely different than everyone in my life. Like maybe the person I am belongs somewhere when I'm around you and Violet."

"You never felt like you belonged anywhere before?"

"With Meems and Sam but that's about it. When I was with them, I felt like I was me. With anyone else, I feel like I have to be how they see me. Or how they want to see me."

"Even Grant?"

"Gawd, especially Grant. Especially since I've changed. He wants me to be the same woman or even little girl he has known his whole life. Even before though, we were nothing like you and Violet. We've never interacted with each other the way y'all do."

She tapped the knuckle of her bent index finger against her lip a few times. "Then why did you say yes to his proposal?"

The ocean pulled me back to it. I watched the waves crash along the shore and noticed the water beyond it to be with calmer currents. It gave the surface no more than a gentle ripple. All one body of water yet different. *Different but the same.*

"Honestly, I have no idea." I breathed in the sea air and felt the salt on my tongue. "I guess I needed something to hold on to. Something concrete, something real. Grant is a constant in my life. Now he's one of the last constants in my life. He was my link to back home. I felt all of this change happening around me. Memaw...Sam...my whole life's plan. Everything I'd grown up knowing was my future seemed to disappear or change in the blink of an eye. I felt like Sam had been this free living, loving spirit. It was all so very intoxicating but in the end wasn't a real possibility for me. She wasn't a real life I could have."

"Who's to say what real life is, Rayne. Shouldn't what's real be about what's best for you?"

"What about you? Were you in love when you said yes? When you got married, did you doubt or wonder at all if that was what you wanted?"

"Yes, I was absolutely sure it was. I loved Zach. I loved him very much." She lowered her legs from the railing and leaned back to peer through the sliding-glass door. "A part of me will always love him and his family. He was my constant too. I'd never loved anyone but him until I met Vi."

"So, you had never thought of women before Dr....I mean Violet before?"

Jazlyn let a small sigh escape her lips. "Nope." She then smiled fully. "Not one single solitary thought."

"Then what? Why?"

She shrugged. "Rayne, the heart can't hide what it wants. Even from its owner."

"What about now? Are you attracted to other women?"

Her smile widened. "I notice attractive women all of the time." She leaned over and nudged my arm. "Present company included, but I don't think of them as far as doing anything with them or being unfaithful to my wife. I'm in love with Vi. She's the only woman for me."

"Do you consider yourself a lesbian then?"

She gave me far more than a snicker and laughed heartily. "Oh, honey, yes without a doubt. But why do you bother putting labels on things?" She tapped my forehead lightly. "Girl, you gotta let go of some of this up here. You don't have to label yourself. You don't have to try to figure it all out in the present. Hell, honey, that's what the future is for. To figure things out. You need to find for yourself who or what turns your body inside out to be with them. Does it really matter if it's a male or female? Be in love. Be in lust. Be whatever. Just feel what it is you want to feel and make no excuses or explanations for it. Don't live a life going through the motions." She stared out at the ocean before patting her thighs and standing up. "Take fifteen minutes to think about what I said. Then stand up, breathe in a lung full of this fresh sea air, and go get dressed." She put her hand on my shoulder and squeezed. "I can't wait for you to meet my friend, Mo. We're going to have a great weekend."

I felt the anxiety build in my gut. It was an influx of nervous energy that quickened my heart rate and would have surely taken my breath had a crashing wave not pulled my attention back out to the surf. The waves had begun to strengthen to create an impressive spray of water as they crashed against the shore. I remembered laughing earlier in the day when the waves lifted my feet from the sand as I stood out in the water. I remembered the feeling of the water flowing through my fingers as I lifted my cupped hand in and out of it. I had lost myself in the crystal blue water, lost myself watching Jazlyn and Violet. They were in synchronicity as they laid on the beach together. They moved without the need for words but yet seemed to know each other's thoughts and needs. Jazlyn would sit up in her chair but before she could reach for the cooler, Violet would hand her a cold drink. She would do the same for Violet. At one point, I noticed Violet turning her head side to side and just as she was about to sit up, Jazlyn stood to adjust the umbrella to shade her face. They shared a smile before returning to their books. Being with them as they interacted so naturally gave me a calmness I badly needed. I knew without a doubt I wanted what they had.

As another wave crashed, I felt the exhilaration in the sound of the surf soak into my soul. I understood the serenity that had shown on Jazlyn's face when it reflected the lights of the Alabama theater. I understood how she was taken away yet brought back as she stood staring at the building that represented her center. I heard her voice in my thoughts. "It's my thing." I breathed in the sea air as she had said and let it wash through me. I smiled broadly because I knew. The water was my thing, whether it was found with waves or ripples…it was my thing.

THE HOT SHOWER stung my sunburned skin as it beat down on my shoulders. I was thankful I had packed a light spaghetti strap shirt and loose linen pants to wear to dinner. It had been a while since I had taken the time to notice myself in the mirror. So much so that my hair was at least three inches longer than I usually wore it. The length had begun to weigh down the light brown curls as they touched the top of my shoulders. No wonder I found myself constantly tossing it into a ponytail. It was either the style I wore leaving the house or the one that happened after a day of fighting the falling strands. I ran some gel through it and decided to let it dry on its own tonight. I tossed my make-up back in my bag and decided to let my sun-kissed cheeks be the only color I wore tonight. I dabbed on a little lipstick and gave myself one final look before opening the bedroom door. My green eyes were a brighter hazel than they had been of late. Maybe it was the bedroom lighting or maybe the hue of my sun-kissed face. I'm not sure what it was but they were definitely brighter.

The smell of garlic and peppers reminded me of what little food I had eaten in the day. I walked into the living area to notice Jazlyn moving around the open kitchen as if she was a true chef. She hadn't heard me come into the room as the steps made with my bare feet had been silent on the dark gray tiled floor. I watched her add ingredients to her pots and skillets as she hummed an unknown song. Her happiness was spreading quickly to me as I watched her.

"It smells fantastic," I said as I leaned against the doorframe of the kitchen.

Her hand flinched slightly which added an extra dollop of garlic to the skillet. "Oops," she said with a smile. "You startled me." She looked down at the spoonful of garlic and shrugged. "Oh well, it'll keep the vampires away."

"It smells pretty damn good to me too," Violet said, walking around the corner. "Hey, babe, what about this one?" She held a bottle of red wine up.

"Perfect." Jazlyn tapped the thin spatula against the side of the skillet and pointed it at me. "I hope you brought your appetite." She quickly wiped her hands on a dish towel.

My stomach growled loudly. So loudly that she obviously heard it because she began to laugh. "I'll take that as a yes."

"I suppose so," I said as I laughed too.

We turned at a knock on the door.

"She's here," Jazlyn said as she sprinted around the kitchen island and headed for the door.

Violet took a side step so as to stand closer to me. She leaned her head over and whispered, "I know you know I'm not comfortable with you being here. I also know you know why that is. Before this trip is over you and I need to find some time to talk but until then, I won't do anything to ruin Jaz's trip. Okay?" She arched her eyebrow at me.

"Okay." I nodded.

"Besides, these two together will be enough entertainment to keep either of us from having to speak to one another too much." She stepped away and joined Jazlyn at the door.

I swallowed hard at the inevitable conversation about Sam. I knew Violet was the one Sam had confided in. I also painfully remembered Violet describing how much Sam had cried to her. My heart couldn't bear to hear of Sam hurting because of me, especially when I knew it would bring back visions of the heartbreak I had seen on her face. I knew this was yet another penance I had to pay.

Jazlyn slung open the door and swooped the smaller figure up in her arms. "Mo! Damn girl, it's so good to see you."

I heard the woman mumble something against Jazlyn's chest.

Mo pulled back from Jazlyn's embrace but held their hands together in front of her. "Sister, you have no idea." She lifted her head in the air. "I know I don't smell your garlic clam sauce?"

"That you do." Jazlyn's smile showed the brilliance of her teeth as she turned to us. "Come in. I want you to meet a new friend of mine." She kept Mo's hand in hers as she led her closer to Violet and me.

Mo dropped the duffel bag she was carrying. "Damn, Vi, you're prettier every time I see you." She pulled Violet against her chest. "Why you ever chose tall and goofy over me I'll never know." She kissed the side of Violet's neck.

"The perpetual charmer." Violet smiled as she tapped Mo's chin. "Which is probably one very good reason for my choice."

"Hey, now. Cut out trying to steal my wife." Jazlyn looked at me with an endearing smile. "Mo, meet my very dear friend, Rayne."

Mo extended her hand. "I've heard a lot about you, Rayne."

"It's nice to meet you." I felt the warmth of her fingers as they wrapped around mine in our handshake. Her grip was firm. Her eyes were a crystal-clear green that reminded me of a field of freshly cut spring grass. I was momentarily lost in the brilliance of them. Although her smile was warm, it held a certain sense of distance.

"I'm at a crucial point in the kitchen. Mo, keep my friend company, won't you? Maybe put on some tunes." Jazlyn talked over her shoulder as she headed back into the kitchen.

Violet picked up the black bag. "I'll take this to your room and then I've got a bottle to attend to."

I realized the warm fingers were still wrapped around mine. Smiling, I released my hand from hers as we both watched the two women walk away.

"What's your favorite type of music?" Mo looked over my shoulder to the stereo. "You can help me pick something out." She reached into her pocket to pull out a thin metallic device. "Let's see if we'll find something like it on my iPod." Her voice held excitement. "Look at this thing. I've got like a thousand songs on it. Is that crazy or what?"

"I've heard of those but haven't seen one yet. I don't listen to a lot of music."

"What? That's very near criminal." She looked at me, shocked. "Why the hell not?"

I shrugged. "I dunno. I guess because I study a lot and music distracts me."

"Oh yeah. Are you in school?" She led us to the stereo system and pulled a cord from her back pocket. "The rental sucked and had no way for me to plug it in. So, school…you were saying?"

"Ummm, yeah, I'm finishing up my plastic surgery residency."

She stopped, turned to look at me, and bobbed her head. "A doctor. Interesting. Okay then, Doc, what kind of music did you like when you did listen to music?"

"Probably eighties music would be my favorite."

Her laugh was deep with a hint of hoarseness to it. "Not sure I have a bunch of that on here." She shook the iPod she held in between her fingers. "How about I do the picking tonight and you make it up to me later?"

"That sounds like a deal."

She smiled. "I'll hold you to that."

She was actually quite beautiful, strikingly so but in a no-fuss sort of way. Her hair was chestnut brown with long, heavy waves that formed around her face. She pulled the long sides over to the side of her neck as she examined her musical selection. I studied a bit of music in school when the curriculum demanded each student choose either band or choir but it was never my thing. Charlie Grace always told me

I couldn't carry a tune in a bucket much less with my voice, so naturally I chose band. I learned just enough to recognize the treble clef sign tattooed behind her right ear. She ran her thumb over the circular dial until something caught her attention.

"Ooooh, I think this playlist should do."

She smiled as a high-pitched trumpet and rolling base drum blared through the surround speakers. A slow and sultry woman's voice joined their song of a lady singing the blues. Mo closed her eyes and swayed her head when the voice turned husky. The sound of tickling ivories played lightly in the background. She shuffled her black boots on the hardwood floor. She wore gray Dickie pants which rode low on her hips. A silver chain with one end attached to a belt loop and the other end leading to her back pocket jiggled as her hips joined the sway of her head. I watched as her body felt the chords played through the speakers.

"Who doesn't love Lady Day?" she said as her hips dipped low and came back up.

"No one I know," Jazlyn said, walking from around the corner. She set a tray down in between us. "Dig in. Wine's coming up."

"How about right now?" Violet walked up behind Jazlyn and handed Mo and me a glass of wine. "I think this'll go nicely with what Jaz has whipped up for us."

Mo swirled the deep red wine until it rose up along the sides. She stopped the twirl of her hand and swiftly brought the glass to her nose. She breathed in deeply before taking a small sip. She swished the wine around in her mouth, swallowed, and then looked at Violet. "Very nice."

Flashes of Sam making those same motions appeared in my mind and took my breath. Sam and Mo's movements mimicked each other's. *Different but the same.*

"Sold. I'll go get our glasses and be right back." Violet disappeared into the kitchen.

I stared at the glass in my hand until I noticed I'd caught Mo's attention.

"It usually has more of an effect if you actually drink it. You know, instead of staring at it."

I found her teasing relaxing and fell into it by letting a chuckle escape. "You know, I think I've read that somewhere before."

Mo smiled and tipped her glass to me as she popped a piece of fresh mozzarella in her mouth. "Sassy. I like that."

"Thanks." I looked down at the wine. "So, why do you do the swirling thing?"

Mo gave me a quizzical look. "Swirling thing?"

"Yeah, you swirled the glass and then sniffed it before drinking it."

"Aw, that." She placed her hand over mine as it held the glass. "Moving around your wrist to let the wine swirl in the glass sets its bouquet free. It oxygenates and releases its aromas." She gently moved our hands. "Now when we stop, bring the glass to your nose and smell." She stopped our hands and urged the glass to my nose but left her hand over mine. I felt her fingertip touch the tip of my nose. "What do you smell?"

I breathed in deeply. "I smell…hmmmm…black cherries?"

Her smile widened. "Yes, very good. Now take a small swallow but swish it around your mouth before swallowing."

I did as she said and felt the room temp wine tingle on my tongue. It left a slight burn along my throat as I swallowed.

"Now what did you taste?"

"Uh, the black cherries I smelled and er…cinnamon. Maybe even a hint of rosemary. Is that right?"

Her smile stretched across her face. Her teeth were gorgeously white and perfectly straight. Her eyes sparkled. "Very good. Now pair it with something off of the tray."

I looked over the food spread out on a granite cheese board. Chalk lettering named each sample. I topped off a piece of aged parmesan with a slice of salami.

"Good choice." Mo did the same. Her eyes kept smiling at me as she chewed.

"My favorite are the olives," Jazlyn said, reaching between us to grab one. She threw her arm over Mo's shoulder. "Damn girl, it's good to see you."

They stared at each other long enough for me to be envious of their friendship. There was no distance between them. They looked at each other as if they could read each other's thoughts and I'm betting they probably could.

Jazlyn broke their stare and changed her glance to include me. "My girl here and I share a love of food and…" She paused to listen to the music. A smile took over her face. "Summertime and the living is easy," she sang and then grabbed Mo's hand as they twirled each other around the living room.

"When those two escape into their little world, you might as well give it up," Violet said, watching them dance.

I didn't know what to say or even if she wanted a comment in return. She spoke in a manner that felt like it was a strain for her to speak to me at all. The tension between us was beyond uncomfortable. She was Sam's friend. I knew that as plain as I knew the nose on my face. I wondered if Sam and Violet were like this when they got together. *Sam.* Feeling the darkness creep back into me, I took a larger swallow of wine. I wasted not in the perfect swish of the liquid and drank for its effect. I couldn't and wouldn't let my thoughts give in to the darkness this weekend. I had to let it go to keep some sanity about me. I watched Mo and Jazlyn spin each other around. I absorbed their happiness to let it be my distraction.

THE CELLPHONE VIBRATED across the nightstand, which woke me from my not-so-restful sleep. The indicator for two voicemails flashed on the screen. One had been left late in the afternoon the day before and the other left early this morning. I held the phone to my ear as I sat up against the large cushioned headboard.

"Hey, sis, dis here Flossie." Silence. "Are you there? Pick up the phone cuz I need to tell you something." I laughed at her lack of understanding as to a cellphone message compared to an answering machine. Damn technology confused an old woman. "Good thing you ain't there. Anyhow, yo' momma done fit to be tied. Grant done come up in here and told'n her you didn't want to come home for the holiday. She had some big barbeque shindig planned up for y'all. Me and Cora been shucking up so much corn my fingers done got blisters on dem. You best be leavin' this here machine on cuz no doubt she gonna be callin'. She was cussin' up a storm when that boy told her." I heard shuffling as if she was trying to figure out how to turn the phone off. "Hey, sis...I'm missing you some kinda bad but I gets why you ain't here. You best be taking care of yoself."

A pain hit deep in the pit of my stomach and rolled a wave of nausea across it. On this weekend a year ago, I felt the happiest I had ever felt in my life. A weekend with Sam, Meems, and Flossie. Now only one of the three remained in my life. How could things change so drastically in such a small amount of time? Fear sprang up behind the pain. If a year had taken so much from me, what would another year take? A woman who once spent all of her days planning for the years ahead was now afraid to look beyond the time at present.

I stood from the bed and walked to the window. A sliver of light rose above the surface of the water but was smothered from expanding any further up by a mass of clouds that rested above it. The phone's screen was the only light in the room. It taunted me with voicemail two. Didn't I know who it was from? I sat in the wingback chair next to the bed, bent my knees up against my chest and pulled my T-shirt over them as I stared at the screen.

Voicemail two.

"Rayne," Charlie Grace said, "I don't think it's asking too much to be notified of your plans when they change." Her voice was strained as if she was choosing her words very carefully and perhaps speaking through gritted teeth. "One minute you're planning a visit and the next Grant tells me you have chosen to go elsewhere for your holiday weekend." Had I told her I was coming home? I couldn't remember. "Consideration. Consideration of others would be a nice lesson to learn. Now I must figure out what excuse I'm going to tell my friends when they arrive to find the honored guest is nowhere to be found. Perhaps you should be more considerate of your fiancé as well as he is celebrating the holiday all alone." She hung up. No goodbye. No terms of endearment. Classic Charlie Grace.

Quietly, I snuck from my room to watch the sunrise from the balcony. The light cast shadows into the darkness of the terrace. The surf's waves greeted me their good morning. I caught the scent of a coffee's aroma as I was about to sit.

"Good morning, Rayne." Violet's voice surprised me both with the sound of it as well as the nature of it. I was reminded of the feared physician of the obstetrics floor.

"Good morning, Dr. Breaker."

Her face was obscured in the shadow but I could see the definition of an arched eyebrow when she looked over her coffee cup at me.

"I'm sorry. Good morning, Violet."

"There's coffee on the table in the corner. If you would like a cup." Her tone was unchanged.

A small French press sat in the center of the glass table with a coffee mug tree adorned with white cups standing next to it. I filled the cup with the black morning's necessity. I didn't want the cream or sugar which sat next to it but I was drawn to rub the bronze fleur-de-lis toppers found on the lids of the glass set. The elegant symbols characteristic of Louisiana seemed out of place among the beach decorations. Yet here they were, proudly displayed beneath the wall hangings of shells and a driftwood sign pointing out toward the surf.

"There's cream and sugar next to the press. If you want it."

"I drink mine black but thank you. I love the containers though."

"Thank you. Sam gave them to us last year. She brought them back from a trip to Louisiana." She took a sip of her coffee. "But I think you already know about that trip."

I didn't move from my position behind her. All I wanted to do was to turn and run back inside but deep down I knew I couldn't. Jazlyn was my friend. She was a friend I had grown quickly to need in my life.

Violet was her wife, her life partner, and a woman she dearly loved. It was time for me to stand strong for the person I am—faults, mistakes, and all. It was time for me to do something not so easy for my future and those I wanted in it.

I sat in the chair closest to her and stared out at the ocean. "Are you sure you don't mind the company?"

She slowly turned her head in my direction. "It's fine." Her tone continued to express anything but it being fine.

The rising sun began to dispel the shadows and glow across her face. When she wasn't wearing her current expression, Violet was a beautiful woman. Who am I kidding? Even with the "I could snap your head off like a twig" look, she was still quite gorgeous. Her complexion had darkened while we were at the beach. The light golden hue of her skin had grown a richer, deeper brown from the hours spent under the sun. She wore her hair about an inch around her head except for the top which she kept it long enough to wear in a fashionable, messy spike. However, this weekend she had mostly left it free to lie across her forehead.

We sat in silence as the sun peeked over the horizon to paint the sky golden as it lay over the crystal blue water which turned to emerald green the closer it came to the shore. I was at a loss for words as I sat next to the woman who may have known more about Sam than I did. She certainly knew more of her in those final days of our time. What had she told her of me? What had she told her of her feelings for me? The sun had risen well above the surface of the water before I gained the courage to speak.

"It truly is beautiful here."

"Yes, it is. Jaz has always enjoyed coming here."

"I can see why. Y'all have a beautiful place here."

"It was her parents. I think she feels closer to them when she's here."

"Was?"

"Yes. They were killed in a car crash when she was a freshman in college." She took the last sip from her cup and stood to walk over to the French press.

"I didn't know."

"No, I doubt you would. She doesn't talk about it." She held the pot up. "Would you like for me to top off your cup?"

I looked down at the partially filled cup. "Yes, please."

"She doesn't let many people get close to her. Acquaintances. Yes, she keeps many of those. Although few get past the wall she keeps up. In fact, until you the only other one was Mo." She sat back down in the chair but faced me instead of the water. "I suppose that's why I know I've got to figure out a way to make this work between us." She brushed at the bangs that had fallen into her eyes. "I love her, Rayne, so you and I need to come to some understanding."

"I would like that. She's become my best friend."

"I see that."

"I don't want to lose her."

"No, and I know she feels the same about you." I felt her stare on me as physically as I did the ceramic cup in my hand. "I didn't have a high opinion of you not so long ago."

"And now?"

"And now, I suppose I'm trying to develop my own instead of holding resentment for things I know. I believe I may have misjudged you."

"How so?" I didn't want to do anything to discourage her from continuing so I sat there as still as I could and waited on her next words.

She took another swallow of her coffee. "Before, I believed you were trying to act out some straight girl lesbian fantasy as a way of sewing some wild oats before you got married."

"I wasn't." I couldn't hold back my interruption because she couldn't have been more wrong. "I swear to you. I wasn't."

"I believe you." Would her tone ever change around me? "I respect the fact that you haven't once tried to get me to talk of Sam or the time she spent with us. I'm not sure if it's my privacy or hers you're regarding. But I do respect the fact that you haven't tried to get me to talk about those days."

The breeze blew the tall blades of dune grass as they reached for the sky that had now turned a fiery red color.

"Both," I finally said.

A tear escaped to trace down my cheek as I thought of the loss of Sam. I remembered the pain of watching her walk away. I remembered the tears falling until my vision was skewed and my eyes fatigued. With all of me, I had fought these tears this weekend. I was so tired of crying. So tired of feeling the pain of watching her leave. So tired of feeling responsible for her pain and my pain. Here they fell freely in front of the woman who no doubt had collected Sam's tears upon her shoulder.

"I never wanted to hurt her," I said between sobs. "Knowing I did hurts worse than the pain of losing her. I can't sleep because when I close my eyes I see her crying in front of me. There was so much I did wrong. So much I could've done differently."

I didn't want the words to keep pouring out of me. I wanted them to stop. She sat across from me and watched as I broke down in front of her but I swear her expression was unchanged. What did I expect her to do? Wrap me up in her arms. Console me after I broke her best friend's heart. After I hurt Sam so much that she left her fellowship instead of staying in a city where she might run into me. No, if it were me, I would probably sit there emotionless as well.

Which is what she did for several minutes before speaking again. "And now? Would you do things differently if given another chance? If faced with the same situation, even if it's not Sam, would your choices or actions be different?"

With a strength I hadn't realized laid dormant within me, I answered without hesitation. "I would. Beyond a shadow of doubt, I would do things differently." What exactly those things would be I did not know, but I had lived enough of my days with Sam out of my life that I realized if given another chance I would do what I could to never feel this way again.

Violet stood and walked to the balcony door. "Perhaps one day you'll be faced with a similar decision. Maybe then you'll remember this feeling you have now and use it to your advantage." She braced her hand against the glass of the door and glanced over her shoulder. "We're taking the boat out today. Why don't you give yourself a day to let those eyes see something besides sadness?"

I looked at her in what I know must have been a look of shock.

"I've seen equal pain in both of your eyes now. I'll tell you like I told her, holding onto the hurt won't bring her back."

"What will?"

She sighed. "She asked me the very same question."

"And what did you tell her?"

"I told her the only thing that will bring her back is her. The same for you. The only thing to bring Sam back to you is Sam. If you two are meant to be together, you will be together."

A breeze caught the curtain of the opened sliding glass door as she turned to walk inside. The material tickled at my shoulder when it flowed across me. The sand had been wiped clean of the footsteps which had marked it the day before. It was a fresh, new surface ready for the day. The drape brushed against my skin once more. I let the tears dry on my cheek and kept the others suppressed. A fresh new surface for the day.

Chapter 9

My FINGERS DIPPED low into the coolness of the water as the sail caught a wind to carry us across the surface of the ocean. I listened to the sound of the wind whipping the sails as the boat skipped across the waves. There was a rhythm to it. A rhythm that soothed my body as it dipped up and down with the hull of the boat. I sat along the side to let the sun warm my face as I looked into the sky with sunglass-covered eyes. The darker the sunglasses, the harder it was to gather which eyes were upon you and which eyes looked away. I saw Mo smiling and wondered if she had caught me staring at her as I tried to make out the tattoos on her stomach. She was stretched out across the canopy that connected the two-small-engine-powered hulls of the catamaran sailboat. The small royal blue bikini she wore did little to cover the ink on her right lower belly. It was a heart ending in a larger treble clef like the one behind her ear. A flow of musical notes passed over the heart and around her right hip. I watched the trail of quarter notes, eighth notes, and two sixteenth notes. I looked back up at her face and noticed her smile had changed. She was obviously well aware of my stare. I quickly looked away as the water broke to spray across the hull. For a brief moment, I was able to ignore her knowing smile but I could hardly ignore when she began patting the canopy beside her.

I moved cautiously across the canvas to sit next to her. I looked down at my one-piece bathing suit with cut-off blue jean shorts and became nervously aware of the difference in our swimsuit choices. It's not that I was embarrassed or ashamed of my body. I had managed not to gain the medical school twenty pounds that afflicted some of my classmates. I still wore the same size six jeans and small tops. Hell, I had even kept some of the remnants of my once-toned stomach by squeezing in a few crunches here and there. I suppose it was a shyness beyond anything else that had me hiding in more material than the three of them combined. Seeing hundreds of nude bodies in the OR should have effectively wiped away any shyness I had. It should have but didn't.

"Are you having a good time?" Mo asked as she cupped her hand over her sunglasses.

"Yes, very. Are you?"

"Are you kidding me? Sun, water, boat? I could live out here."

Sitting up close to her, I could make out the tattoo underneath her left collarbone. In two separate lines was written, "When the pain penetrates the music resonates." Small birds inked in black soared across her shoulder. *Pain*?

Violet sat next to Jazlyn as she steered the boat along the water. Her hand rested on the small of Jazlyn's bare back. I marveled at the contrast in the color of their skin. It wasn't like a separation or difference in them but rather a stronger bond. They blended. They became one. Her thumb traced circles along the bikini bottom line of Jazlyn's suit.

"Sort of makes you want to fall in love, doesn't it?" Mo was watching the same expression of tenderness I was.

I smiled.

"If you go for that sort of thing." She winked.

"Does that mean you don't?"

"What? Falling in love?"

"Yes."

"Nah, it sort of takes all of the fun out of it to me."

Jazlyn stopped the boat when we pulled into a small alcove. "We're here," she said as she dropped an anchor into the water.

"Race you in." Mo stood up and tackled Jazlyn into the water. The force of them hitting the water in a ball of arms and legs rocked the sailboat and sent a spray of water onto Violet and me.

"Oh, I'm so getting you now," Jazlyn screamed when her head popped up out of the water. They became a tangled mess of splashing arms and girl-like screams as they wrestled in the water.

"Those two will go at it like this for hours if we let them," Violet said.

I laughed as I watched them frolic about in the water. "How long have they known each other?"

"Hmmmm, let's see." She tilted her head upwards as if calculating. "We've been together for ten years, so I guess close to eleven."

"So, she knew Mo before you?"

"Not exactly." Violet squeezed some sunscreen into her palm and then handed the bottle to me. "You're getting a little pinkish." She rubbed the lotion onto her shoulders, which gave her darker skin a whitish tint. "She'd met me before Mo. You could probably say Mo is the reason we're together. If it hadn't been for her, I doubt Jaz and I would've made it past our own shit. I suppose, if we're being completely honest, I should say I doubt we would've made it past my own shit."

"She told me she was married when she met you."

She made a sound of something between a puff and a sigh. "I thought she might. She told me you needed a Mo like she had needed years ago. She wants to be that for you and asked I not stand in the way."

"And how do you feel about it?"

For the first time, she gave me a smile meant solely for me. It wasn't a huge smile but it was a smile nonetheless. "I'm warming up to it."

Cold water splashed across us again. "Are you two coming in or what?" Jazlyn yelled. Mo was riding her piggy-back style.

"In a sec." Violet waved as if to shoo them away. "I was so in love with Jaz when we met that I couldn't see reason. I couldn't see anything beyond wanting to spend my every moment with her. I knew she loved me too so I didn't understand her indecisiveness in divorcing her husband. To me, it was simple. She wasn't in love him. She was in love me. I didn't understand why she struggled so much with leaving him. So, I left her. I wasn't going to be the mistress who waited for her lover to leave her husband. That's all I saw. I didn't see the rest."

"The rest?"

Violet looked at me. "Yes, the rest. Her side and apparently what is your side. The side that loves the men in your lives yet know it isn't what will sustain your happiness. There are different forms of love, of commitment, and of loyalty. Jaz met Mo when she was pretty messed up over it all. Mo helped us both see the other's side. She sat down with us and showed us the way to work through it."

I looked out at Jazlyn who was laughing a full belly laugh in the arms of her best friend. Her laugh was the kind where her whole face lit up and her head fell back. Her mouth was open wide as the laughter billowed out.

"You see, Rayne, it took time for me to realize that loving Zach and feeling the loss of him in her life didn't take away from the love she felt for me. Zach was all she had when her parents were gone. It was her constant. The one thing she knew would be the same beyond all else. It was hard for her to give that up. Plus, his family had become hers. Besides me, Zach and his family were all she had. When I ended it, she was devastated because she felt she had chosen them over me. Zach was a good man. It felt wrong to hurt him. I, for all practical purposes, was a good woman. It didn't seem right to hurt me either. She didn't know what was right or wrong anymore. Someone would be hurt. Someone's life would forever change. I made the decision for her and ended it. Mo helped us both see the only clear choice for us."

She brushed at the water sprinkles that Mo and Jazlyn splashed onto us.

"Mo helped me to understand how I needed to be there for Jaz while she did the wrong she felt was the only right decision for her. So, I was there with her every step of the divorce. I let her cry. I let her grieve his loss. But I had to let go of my own hang-ups before I could do that."

Yes, the constant. The one thing I always thought would be the same.

"Jaz suspects you may be in the same boat as she was and that

Sam was where I was. She could see it clearly when Sam was with us. I suppose I had let the last ten years let me forget about the most painful time in my life and didn't want to bring it all out again when you started coming around." She held her hand over her eyes to look at me. "I'm sorry for that."

The boat rocked to the weight of Jazlyn climbing up over the hull. Her tall frame crossed the distance of the catamaran quickly. She stood in front of Violet and shook her head violently. The wet shower from her long hair drowned Violet in a spray of water.

"Okay you. Either jump in on your own or I'll throw you in," Jazlyn said.

Violet laughed as she shook her finger at Jazlyn. "You wouldn't dare."

"Don't test me." Jazlyn pushed Violet onto her back and covered her with her soaked body. She wiggled on top of Violet until Violet emitted a loud cackle. I must say it was not the laugh I ever expected from Dr. Breaker.

"Am I going to have to threaten you the same or will you come quietly?" Mo had raised her body up along the side of the boat to cross her arms over the hull closest to me. Her smile was mischievous.

I put my hands up in defense. "No, no. I'll come quietly."

"Well, damn, I never thought I'd be happy to hear a woman say those words to me."

Wait. What?

I felt a strong blush fill my cheeks and hoped like crazy she mistook it for a sunburn. I also hoped she was fooled into thinking I actually nearly stumbled on something other than my own clumsiness as I stepped toward the side of the boat.

WE SPENT THE large part of the afternoon playing in the water of the alcove until our hunger insisted we return. Jazlyn opened the sail as the wind picked up to carry us quickly back to the shore. I let the sun and sounds of the water hitting the catamaran carry me away into thoughts of nothing but the warmth on my skin. The heaviness in my chest rose to be carried away within the sails. I was having fun. I'd laughed. I'd splashed. I'd forgotten.

I stretched my head further back to see Violet and Jazlyn sitting together. Turning my head to the side, I saw Mo watching the same. She winked at me as our eyes met. Another wave of happiness swept over me. I liked her. She had this carefree way that made me feel as if she had no worries in the world.

Once the sailboat was docked in the boat slip, we made our way along the sidewalk that paralleled 30A. 30A is as much of a culture as it is a connection between towns along the Gulf of Mexico. Tourists and locals alike ride around in cars with open sunroofs, convertible tops lowered back, or Jeeps with little to no barrier between the passengers and the open air.

"I'm feeling me some fish tacos." Mo stepped ahead of us as we walked along the sidewalk. She had pulled her long hair into a ponytail that swayed as she walked and revealed yet another tattoo. Just at the base of her hairline was a circular design of a deep blue sky dotted with stars on one side and a quarter moon on the other. A three-dimensional narrow rainbow was wrapped around the moon. Below it was linear writing in cursive print that traced down between her shoulder blades. Its full passage was hidden underneath the scoop-neck white T-shirt she wore. For a brief moment, an image of me lying on my side next to her body as I read the writing flashed through my mind. I shook the image and the shock of it from my thoughts.

Mo shuffled her feet and spun around when Van Morrison's Brown-Eyed Girl song began to play from the speakers hidden in the small palm trees that lined the sidewalk. The smile she gave Jazlyn when she held her arms out for her shined brightly underneath the string lights hanging overhead. The tiny clear bulbs joined the line of silver Airstreams that had been converted into food trailers. There was everything from ice cream to full meals available.

"My brown-eyed girl. You my brown-eyed girl."

Jazlyn picked up her pace to take Mo's hands. They danced in the middle of the sidewalk with Jazlyn spinning Mo around as I remember seeing Charlie Grace and Jacques do many times before.

"Sha la la, la la, la la, la la, l-la te da," they sang slightly off key.

Violet stepped closer to me as we followed behind the dancing queens. She smiled and shook her head. "I so love to see her this happy. Mo brings the little girl out in her. She grew up too fast after her parent's death. It's good to see her this way."

Violet was smiling as widely as Jazlyn who was now dancing back to her. "Makin' love in the green grass," she continued to sing as she picked Violet up in her arms.

Violet laughed as Jazlyn carried her off toward the Airstream boasting the best grilled cheese sandwiches on the Emerald Coast.

"You can have a piece of bread with cheese melted between it or you can come with me to taste something truly delicious." Mo raised her eyebrows in excitement.

"Fish tacos you say?"

"I sure as hell did. The best you've ever tasted."

"That won't be too hard to master because I've never actually had them."

"Follow me and we can change that." She grabbed my hand and led me to the last Airstream on the corner. "Do you have a preference of fish? Or do you want me to order for you?"

"I trust your judgment."

Mo looked at me and smiled. "Hmmmm, can't say I hear that too many times." She laughed.

I watched her face as she studied the menu. She furrowed her eyebrows as she considered the options. Her eyes were a brighter green under the red-and-orange lights hanging above the Airstream's window. She was even more striking with her sun-kissed cheeks.

A young girl who looked to be not much older than legal stepped in front of the older gentleman as Mo came to be next in line.

"Hi, there."

"Hi." Mo looked at the row of toppings displayed to the side of the girl.

"What can I get you, doll?" The girl smiled.

Doll? Isn't she a little young to be calling someone doll?

Mo gave her a million-dollar smile. "Off the menu…" She winked at the girl. "I'll have four grilled Mako fish tacos topped with jalapeno coleslaw and avocado." She directed her attention back to me. "Good?"

"Yes. Good," I said, shaking my head.

The girl followed her eyes to me and frowned briefly before turning to prepare our order.

Mo peered around those in line to look at the open grassy amphitheater. She smiled a much different smile as she watched some kids playing Frisbee with a border collie. She motioned for me to look at them. One of the little girls got tangled with the puppy and tumbled down the small hill. Mo matched the girl's childish giggle with her own. The puppy popped up and wagged his tail so fast his backend shook with a frenzy. Mo laughed again.

Oh yeah, I like this woman.

"Here you go," the girl said as she returned to the window. She handed the wrapped packages to Mo but held onto her hand as she collected the money from her. "Nice ink." She tapped the bass clef tattoo on the inside of Mo's wrist before releasing her hand.

"Thanks." Mo gave her the same smile she had given her before.

I imagined she had many women flirt with her. I wondered if this was the smile she was used to showing when it happened. I decided it was a smile I hoped not to see in my future.

The unsolicited flirting reminded me of watching women openly flirt with Sam. Either these women knew both of them were lesbians or in the very least they must've thought they would respond to their flirtations. How did they know? What aura did they give off?

Mo waved at Jazlyn as she stood above the seated crowd. She was pointing to an empty table Violet had snagged for us.

"What did you two get?" Violet asked as she was wiping off debris from the sea-foam-colored table. The palm leaves hung low over the table and very nearly touched her head as she bent over.

"Fish tacos of course." Mo set the paper basket containers down and pulled two orange Adirondack chairs away from the table. She pointed to the one next to her before taking a seat in the oversized chair.

"Rayne, did Mo even give you a chance to choose something else besides her beloved fish tacos?" Jazlyn asked.

Mo was already one bite into her first taco. "What? Of course, I did." A few shreds of cabbage fell from the soft shell onto the paper packaging. She quickly picked them up not to let a single bite escape her mouth.

"She did. But she was pretty insistent this was the best choice." The heat of the jalapeno coleslaw lingered in my mouth. "I'd have to say she was dead on. These are amazing."

"Damn straight they are." Mo gobbled up another bite.

"You may change your mind once you see my grilled cheese," Violet said as she set four bottles of cold beer in front of us.

"Where're you headed next?" Jazlyn opened her wrapper and nibbled on a large sourdough sandwich filled with melted white and yellow cheese.

"Key West, Florida." Mo took the last bite of her first taco and chased it with a few large swallows of beer. "There's a slammin' new club opening up."

"Key West. Nice," Violet almost hummed.

"Like way nice. These girls do it right too. This is their third club. They have one in New York, Las Vegas, and now the Keys. They're putting me up for the first month they're open."

"A month in the Keys?" Jazlyn tipped her beer toward Mo. "I hope you've worked on your exercise tolerance."

Mo held her palm against her chest as if innocent to Jazlyn's accusations. "Who, me?"

The three of them laughed at what had to be a private joke. After seeing the Airstream girl's obvious flirtation, I didn't have to stretch my imagination too far to understand their laughter.

We sat under the rustle of the palm leaves and let the breeze off of the ocean sweep away the humidity of the day. We took turns making trips to retrieve fresh cold beers. We watched the crowds continue to appear even with the passing hours of the night. We laughed at the parents who showed noticeable fatigue as their children pranced around them with energy that did not seem to be diminishing anytime soon.

Jazlyn and Mo slammed their hands down on the table after a few chords of a calypso steel pan sounded above us. They pulled their chairs closer to sing together about wasting away again in Margaritaville.

"Salt. Salt. Salt," they sang loudly with their beers held high in the air. They were Jimmy Buffet's back-up singers as he crooned for his lost shaker of salt.

"Some people claim that there's a woman to blame," they sang together. Except this time Jazlyn looked at Violet and Mo looked at me. She raised her eyebrows as her lips curled into what I would call an impish smile.

Yes, it was a very good day.

"What are you talking about?" I heard Mo say as I was about to turn the corner into the kitchen.

"Don't play dumb with me," Jazlyn said in a playful tone. "I've learned to read that look in your eyes."

"Okay, okay. But you have to know she's pretty damn hot."

I stopped abruptly and took a small step backward as to not be seen in the doorway.

"Yes, she's a very pretty woman."

"Hot. I believe the word you're looking for is hot."

"Come on, Mo," Jazlyn whispered. "She's my friend."

"You know what makes her even hotter? She has no idea she is. She doesn't seem to sense it at all."

"Which is exactly why you don't need to mess with her. She's not in a place to be able to handle—" She paused and seemed to stutter to find her words. "Well…you."

"Me? And what exactly do you mean by that?"

"A good time. Honey, you know I love you like the sister I never had, which is why I can talk to you openly. Rayne's in a really bad spot right now."

Rayne? Wait. They're talking about me. Did she call me hot? I felt my heart rate speed up as the heat of a blush sprang to my cheeks.

"I'll let her share the details if she ever wishes. To sum it up, think of me when I met you. Would you have been good for me at that time in my life?"

"I was good for you."

"Not like that. You didn't find me *hot* or want to bed me down."

"Who says?" Mo said as she began to laugh.

Jazlyn laughed too. "You're incorrigible. What in the world am I going to do with you?"

"Love me and be my best friend for all of my days?"

"I suppose I could do that."

There was silence for a moment before Mo spoke again. "I get your point though, okay? I understand what you're saying."

"Thank you."

I listened to them move around the kitchen and waited a few minutes before walking in. I didn't want them to think I had heard their conversation.

"And what if I think I like her?" Mo said.

The coffee grinder stopped. "Then I say let's talk again when you feel something beyond thinking you like her."

No longer thirsty for a glass of water, I turned and quietly walked out of the condo.

THE FULL MOON was bright in the sky. Not a single cloud shadowed its brilliance. I followed its path out onto the beach. The sand cooled by the night air made a distinctive sound as I walked across it to the surf. A stretch of the imagination and I was back home on the bayou with the moon's light sparkling atop the water and the gravel crunching under the weight of my footsteps. Yet it wasn't the bayou. The darkness wasn't able to steal the salted air I breathed in. Nor could it keep me from feeling the sea air on my skin or the thickening of my curls with the wetness in my hair. The growing waves wet my legs and shorts as they crashed farther up the shore to where I sat. A stray beam caught the stone upon my finger. I stretched my hand out in front of me and watched the beam dance upon the cuts of the diamond. Fingers flexed into a fist didn't seem to dampen the reflection. I turned the ring around my finger to crush the stone in my grip. I tightened my fist until I could feel the pain of it digging into my skin.

This damn ring. I cursed it for everything it meant and stood for.

"You stare at that a lot, you know?"

I jumped.

Mo walked around from behind me, sat next to me, and stared out across the water.

"Actually, I hadn't noticed."

"Well, you do. I'm assuming it's from a man."

"Correct."

"And I take it this man's not here."

"Nope."

From the corner of my eye, I saw her shift her weight to face me. "Why wear it then? He's not here. You're with your friends. Why not leave it off if it bothers you so much?"

"That's a good question."

"And your answer is."

I picked up a handful of sand and let it slowly drain from my palm. "I suppose to remind me. Remind me of the past."

She scooted across the sand to sit closer to me. I wondered if I wasn't talking loud enough for my voice to carry over the sound of the waves.

"Remind me of what's ahead," I said louder this time.

"I don't know much about what's in your past but what lies ahead is still open for change, isn't it? I mean, it hasn't happened yet, so how can you say it's a done deal?"

"Sometimes the decisions we make are what makes it a done deal. The consequences of those decisions prevent change."

Mo placed her hand on my arm. "Do you really believe that?"

"Yes."

"Well, no wonder." She leaned back on her hands stretched out behind her.

"No wonder what?"

"No wonder your eyes look so defeated. You've given up."

I watched the moonlight reflect her face to me. She had this look of sureness to her as if the world was laid out in front of her to read. *Different but the same.* The waves became louder as they grew and rolled into us. The force of their current lifted our bodies and pulled us closer to the water.

Mo laughed as she gave into the water's pull. "We're already soaked." She stood up, pulled her long hair back into a ponytail, and extended a hand to me. "What's say we go in?"

I felt like the young girl who waited on us at the taco stand. I couldn't resist her magnetism. I held her hand as she walked me out into the waist-high water. I let my fingers tighten over the warmth of her hand within mine.

"Why do you say I've given up?" I stood close to her as the waves rocked us unsteadily off of our feet.

"Haven't you?" Her tone was matter-of-fact as if I was now part of the world laid out in front of her to read.

"You don't know what happened. I didn't have a choice."

Mo stepped closer to me and placed her hands on my sides to keep our balance together. "It's about perspectives, Rayne. Look around you in this darkness. Earlier today, we could see all the way down to our feet but now look." I followed her eyes down as our waists disappeared into the depth of the water. "Same water, same feet. Different perspective. Maybe you should start with changing your perspective."

"I don't understand."

She removed a hand from my waist and glided it down my left arm until she found my hand. "Don't you?" She pulled our hands out of the water. "Is this who you are?" She tapped the diamond on my finger. "Or is this just a part of your path and your decisions on this one path? Nothing about this ring changes who you are or who you can be. It's merely a stepping stone of your life. What you do with it is up to you."

I watched my hand disappear under the surface of the water as I lowered it from Mo's grasp. The stone's sparkle was lost in the cloak of darkness. Perspective.

Chapter 10

"HEY, YOU." Mo's throaty voice strangely lifted my spirits the moment I heard it.

"Hey, yourself. How's Key West?"

"Girl, it was some kind of wild." Her voice carried the smile I knew she must have been wearing. "But I'm headed back to the real world soon."

"And what exactly do you call the real world?"

"Ha! In this case, I would call it Atlanta, Georgia."

"I s'pose that's real enough."

"So, I've got a gig up there weekend after next. Jaz is coming. I was hoping you would tag along with her. Y'know, see me in action."

I pushed the doors open to the emergency room and held my finger up when I saw Angie waving from behind the nurse's desk. She gave me the okay sign before returning to her charting.

"Would your silence be a no?"

"What? Oh no, sorry. I was looking to see if I was on call that weekend." I felt the lie stain my lips the moment I let it pass. I already knew I wasn't on call as I had checked the schedule last week when Jazlyn asked me to go with her.

Mo and I had spoken several times on the phone after meeting in Seaside. I enjoyed the conversations very much and found her to be a charming distraction from my thoughts of Sam. She had never ventured into what I would call serious flirtation or beyond a friendly conversation; so, the company was both enjoyable and comfortable. But this was entirely different. This was seeing her again. Seeing her in her own element meant at a lesbian club, not a private beach gathering.

She read me when we sat on our sandy seats the night on the beach. Wasn't I nervous to see what else she may decipher in me should I see her again? I knew after that night, I still held a glimmer of hope Sam would return. Somehow, I dreamed she would walk up to me and tell me we would figure things out together. Mo never asked about Grant or my family. I'm not even sure she knew his name. She let me carry our talks where I wanted them to go. Not once did they include him.

"How about this? How about you look at your schedule then get back to me? I've got to run to do a sound check before the show. I'll talk to you later."

"Okay, have a good show. We'll talk soon." I ended the call and tapped the receiver against my chin.

Angie met me at the corner of the desk. "Hiya, Doc. Whoa, what's got you all flushed?"

I touched my hands to my cheeks. The blush was warm against my palms.

"Got one for you in exam room three." She handed me a chart.

"I appreciate it, Angie, but I'm not on call for the ER today."

"This one here's a special request." She used her pen to point out the name on the chart.

"Tyler Richard? What happened to her?"

"She fell down and went kaboom." Angie smirked. "Got her a nasty cut on her pretty little chinny chin chin."

"Did anyone call Dr. Richard?"

"You mean Dr. Dick? Yeah, we called him. Little bastard had the nurse tell me he was in a case and to call you. Besides, Doc, you sew much prettier than he does."

"That may be, but he's her husband."

"Tell him that. Gotta' run, Doc. Got you all pulled in there. Laid out a bunch of different sutures for you. Make her pretty again." Angie headed down the hallway toward the trauma rooms. She turned and walked backward. "Oh, and Dr. Breaker should be in here in a bit so you'd better hurry if you want to beat her in there."

"Dr. Breaker? Why is she coming?"

"Cuz she's knocked up. She passed out so OB has to check out the baby."

I pulled back the curtain leading into the examination room. "Hey, Tyler, what happened?"

The vibrant woman I had shared dinner with on a few occasions sat on the side of a gurney like a scorned child. She lifted her head barely enough for me to see her eyes. She kept her hands clasped in her lap.

"Hi, Rayne." Her voice was subdued. "I'm sorry they called you."

"I'm not." I sat on the edge of the bed to lift her chin so I could study the cleaned cut there. Angie had done a fine job. Careful not to touch the wound, I gently moved her face to the side to get a full visualization of it.

Her eyes caught mine to hold them within her stare. "Do you treat all of your patients like this?" She looked back and forth between the side of the bed where I sat and the small stool left rolled up next to the bed.

"Oh." I started to stand but she caught my wrist with her hand.

"No, please. It's nice."

I felt a wave cross over me from the combination of sincere warmth and sadness in her eyes. She moved her hand from my wrist to my hand and held it gently before pulling it up to rest against her forehead.

"Oh, Rayne." She sighed deeply. "What am I going to do?"

"About?" I felt as if I could do no more than whisper as I watched her wrestle with her feelings. Her breath against my arm left tingles upon my skin. *What the hell?*

"Did you hear I'm pregnant?"

"Yes." From her expression, I didn't feel congratulations were in order or even warranted.

"Don't get me wrong. I love this baby, but now I'm tied to him forever. And look at him. Where is he?" Tears slowly fell from her eyes. "He couldn't care less I'm here. Look, he even sent you to take care of me."

I wiped her cheeks with the thumb of my free hand but kept my other hand where she seemed to need it most. "I'm glad to be here."

She forced a smile.

"What did he say about the pregnancy?"

Her smile turned into a sideways smirk. "That it's my fault and I should've been more careful."

Dick.

"He said he was going to be too busy to take care of a kid and I would have to figure out how to manage without him. I mean, the pregnancy will be fine while he and Grant are gone to New York, but if he gets accepted for that year program, I don't know how I'll manage a baby alone. I can barely afford to take care of us on my salary. I don't know how I'll pay for childcare."

"Wait. What?" I was having trouble keeping up with her because she was speaking rather quickly but I knew for certain I hadn't heard anything about a year program. "What year program?"

Her eyes widened in surprise. "You know, the chance to train under that hot shot vascular surgeon up there? He's taking two residents from UAB."

"No. I don't know about that." I pulled my hand from hers as I shook my head. "Grant told me about the rotation but I thought it was like for a couple of months or something. I didn't realize it could turn into a year."

"Well, yeah, the first stint is. A group will go up from August to the end of October or early November. I can't get a straight answer out of Paxton. But then they're supposed to choose two residents out of that group to go back for a year."

I felt myself take a step back and rock on my heels. A year? He could be gone a year and I knew nothing about it? Why didn't he tell me? It seems we were both having possible changes in our lives that neither one of us was sharing with the other. I began to feel an uneasy discomfort of this being my life—pregnant by a man I didn't truly love and living separate lives because there were pieces we didn't want to or couldn't share with one another.

Tyler put her hand on mine. "Rayne, I had no idea you didn't know."

Her need to console me brought me back to the reality in front of me. This wasn't the time or the place to think of such things. "It's fine." I patted her hand. "That's not of our worries right now."

"Then what is?"

I looked at the tray of supplies. "Fixing this nasty cut. I'm afraid it's going to need stitches."

She smiled a real smile this time and laid back on the gurney. "I'm in good hands. Have at it, Dr. Storm."

"This should heal really well," I said as I tied off the last of the nylon stitches. "I put a few absorbable sutures underneath. Come back in seven days so I can remove these nylon ones. They're just here to keep the skin edges together but I don't want to leave them in too long or they may scar."

"Can someone tell me who on God's green earth thought this ultrasound would be effective outside the patient's room?" Violet's voice was loud and left little doubt that the entire emergency room hadn't heard her.

Tyler flinched. "Who the hell is that?" she asked.

The curtain pulled back quickly. "Hello, Mrs. Richard, I'm Dr. Breaker from OB. Let's have a look at this little baby." She saw me and stopped pushing the ultrasound cart. "Dr. Storm."

"Dr. Breaker."

"I'm sorry. I didn't realize Mrs. Richard had someone with her."

"Call me Tyler." She pointed to the fresh black sutures on her chin. "I cut my chin when I passed out. Dr. Storm had to sew me up."

"Aw, I see." Violet looked around the room. "You have got to be kidding me?" She pulled the curtain back again and nearly ran head first into a nurse who was quickly rounding the corner.

"I'm sorry, Dr. Breaker. I'll have you ready in a second," the young nurse said as she finished wheeling the cart next to the stretcher. Her hands shook as she plugged the electric cord into the wall.

"Do you see anything else missing?" Dr. Breaker's eyes threw daggers at the nurse. "Well don't look at me, nurse. Look at the patient. What is missing?"

The nurse bit her lip as she searched over Tyler. Tyler looked nearly as frightened as the nurse did. "Umm…"

Dr. Breaker sighed deeply and rolled her eyes. "Let's see. You page an OB doctor because you have a pregnant female who suffered a loss of consciousness, fell, and sustained a laceration. A pregnant female. Oh, dear Lord in heaven. A monitor. Wouldn't you think a fetal monitor would be good for this patient?"

"Oh, yes, ma'am." The nurse dug into the drawers of the cart as she tried to find the monitor.

I was having a hard time not leaping in to help the poor girl but I had no idea where the monitors were kept. Yet I felt pretty certain they weren't in that slim drawer she was searching in.

Dr. Breaker stepped in between her and the cart. She raised her hand in the air. "Just get out of here and find me someone who knows what the hell they're doing."

The young woman wiped away a tear as she brushed past me and disappeared behind the curtain.

I turned around.

Dr. Breaker was looking at me. "Were you finished, Dr. Storm, or do you need more time?"

"Oh no. I'm finished." As if I was going to say anything different to Dr. Ball Breaker. I'd completely forgotten she was Violet and wondered if she too had forgotten or rather regretted the friendship we had started developing in Florida. Could she feel it a betrayal to Sam? I ignored the image of Sam as it appeared in my thoughts.

I peered around Violet's shoulder to Tyler. "The nurse will bring you an instruction sheet as to how to care for the wound." Tyler looked at me with begging eyes and I knew she didn't want me to leave her with Dr. Breaker. *Sorry, chick. You're on your own here.* "I'll see you in seven days." I turned to Violet. "Dr. Breaker."

She nodded. "Dr. Storm." Then she winked and mouthed the words, "Nice seeing you."

I walked from the room and wondered how she could do that. How can you bless out a sweet young nurse and then smile a second later?

"I'm going to need a shot of something strong after this night," Angie said as she passed me while wheeling yet another cart into the room. "Dr. Dick's wife and Dr. Ball Breaker all in one room. Being charge nurse sucks dirty ass. Do you hear me? Dirty ass." She held back the curtain. "Dr. Breaker," she said in a more pleasant voice. "I apologize for us not being better prepared for you. I'll be your nurse from here forward."

Angie had a point though. Tonight called for a shot of something very strong and I knew just where to go.

"HEY, YOU." JAZLYN was adjusting the sound board as I walked into the Pineapple Post. "You're cutting it close tonight. Women should start coming in very shortly."

I wondered if she ever considered I might choose to stay one night. So far, I hadn't. "Got tied up in the ER. Some fiery OB/Gyn came in raising hell. Had the whole ER buzzing."

Jazlyn gave a hearty chuckle. "Uh oh. Did she turn into Dr. Ball Breaker tonight?"

I blinked at her surprised that she knew Violet's nickname. "You know about that?"

Jazlyn stepped down from the deejay area. "Oh, hell yeah. Vi's sort of proud of the nickname."

"No shit."

"Are you kidding? She loves it. She says people respect her more if they're afraid of her."

"Well, then she was gettin' a whole lotta' respect tonight." I followed Jazlyn to the bar. She reached into the ice bin to pull out a beer. "Not tonight, my friend. I think I need something a little stronger."

"Oh, really? Been one of those days?"

"You can say that again."

"Pull up a stool. I've got just what the doctor ordered." She pulled a bottle from the shelves behind her and poured a clear liquid into two shot glasses.

I recognized the Patron bottle the minute her hands gripped the neck. I closed my eyes to the memory of Sam's hands over mine as she instructed me on the art of shooting tequila. She'd given me a swarm of butterflies that night. Butterflies that drowned in the warmth of the tequila buzz. My lips loosened to let spill the intoxication of her smell as I fell into her arms.

"Hey." Jazlyn's hand was on my arm. "Where'd you go?"

I shook my head. "I'm sorry."

"Don't be." She pushed the shot glass toward me. "I've learned that only one person brings that look on your face."

I slammed the liquid back and hoped the burn would ease the hurt in my heart. Unfortunately, it only managed to make me cough. I slid the empty glass back to her. "Again."

Light poured into the darkened club as the entrance door opened. Jazlyn squeezed my arm to steady me. I realized I must have jumped.

"Hey, girls. Come on in. The pool table's all set up for you."

"Thanks. Can we have a pitcher of whatever you've got on tap tonight?" one of the four girls said as they walked to the pool tables.

"Sure thing. Got a light and dark. What are you in the mood for?"

"Make it a dark." She held the hand of the shorter girl next to her.

Jazlyn gave me two more shots in the time it took her to fix a tray with a pitcher of beer and four mugs. She pointed at me as she walked around the side of the bar. "Stay. I'll be right back."

I watched Jazlyn as she talked to the four of them. They looked young, alive, and full of uninhibited smiles. I felt a heavy weight on my shoulders at the irony of me describing the girls in that way. They were probably a mere couple of years younger than me. Yet I felt at least ten if not fifteen years older than them. Two of the girls giggled as they had found an escape in one another. They playfully tugged at each other's body as they leaned against the side of the pool table.

I rested my head in my hand as I propped my arm up on the bar. The empty shot glass sat in front of me. "I don't remember the last time I giggled," I said to Jazlyn as she walked back behind the bar. "You know, giggled." I rubbed my fingertips in circles around my temples. "I feel so old. Like a woman who has watched her life go by."

Jazlyn placed her finger under my chin and raised my eyes to her level. "But see, that's the beauty of it all. You aren't old and you haven't let your life pass you by. You're young and fully capable of changing anything about your life you want."

I tapped my finger on the rim of the empty shot glass. "Why don't you ever ask about him?"

She filled my glass. "Because he has no bearing on our friendship. And he's your story to tell. Figure when it's us—it's us."

"She used to ask about him all of the time."

"That's because he had a huge bearing on yours and hers. Sam wanted you from the get-go. He was who had you."

"Not really." I drank the tequila hard and fast. "He's never had me the way she did. Why couldn't she see that?"

"She was too close."

I thought of Tyler. I saw her tearful eyes looking into mine, searching for answers I'm sure she didn't find. The tequila rose in my throat with a soured taste as I thought of Paxton and Grant's plans. Not once had he mentioned the possibility of the year extension. I thought of her sitting alone in an emergency room. But in all reality, she wasn't alone. She was sitting there with their unborn child. I thought of her feeling pregnant, alone, and trapped in a marriage she didn't want to be in any longer.

"I don't want this life." The glass had magically been filled again but this time I felt the spinning of my head as I leaned back to drain its contents. My vision had to catch up to the position of my head as I looked back at the giggling girls. "I want that."

"Whoa, sister, you're going to have to slow down. That last bit came out a little slurred."

"No." I held my glass up. Or at least, I think I held my glass up. "Please give me another. I don't want to think right now. Please."

I opened one eye to notice dimmed recessed lights above me. The room was a quick blur as I lifted my head to look around. Damn tequila. At some point, Jazlyn must have helped me up the stairs to their loft. I pictured a distorted image of her leaning over me and telling me we'd work all of this out together. That must have been when she deposited me on her couch. I dug my cell phone out of my back pocket to send a text before rolling back on my side.

Text Message to Mo at 1:55am: "I'll b there."

Text Message from Mo at 2:10am: "Gr8!"

Chapter 11

"**S**EE, WHAT DID I tell you?" Jazlyn screamed over the crowd. I had thought the Atlanta club would be crowded but I'd never imagined this. The club was at least twice as large as the Pineapple Post and I dare say there wasn't one single spot of flooring not covered by feet.

"I'd kill to have a place like this."

Or at least that was what I think I heard her say over a multitude of voices drowned out by sounds of music pumping through the speakers. Then it occurred to me, no one here knew me. I could be who I wanted to be without anyone back home the wiser. I could absorb the scene around me yet not have to talk or be nervous or even dance as there was little room to do any of it. I didn't have to worry about expanding out of my own thoughts as it was too loud to do anything but feel the bass vibrating my chest. A little over two hours from Birmingham and here I was standing in a club full of gay women. Their bodies leaned into each other as they strained to hear one another. Their casual touches of hands on arms, shoulders, smalls of back were a sign of attraction or comfort between them. A sign they didn't try to hide or dampen. They were open to everything they wanted to share. And here I was, standing in the middle of them, grinning like a fool.

I caught Jazlyn looking at me with a huge grin on her face. "See. This is why I kept asking you to stay at my club instead of jetting before the ladies came."

"Yes, but no one in this crowd knows me."

She smiled in understanding but was suddenly distracted as she looked up over the crowd. "Come on. She's about to start." She pulled my arm to move us closer to the large deejay box. "We need to get closer."

The lights dimmed to black as the masses of voices around me quieted. The music of a single violin began to play. The crispness of the speakers made the music sound as if it had taken the stage before us. Its notes streamed together in a near torturous song of shyness seduced by pain and sadness. A soft, falling rain filled the wall-to-wall screen behind the deejay's booth. The violin's scream became stronger, confident, and powerful as the raindrops strengthened into a storm. A flash of lightning erupted across the wall as the lights above us turned on bright all at once and then faded again into darkness. The intense energy of the room was electric from the music and created a storm. My senses were intensified to everything around me. A synthesized beat joined the violin. Another flash of light and lightning.

"Can you feel it?" a sultry voice, deep and low was heard over the electronic music. "Come on, ladies. I said, can you feel it?" The voice held the last words to linger over the sound system before they faded into song.

The lights lit up one by one over our heads. A keyboard's notes teased into a slow crescendo.

"Say my name and you can dance." That voice. The voice I had grown to know as a friend sounded much different than the one I had heard over the phone.

The crowd erupted in a scream. "Mo!"

Boom.

The bass exploded with one final lightning strike. I could feel the beat pounding in my chest as laser lights danced around us. Strobe lights flashed until they centered on the female standing in the deejay box.

The crowd roared in unison as they sprung up and down on their feet. One beat. One crowd collectively dancing to that one beat.

She held her hand up in the air as she danced with them to the music. She adjusted the oversized earphones until only one covered her ear. "The night is ours!" She moved her hands along the large instrument panel until the beat faded into an even faster paced rhythmic collection of strings, keys, and beats. "Now dance your beautiful asses off."

Jazlyn's face was as energetic as the bodies moving around me. "Isn't this friggin' amazing?"

And it was. I was held captive by Mo. Her body flowed and became one with the music. She raised her hand in the air and swayed to the beat as the other hand deftly moved across the panel—pulling, pushing, or spinning the device to will her tunes. Her hands created their own rhythms as they moved from the panel board to adjust the headphones from her ears to her bare neck. I wondered if she had cut her hair as I couldn't imagine that much hair staying tucked in the newsboy cap she was wearing.

The beat she created enticed my body to sway with hers. I was under her spell as much as anyone surrounding me. She didn't release any of us as her music streamed unbroken. Her voice called to give our bodies freely to her, reassuring us she was in control tonight. Women shouted their submission to her as their bodies moved together. Heads bobbed to her cadences, they bounced on their toes to her tempos and swayed their hips to her pulses. I was no exception although my screams were silent. It was a seductive trance she had us in, undulating our bodies to her creations. Sweat gently rolling down the small of my back. She was as erotic as the music she was vibrating through the women…through me.

The strobe and dancing lights kept the faces darkened from me. Only rarely would one hit a face just right for me to make out their expression. Flash, beat. Flash, beat. The faces of women all strangers to me spun around in the light. Was I so oblivious to think I would see one type here? Had I not considered women of all shapes, sizes, races joined together for one night. Feminine. Androgynous. Casually dressed. Sporty dressed. All strangers to me. The lights flashed on and off to the beat.

Sam.

Off.

On again. Sam's face.

Sam?

Off. I looked at Jazlyn.

"What?" Jazlyn mouthed. "You okay?"

I nodded. *Couldn't be. I'm seeing things.*

The music lowered. "Ladies. You're killing me. You look too damn good for me to stand up here all night." She moved her hands across the panel one final time before she took her earphones off and walked down the stairs. The screams were the loudest I had heard yet.

Mo made her way through the crowd. Not an easy feat as she was stopped multiple times. Her clothes didn't do much to hide the body underneath. She wore a white tank top which fit snugly against her chest. Her lean, long arms were adorned with bracelets. Her hips were covered with blue jeans tied together by leather straps instead of a zipper and button.

Jazlyn swooped her up in a hug the moment she came to stand in front of us. "Girl, you're freakin' killing it tonight!"

Mo grinned ear to ear. "This crowd is too crazy. I don't think we could fit another woman in here tonight."

"You just make sure you bring this sort of crowd out when you come play at the Post."

"No doubt." Mo diverted her attention to me and smiled the one I did not see when she talked to the young girl at the taco stand. "Hey, you."

"Hey, yourself. You're amazing."

Mo leaned in to hug me. "I believe you owe me a dance." Her voice and the breath that followed it tickled the hairs of my neck.

I let my lips find her ear, hoping mine would maybe have the same effect on her. How could it in reality? Any one of these women could be hers. "I believe I told you I don't dance."

She leaned back, raised her eyebrows with surprise, and grinned. "But what if it was your favorite music?"

The music suddenly changed as another electric violin played, followed by the undeniable voice of Annie Lennox singing, "Sweet Dreams Are Made of This."

I could do nothing but smile in my defeat. Mo's face brightened in the flashing strobe light. She shook her hair free from the newsboy cap and handed it to Jazlyn. Thank the Lord she hadn't cut it.

"We'll be back." She grabbed my hand and led me out into the crowd of staring women. Their faces were visible to me in the flashes of the strobe lights. Thankfully, I still did not recognize a face, although many of them carried the same recognizable expression. I felt like the envy of each of them as they watched the woman who'd taken over their bodies guide me to center stage.

The music changed. The opening of "You Spin Me Round (Like a Record)" started to play. She had made a collection of popular eighties songs. She turned to me and walked backward as she sang. She swayed her hips.

"I'm serious. I don't know how to dance," I yelled over the music.

Mo smiled. "Look around, love. There isn't room to dance." She held her hands in the air. "Feel the music." She leaned into me and breathed into my ear. "Feel me."

I felt my heart skip. This time, the vibration came from Mo, not the bass. Her hands slowly skimmed down my arms and around my wrists as she placed my hands on her hips. She followed with her hands on my hips. I felt the pressure of her grip urging my movements to and fro with hers. She uttered not another word. Yet her eyes spoke volumes to me in her unreleased stare.

I immediately recognized the lyrics of "I Melt With You." It was one of my favorite songs from the eighties.

"Moving forward using all my breath," I sang along to the music.

I became unsteady in the sensation of her body morphing into my own. Her hips against mine ignited me. I wanted to stop the world and melt into this moment. I envisioned no one but us in the strobe-lit darkness. The grip of her hands soft yet determined as they held me tighter against her. I felt the heat of her palm against my skin as she slipped her hand under my shirt to lie against the small of my back. The strength of her hand pushed me into her thigh as her leg interweaved between mine. She smiled as she nestled my thigh tightly between her legs and used the strength in them to lower our hips rhythmically together.

So many of my favorite songs from the era filled my ears as the back of her fingers, warm and sensual, traced a pattern along the inside of my jean's waistband. A clip from "Don't You (Forget About Me)" started playing. I knew the feeling of her hands on my skin was one sensation I would not forget for a very long time. Her hands reached the front of my jeans where she gripped them tightly and pulled me all the more into her. Perspiration of desires not awakened for so long broke out in beads of sweat along the back of my neck. Her hand found the dampened curls there as it traced a pattern up my back.

Each pulsating beat tore me down from the inside. She was taking my breath away just as the lyrics of the song described. Her eyes held me in a locked trance as they drifted from my eyes to my lips and then back again. Her hair tickled my cheek as her body melted into me. My breath was as the song described—taken away. I wondered how she picked so many of my favorite songs. Dizziness filled my head within the fog of curtain smoke as her chest, heavy with her breaths, rose and fell against mine. The closer she brought our bodies together, the more I felt the pressure of her breasts against me. Excitement…intrigue… arousal. Each completed me in equal proportions to the very core of my body as it was held in the gravity of her arms. Breaths escaped and retreated in labored fashion as her hand found a new tempo along the skin of my stomach. My body was hers for all she wanted it to be in that dance. The last lyric played told me what I wanted to feel in this moment. Even if only for today, if only for this moment, couldn't I be unafraid?

Returning to Jazlyn, I was more aware of the faces in the crowd as they seemed to be watching me in the midst of Mo's return to the deejay booth. Jazlyn said little. No doubt she was remembering a conversation warning Mo to not mess with me. I know I was remembering it and was left to wonder if that dance would be termed beyond friendly.

One by one, I searched the faces around me. I watched to see if their dances mimicked the one I had experienced. Blondes. Brunettes. Gingers. Dancing.

Flash of light.

Sam.

Off.

On. *Sam?*

Off.

On again. Sam's body moved through the crowd.

Off.

On. Sam stood in front of me. I felt her hand grab and clasp around mine. My pulse raced as she tugged me through the crowd. The music trailed behind us until it was a deafened noise locked behind a closed metal door. She pulled me out of the club and into an alley. She maneuvered me through groups of mingling women and traffic until we were nearly a block away. We entered a park at the corner of Piedmont and Tenth Avenue. Sam didn't slow her steps until we were standing next to an empty park bench sitting by a small body of water. I felt my heartbeat pounding in my ears at the sight of Sam's face staring at me in the moonlight.

She was silent as she glared at me. I cursed the sweating of my palm held within hers as I felt her grip loosen to release it. I squeezed in an attempt to hold on tighter so she couldn't let go of my hand.

"No, don't let go," I begged her.

She bit the corner of her lip and I felt myself melt in the memory of all that was her. "What are you doing here?"

"Jazlyn invited me."

"I know the simplicity of what brought you here. I'm asking why you're here."

The sharpness of her tone caused me to recoil. "I don't know."

"Figured you'd say that." She briskly pulled her hand from mine and turned to walk away.

"No, goddammit, don't you walk away from me." I felt a wave of nausea course through me.

Why? Why had I said the profanity I never say? I felt the sickness in my mouth from the heated anger of it. Hadn't I blamed my faith as much as anything for the reason I was where I was now? Wasn't my scorn for the decision I had made somehow turned toward the religious teachings which had been shoved down my throat since I was old enough to sit in church with Charlie Grace.

Sam turned to me with anger in her eyes. "Tell me one good reason why I should stay?" The tone of her voice was equal with her expression.

"Because I die a little every single time you walk away from me. And honestly, I'm not real sure how much of me is still alive at this point."

"You looked pretty alive a few minutes ago."

"Sam, please. Please don't go. For some reason, you found me in that club tonight. For some reason, in the mass of all of those women, you saw me. Can't we at least just acknowledge that?"

She studied my face. "We can acknowledge that I would've never imagined you'd dance like that with a woman. You've gone from not knowing who you wanted to be to practically making out with her in front of everyone. And with her. After everything, you get with someone like her."

"I didn't get with anyone. I'm not with Mo. We're just friends."

"That dance was anything but friendly." She shifted her weight on her legs and looked away from me. "Whatever. What does it matter to me now anyway?"

"Don't be like that, Sam. We're just friends. Please, let's sit down and talk."

She brushed the overgrown shrubbery off the back of the bench and sat down. "I really don't think there's much to say."

"Can we try?" I sat beside her and took her hand. The fingernail moon was but a sliver deep in the darkened sky. Oh, how I yearned to get lost in the blueness of her eyes. I felt the warmth of her hand in mine as I stroked my thumb against the tip of her finger. I watched her as she looked down at our hands. The street noise was all but drowned out by the call of the insects in the night. Their song took me back to a night with our toes dangling in the bayou water.

I looked over her shoulder into the rolling hills of the small park. "The noises." I waved my hand. "Reminds me of being back home on the bayou with you."

She looked up and around the park. "Yeah, but they sound different." I saw her catch a glimpse of the charms hanging from my neck. I heard her swallow hard and wondered what she was thinking when she saw the combination of the cross and cicada looped together along the golden chain. I hope she knew I wore the chain daily but I doubt she let herself think of the way I touched them constantly when I thought of her or Meems.

"The cicadas don't sound the same here," she said flatly.

"I think those are katydids."

"Katy dids?"

"There are a thousand different species of them. They say they're named because they sound as if they're saying 'Katy-did.'" I was nervously rambling about a silly insect fact. "Meems would tell me..." I looked out into the water. I'm not sure if it was a reflex or intentional but Sam's grip tightened on my hand. "One of the folklore stories is that there was a woman named Katy who was madly in love with this man. But he left her to marry another." Her grip loosened. "They were found dead in their honeymoon bed the morning after they'd married. It was said they were poisoned but no one saw the crime. Well, no person saw the crime. They say the bugs saw what happened as they had been watching from the window. On hot summer nights, it's said they shout from the trees to tell us who committed the crime. 'Katy-did, Katy-did.'"

Sam stopped a smile that tried to curl the corners of her lips. "I should've known you'd have a story about them."

I shrugged. "Guess I'm weird like that."

"Not weird. Different." She faced the park. "So really, what are you doing here?" she said with a softer tone than the one she had used earlier when she asked.

"Jazlyn invited me. Violet had to take call this weekend so she asked me to come with her."

I'd hoped she would look at me but instead she turned her head away even more. "And how'd you two become friends?"

"I met her when I went to the Pineapple Post."

She snapped her head back and stared at me. "Why were you there? Why did you even go there?"

"I overheard Kylie talking about it."

"Oh? And what? You hear the Queen Lesbian Conqueror talking about a lesbian bar and you just have to go. Please tell me you didn't get with her after I left."

"Why do you say that? Why do you keep assuming I've been with another woman?"

"I do believe lesbian bars are filled with lesbians. Why else go unless you're looking for one?"

"I wasn't looking for another woman when I went." I looked down at the bench. "I was looking for myself."

"It didn't look that way to me. Looked like you were trying to sew some wild oats before the big wedding day. You were nearly making out with Mo on the dance floor. Geez, Rayne, why don't you try to have some decorum and keep your little lesbian trysts discrete."

Bitterness. That's what her tone held for me.

I swallowed the lump in my throat and stared out into the tiny moon's reflection. The glow of the skinny moon was barely enough to cause a sparkle across the small pond. I couldn't speak for the fear of the tears toppling over so I held my words for more than I had anticipated. I felt her hand loosen to release mine. I didn't fight it this time.

"It's not like that," I finally said.

We sat with the silence building between us. I turned to her and bent my knee to lay it on the bench. "Sam, I don't know what all of this means. Why I'm here. I see these women being together so openly and yeah, it makes me know there is something beyond what I've always been taught it would be like. I understand why Jazlyn wanted me to come but it doesn't change what I feel."

I watched her profile as she continued to stare out at anything but me. She looked thinner than I remember. The shirt she wore was baggy over her shoulders and chest. A large brown belt adorned her blue jeans and I struggled to remember seeing her in a belt in the days we had spent together. She tried to brush a strand of hair away from her eyelashes but the shortened length didn't stay tucked behind her ear. I wondered how long she'd had her highlighted blonde hair cut this short as it rested just above her shoulders. I wanted to run my hand along the side of her head and let the defined layers flow between my fingers.

"It doesn't change that it's still only you."

She looked at me surprised. Her mouth was slightly open with an arch of her lips.

"Among all of these women, it's still only you." I picked her hand up and rubbed the back of it across my face. The taste of her skin as my lips parted against her knuckle sent a wave of butterflies through me.

Butterflies.

I searched her eyes. Her eyebrows softened as I traced my thumb across her jawline. The layers did fall softly between my fingers as I ran them along the back of her neck to pull her lips closer to me. I closed my eyes to the thumping of my heart with her breath upon my lips.

Eucalyptus mint. I smiled to its scent and closed my eyes to fall into her kiss. Instead of her lips, I felt skin and opened my eyes. She held her finger against them but left her forehead to rest against mine.

"I can't," she whispered.

"Why?" I kissed her fingertip until she dropped it from my lips.

She inhaled deeply. "I barely survived our last kiss, Stormy. I dare not tempt fate and try again."

"I'm so in love with you that I can't breathe when you're near me." I felt the pleading in my words. I wanted badly to feel her kiss again.

She moved on the bench and grabbed the hand I had resting across the back of the wood. "And this?" She tapped the ring on my left hand.

Damnit all to the hell. That fucking ring. Why in the hell did I wear that fucking ring tonight?

"Aren't you engaged to Grant?"

"Sam…don't. Don't bring that up right now."

"Why not, Rayne?"

"Because." I looked up at the moon. "Because I know I'm not marrying him."

"Does he know that?"

I placed my hands across her face and urged her to look into my eyes. To read them as I knew she could. "I'm telling you I love you. Please don't do this. I need time. We need time. Time to get it all worked out. It's not easy for me and I know it's not easy for you."

"But you said yes. You didn't have to say yes. I was there. I was in that room when he proposed. You had me but you let me go and you said yes."

I shook my head vigorously. "No, no. That's not true and you know it. I didn't let you go that night. You left. There's a big difference. I know what I asked that night wasn't right. I know my mistakes but I needed you to stay and help me work it all out. Be with me and support me while I did. But you said you couldn't. It broke every single part of me when you left. Not a moment goes by that I don't think about you." Reflexively, I reached up and rubbed the cicada charm. "I didn't say yes. I didn't say anything. He and Charlie Grace started planning things as if I had. I was just too broken and numb to argue."

"Rayne, you wanted me to fit into your perfect picture. You wanted me to guarantee you what it would be like so you could plan it out just like you plan everything in your life out. But life's plan isn't a guarantee. It's ever changing and you have to be ready to make those changes. I couldn't and wouldn't be that for you. Don't you get it?"

"No, not really. We could've been together while I made those changes."

"But I needed you to make the changes on your own. I needed you to realize who you were without it being dependent on me."

I dropped my hands in my lap. "So, I'm to blame for losing us because I wasn't ready or because I didn't know who I was. I don't think that's fair. You showed me a life I'd never imagined. Loving you changed everything I had ever seen my future to be and you left because I didn't accept all of those changes immediately. As if something like that wouldn't take time to adjust to."

"No, it's not fair and it's not entirely you. I let you take the blame for it. I'm sorry for that." For the first time, she reached for my hand. "Stormy, you changed me too. You changed everything I saw for my future too. I saw you. I saw us. I wanted us so bad. For as hard as it was for you, it was equally hard for me. I didn't know who that person was or how to even be someone's girlfriend. I ran."

"But you're here now. It's not too late. We can have another chance. We can work it all out together."

"I can't, Stormy. I'm not back." She stuttered on her words. "And…I've got someone I need to get back to."

"Oh." I let go of her hand and tucked mine between my thighs. "I see."

"No, you don't." She pulled her knee up against her chest. "Because I still don't fully see myself. I'm still trying to figure out me. In much the same way as you've been trying to find you, I've been trying to find myself. I didn't know what I truly wanted until you showed me." She pulled at the frayed strands of the hole in her jeans. "I didn't tell you why I was here. My parents are getting a divorce. Mother finally asked the old bastard for a divorce. I'm here for her. See, Rayne, he had it all planned out too. His whole life, her, me. We were all according to his plan. And then one day we weren't. I don't want to be my mother. She stayed in his plan until the day she couldn't breathe. I want my own plan. I want to know my own path. You showed me how much more of life I wanted. I fell so hard for you that I forgot the reality of the situation. I wanted the fairy tale."

She faced me and wiped a tear from my cheek that I hadn't realized had fallen.

"Falling in love with you made me realize I wanted more than sex, more than one-night stands. I want it all. I want love and sacrifice and commitment. I want the woman who loves me to fight against all consequences of what it means to do so. Maybe if you hadn't changed that in me then I could be what you're asking of me. But I can't. I can't wait on the sidelines or hide in the closet loving you in secret while you pretend we're only friends. Even if it isn't about just Grant. You're not ready to live in anything but secret. I'm sorry. I want the fairy tale. But the truth is, the fairy tale is mine to make. To me, it's all about timing. We weren't ready for one another. We still aren't." She stood, ran her fingertips underneath her eyes, and brushed the bench dust from her jeans. "But that doesn't mean I don't love you. I will *always* love you."

"So, this is goodbye again?" I could hardly get the words out as I was desperately holding back a volcano of sobs.

"I hope not." She turned and walked away. The silhouette of her in the darkness all but disappeared until I saw it change direction. She stopped walking as she passed under a sidewalk lamp. She leaned her back against the pole and stood still for several moments. I thought I saw her head turn back in my direction but I wasn't sure. I sat on the bench, hoping she would start walking back for me. I ached for her words to not be truth and for her to run back to me filled with regret for saying them. She didn't. I never dreamed it possible to hurt as much as I did the night she left me after Grant's proposal.

No. This time, I wouldn't sit waiting for her to come back to me. This time, I would go to her. I stood from the bench and began sprinting toward her. For a moment, I believed she was waiting for me at the light. But then she raised her hand in the air for me to stop, pushed her back off the post and hurried out of the park. She didn't look back again.

Chapter 12

"Mo, you were slamming tonight. I mean slamming." A brown-headed girl who looked to be all of twenty-one stumbled over to our table.

A friend of hers followed closely behind and pulled at her arm as she tried to rein her back to their table. The drunken girl braced herself by grabbing the edge of our tabletop.

"I danced my fucking ass off," she said far too loudly and with a bit too much slur to be appropriate in the IHOP diner.

Mo's eyes widened before she placed her hand on top of the girl's. "Thanks. Glad you had a good time." She waved to the waitress as she walked by a table closest to us. "Will you bring them a pot of strong coffee and put it on my tab?"

"Yes, ma'am. I sure will."

"I'm so sorry," the soberer of the two said as she reached the table. "It slipped up on her tonight." She wrapped her arms around the other girl and motioned her to come back with her to their table.

"What? Huh? Where we going?" she slurred as she tumbled into the girl's arms.

"No worries." Mo smiled.

"Thanks for the coffee," she said as she pulled her friend back.

"Anytime. Get her home safely."

"Will do."

Mo removed the newsboy cap, tossed it into the seat next to her, and shook her hair out with her fingers. The long locks tumbled over her shoulders.

"New addition?" I pointed to the streak of blue-dyed hair that was about two inches wide and ran from the root of her scalp down to the tip of her hair.

I hadn't noticed it before when we were dancing. Had I really noticed anything other than her piercing stare as her body molded into mine? It was hard to think about anything, especially our dancing, with the sadness of watching Sam walk away weighing so heavy in my thoughts.

The bass clef tattoo disappeared into her tresses as she ran her fingers through the blue-colored streak. "Yeah, pretty new." She leaned over the white Formica table. "Don't change the subject."

I sat back surprised. I knew my attention was half-assed but I didn't realize I had changed any subject or even that there was a subject to change. "I didn't think we had a subject."

"Your eyes say differently."

What did my eyes tell her? I knew the thoughts behind them. I felt the sting of tears I'd been forcing back ever since my time with Sam in the park. The dance club had kept them shadowed but here under the bright fluorescent lighting, I suppose they were visible for all to see… particularly the woman sitting across from me.

I shifted in my seat until I could see over Mo's shoulder to Jazlyn who was standing outside talking to Violet. She had called right before we sat at our table.

"Is it because we danced or is there something else?"

Mo held concern and worry on her face as she looked at me. "It's not because of the dance."

Relief washed over her expression. "You had me worried. Thought I'd stepped out of line and made you uncomfortable."

"No, it wasn't you."

"I don't care about that, you know?"

I looked up to see her eyes on the ring finger of my left hand. I felt the restaurant around me fade to black as I focused only on the sparkle of the diamond against the harsh lighting. I clinched my hand into a fist.

This damn ring.

Instead of her next words to me, I heard only the sounds of ceramic cups as they struck against ceramic saucers, the scrape of cheap metal forks across plates, and voices carried in conversations. Maybe it was easier for me to focus on the noise than to hear clearly the words spoken mere inches from me.

"I'm sorry. What did you say?" I couldn't look at her. I couldn't look at anything but the prism of reflected light on my finger.

"I said, I don't care about that ring on your finger. I wonder if you study it this way when I'm not around. But like I said before, that piece of jewelry doesn't define you to me. So why don't we let it be what it is when you're around me?"

"I don't know if I can right now."

"Why?"

"I'm engaged. I said yes to a man who asked me to marry him." The plates, the cups, the chatter were all so loud. I felt the chaos in my head and fought the urge to escape. Fought the need to run out into the night and far away from the noise of everything in my life. Far away from Sam's words in my head when she told me she needed me to choose her. Not only choose her, but also be open about that choice. Had she really told me I had to do it all at once? Accept who I am? Accept who we are and in a moment's breath tell the whole world about it? If I had heard it right, it didn't seem like she was giving me much of a chance to be the woman she needed.

Mo reached across the table and buried her hand underneath mine. "And that means what?" she asked. "Does it tell me who you are? Does it tell me the woman inside of you?"

I stared at the bass clef at her wrist. The noises around me began to still and slightly diminish.

"Rayne?"

I was startled at the clarity of which she said my name. She didn't have a nickname for me like Sam did. I'd missed being called Stormy. I'd missed the way it made me feel when Sam used it. But Mo called me by my given name and it elicited similar feelings the nickname had once given me. I looked up into her eyes.

Her eyes were searching mine like no time I had ever seen before. She squeezed my hand gently. "If it doesn't define who you are or the woman you have become, then it doesn't matter to me. I couldn't care less about that piece of jewelry on your finger. All of that is for you to figure out on your own. Now…" She paused. I hadn't realized my eyes had drifted from her until she stopped talking. "The two charms on your necklace may be a whole different story." Nor had I realized I'd grasped the charms between my fingers. "Something tells me those," she pointed to the necklace, "little doodads may very well define the woman sitting across from me. The woman I want to get to know better."

I felt my hand flinch and try to recoil from hers. She held it still with a stronger grasp.

"Damn, did my girl ever have a bad night of call. It's three a.m. and she's just now crawling into bed." Jazlyn stopped and looked at us.

Mo released my hand and slid over for Jazlyn to sit down. "That sucks, dude. Was she beat?"

Jazlyn gave Mo a sideways glare. "That's an understatement." She gazed at me. "Am I interrupting something?"

"No, not at all." I motioned the waitress over to our table and hoped she would be brisk enough to change the conversation.

A STEADY FALL of rain fell on the top of Jazlyn's Range Rover as she drove us back to Birmingham. My lids became heavy as I watched her hands change positions around the steering wheel. Her long, slender fingers wrapped easily around the wide wheel. They changed positions multiple times as we traveled with nothing more than the sounds of raindrop splatters and light acoustic music from the radio. I felt entranced as I watched both her and the blurring white lines as we sped along the interstate.

"Do you want to talk?"

Her voice sprang the fatigue from my eyes. "Huh?"

"I asked if you wanted to talk but maybe what I should've said was *can* we talk?"

"Sure. We can talk. What do you want to talk about?"

"How about you and Mo?"

I shifted nervously in my seat. "Okay."

"You're a grown woman. Both of you are. And it's probably none of my business but you're both my friends so I think I should tell you some things about Mo." She ran her hands over the steering wheel before adjusting the volume control with her thumb. "I may be way out of line here. It's just you two seemed...I don't know...close. Like that dance and then walking up on you in the restaurant. She was holding your hand." She ran her hand through her hair.

"It's okay. You can tell me what's on your mind." I hated seeing her nervous to talk to me about anything. I didn't want that in our friendship. "You're my best friend, Jaz. I don't know what I would do without you. You can talk to me about anything...especially if it's on your mind this much."

She gave me an appreciative smile. "Thanks. I value our friendship more than you know and I don't want to see you hurt anymore. Mo is like my sister. I love her dearly. She's a wonderful person and a true friend. Not once did we ever have an attraction between us. We were friends straight away without that ever interfering." She adjusted the defrost on the dashboard as the temperature change from the rain had given the windshield a nice opaque covering. "I wanted you to find what I had found in her so many years ago, but after watching you two tonight, I'm afraid that isn't going to be possible. You both have the attraction part to deal with." She peeked at me. "Or am I wrong and it's just her?"

That last part caught me off guard. "Why do you ask that?"

"Well, you ran off after you two danced. I figure it made you uncomfortable so you jetted."

"No, that wasn't it."

"Then what was it?"

I rubbed at my nose. The faint smell of old cardboard filled the interior of Jazlyn's SUV. I suppose she would have to use it to cart boxes needed for her club. I wasn't sure if the smell was the cause or if the tears that lurked in the shadows of my mind brought the tickle to the tip of my nose. When would I ever not feel this with the thought of Sam? Would I ever not feel it?

"Sam." I sighed deeply. "Sam was there."

"What? She was there?" Her voice was raised. "I didn't see her."

"Neither did I until she grabbed me and took me outside."

Jazlyn glanced at me as if encouraging me to go on.

"We walked over to a park and talked." Nope, it was the impending tears as they now freely flowed down my cheeks. Damnit all to hell. When would I stop doing this? I angrily wiped them from my face.

"I take it things didn't go so well."

"Not the way I wanted. No." The trees along the road were nearly hidden behind a sheet of rain. "Gawd, I love her so much."

"But?"

I clenched my fist tightly until I could feel the ring cutting into my skin. "It's not enough. I hurt her. She doesn't want any part of me."

"I don't believe that."

"You weren't there. You didn't see the way she looked at me. It was like she hated me."

"She doesn't hate you, Rayne. The woman I know could never hate you. Was she hurt and heartbroken? Yes. But hate? No." She touched my hand as it rested on my thigh. "But I'm thinking that hurt is a two-way street. Hmmmm? I've not been around you a day that your eyes haven't shown the same kind of pain hers did."

I wiped more tears from my cheeks.

"So, where did you leave it?"

I felt the words stick in my throat unable to pass. Unable to speak. I gripped my jeans with my free hand and squeezed hard. "It's over. Done. She's not a part of my life anymore. Not a consideration when I think of the future. Before, I guess I hoped she would be. Hoped we would find a way to be together. She would come back and we would tackle all of it together. But looks like anything I do from here, I do alone."

She held my hand tighter. "No, not alone. Never alone." She pushed the blinker on her steering column up and slowed her speed. "I need gas and this one is covered. I'm not in the mood to become a drowned rat." Her laughter eased the tension.

"I can tell Mo's attracted to you," she said as she climbed back into the SUV. "Where she'll take that I have no idea. I asked her to leave you be."

"Yes, I heard."

"You did?"

"The night at the beach. I overheard you two talking."

She pulled her knee up into the seat as she turned to face me straight on. "It was nothing against either of you. Nothing at all. I think both of you are incredible women. It's just…" She tapped her finger on the gear shift that sat between us. "Mo is a wonderful woman and friend. As long as you care for her for who she is and not what you want her to be, it will be fine. She lives life by her own rules. I may talk to her for a month solid and then bam, she's gone. It may be a month or two before I hear from her again. With women she is interested in, I've seen her show them attention to where they feel like they are on a pedestal. And well, they are. Her feelings for them are real in that moment. But it's just in that moment. Once the moment is gone, so is she. She won't want to hurt you but if at any moment you start to let yourself believe it is more, then you will be. I didn't want her messing with you because it will be hard to keep yourself in check with a mending heart when someone is making you feel like you're her every desire."

"I get it."

She straightened in her seat, turned the ignition on, but then turned back to me. "She's not girlfriend material, Rayne. God knows

I love her. I do. But she isn't girlfriend material. She changes women more than I change my underwear." She tried to force a laugh. "I don't see her changing. She's happy with who she is. Free to live. Free to love. I doubt she'll ever live in one place long enough to set down roots." She looked out the windshield and shifted the SUV into drive. "I don't want to see you get hurt again."

Her concern for me with her true friendship made me smile. She was protecting me. There it was. The rainbow of happiness shining through the grayest of rain clouds. I breathed in the scent of old cardboard. For the first time, a scent of sand, surf, and sunscreen lingered behind it. How had I missed her air freshener until now?

"Thanks." I patted her thigh. "Thanks for being my friend. No worries. It was only a dance."

The words brought a swift reminder of the sensation a blue jean-clad thigh pressed between mine had caused.

Chapter 13

"**S**ON OF A fucking bitch!" Grant screamed from the bathroom. "What the hell is wrong with you?" I burst through the door, agitated with his vulgarity.

To be honest, I had been struggling to keep from being agitated with everything about him. I'd hardly slept a wink the night before. The mere sound of his breaths as he slept kept me from finding my own sleep. It wasn't his fault and I knew he didn't understand why I had been so short-tempered with him. I was trying to be more patient and attentive to him but I was failing miserably. The timing of his acceptance to go to New York couldn't have been better. I needed to be alone.

I realized I was standing in rising water as it filled the bathroom floor and spilled out into the hallway.

"Shit. Shit. Shit." He frantically fought to reach the water shut off valve behind the commode. The picture of his naked butt as he bent over was not the sight I wanted to see before my first cup of coffee.

"I don't have time for this shit this morning." He stood up to face me.

I believe I may have winced as I held a towel out in front of me. "What happened?"

"Do I look like a plumber to you?"

"No, actually right now you look like an asshole to me."

He snatched the towel from my hand and wrapped it around his waist. "Nice, Rayne. Very nice." He sloshed pass me. "My plane leaves in three hours. I'm going to my place to get dressed."

"Are you serious? You're leaving me like this?"

He turned in the hallway. "What do you expect me to do?"

"Hey, I don't know. Here's a novel thought. Why don't you act like a boyfriend and stay to help me get my plumbing taken care of?"

"Maybe if you acted like a girlfriend sometime, I would feel more impelled to act like a boyfriend." He walked into the bedroom but stepped back to peer around the doorjamb. "Or, hey, better yet since were fucking engaged, maybe you could act like a fiancé sometime. Wouldn't that be a grand idea?" He shed his towel and jerked his clothes on over his body.

"What the hell does that mean?"

"I'm leaving today for three or maybe even four months. I spend my last night with you thinking…I don't know, that we may act like a couple about to be separated for three months. You're so freakin' frigid all of the time that even last night I couldn't get a little."

"Get a little? Did you seriously just say that to me?"

He stepped quickly to stand in front of me. "I sure as hell did." His breath was hot against my face. The smell of toothpaste followed. "I can't even remember the last time we've had sex. You act repulsed when I touch you but I thought last night, surely last night, we could be together. I shouldn't have to jerk off as much as I do when I have a fiancé."

"Well, what do you know, folks. Dr. Dick number two is in the house." I stormed down the hallway to the kitchen and hoped he would leave instead of following me. A sharp pain shot through my jaw as I gritted my teeth. "Ass!" I screamed over my shoulder.

A fully dressed Grant followed me into the kitchen by the time I found my landlord's number. His face was solemn. "Rayne, I don't want to leave like this. I don't want to fight." He sighed deeply as he rubbed his hands up and down his face. "I just don't get what has happened to us. I don't. You act like you can hardly stand to be with me in the same room sometimes. What has happened to us? Please tell me what I've done. What I need to do."

I leaned against the kitchen counter but wrestled with any words to say to him. He looked defeated and lost. I had done this to him. I had brought him here.

He kept his ground and didn't step closer to me. "I'm leaving in a few hours and we're fighting. This isn't us, Rayne. This isn't who we are." He scratched at the whiskers on his chin. "I don't know what to do anymore. Should I not have signed up for this rotation? Is that it?"

"No, it's not your rotation. It's not."

He held his head down. "Then what is it? I just don't know what has happened to us. I know I get distracted with school. I'm sorry I got so distracted with this New York thing. I'll stay if you want me to. I won't go." He closed the distance. His sad eyes drew my attention to them. Above the left eye, I saw the small separation in his eyebrow. I pictured a young Grant running to his mom after he fell from his swing and landed on a fallen branch. My heart took him in as it had a way of doing. When I let go of the confusion which easily manifested into anger, I was reminded of the little boy I had grown up knowing. I was reminded of my friend.

He put his hands on my hip. "We're so distant. It's like I don't know you anymore."

"Grant, we're both changing. Have you ever wondered if we were growing into different people?"

"No, not different. I'm not different. I want to get all of this behind us." He wrapped his arms around me and pulled me against him. "Get it behind us and start our life together. Start our family."

An image of Tyler's quivering lip flashed across my thoughts. Pregnant. Trapped. Unhappy.

He nuzzled his face against my neck. The whiskers scratched my skin. "I love you so much, Rayne." His breath was warm. His lips dry and rough as he kissed me. "I'm so sorry I said those ugly things." His kiss on my lips was forced. The coarse hairs pricked like small needles on them as he deepened his search for connection.

A wave rolled over my stomach. Not a butterfly.

His kiss scrounged around and over my lips for any shred of acceptance or encouragement. He left them to let his mouth explore my neck and pulled me closer against his chest. I felt his excitement in our togetherness grow against me.

Far from a butterfly.

His fingertips dug into the skin on the outside of my thighs as his hands raised my robe with their travels. I felt the strength of his hips push me against the counter when his pelvis responded to the urges his body was showing me he felt. The pressure gave me nothing of the feelings the last time another's body was pressed against me. Another roll over my stomach.

I can't do this.

Another thrust of him against me. The tie of my robe was loosened and tickled the side of my thigh. The denim of his jeans felt coarse against the thinness of my satin underwear.

No. I can't do this.

The sound of his zipper was like a siren in my head.

No! Stop.

I stilled his hand as he tried to pull at the satin waistband. His eyes caught with mine. They held sadness but no longer the traces of anger I had seen a few moments ago.

"I get it." He gave me a small smirk as he refastened his pants. He kissed the tip of my nose. "When I return, we'll do this right." His smile was strained. "Something to look forward to. I do love you, Rayne." He kissed the back of my hand and let his whiskers rub across the skin of my knuckle. "I'll miss you."

"You're kidding me?"

"I wish I were. I have a pond in my bathroom and hallway now." I held the cell phone against my cheek and studied the mess in front of me. "The landlord says he'll have someone out in a few minutes. I'm packing an overnight bag now to go stay at Grant's."

"Ah. And is that where you want to stay?" Jazlyn's voice was as if she knew my answer already. From the time I had met her, she seemed to know my wishes sometimes quicker than I myself did.

"No, not particularly."

"So, come stay here."

"I couldn't do that. I'm in your hair more than I need to be as it is. This may take all weekend to repair. You don't want me staying on your couch the entire weekend."

"Nope. I wouldn't dream of you staying on the couch that long. You can have the bed."

"Ummmm....what?"

Jazlyn's laugh was throaty. "We're going out of town, crazy girl. We're jetting as soon as Vi comes in from the hospital. You can stay here. It's no problem. Totally up to you though."

I walked into the living room and looked around the room. A change of scenery from my everyday life would very nearly be like a vacation to me. One that couldn't be found if I went from this place to Grant's. The memories would only follow me there. "Are you sure you don't mind?" I asked as I sat on the arm of the couch.

"Not one bit, honey. I'd be happy if you stayed here."

"Then I will. I can't thank you enough. It would be great to have a different atmosphere for a while."

"Excellent. I'll have the place ready for you."

I felt the sting of Grant's whiskers on my lips and noticed I had reached up to rub at my bottom one. I felt the wave of nausea run across my stomach as I remembered his hips pressed against mine. "Hey, Jazlyn?"

"Yeah?" Her voice was dampened against the sound of glass bottles clinking against one another.

"You sound busy. Are you?"

"Not at all. I'm just picking you out a good bottle of wine. What's up?"

"Gawd, sometimes I feel like all I do is ask you a thousand questions. I'm afraid you're going to become sick of me soon."

"Not going to happen. If you haven't figured it out yet, I kind of like ya'. Besides, my brain needs a good picking every now and then."

I slid off the arm of the couch onto the sofa cushion. I never found it easy to talk to anyone about sex and this conversation would be no exception. Maybe talking over the phone would be easier than sitting across from her at the bar. "It's kinda hard to talk about actually."

"Ooooh, this one sounds juicy. Let me grab a seat." I heard chair legs slide across the floor and figured she was sitting at the dining table.

"Did you...?" I stuttered for my words. "I mean what was it like with Zach? Like in a sexual way." I felt my teeth biting into my bottom lip. "Did you like it?"

She was silent and I began to wonder if my question was too personal.

"I'm sorry. If that's too personal, you don't have to answer. We can forget I said anything at all." I pulled the sofa pillow across my chest and held it tightly against me. I was immediately regretful I had asked the question.

"No. It's not that. You can ask me anything." She took in a deep breath. "It's just that this has to be between us. If I speak openly, it can't be repeated. Would you be okay with that?"

"Of course, I would."

"Whoa, okay. I've not thought about this in so long but here goes. Yeah, I did enjoy sex with Zach. I actually enjoyed it a lot."

"You did?" I asked so quickly that my filter didn't have time to catch up with me.

She laughed one of her belly laughs. "Yes. I did. You sound surprised."

"Well, yeah...I mean..." I thought about what I wanted to say next but nothing really came. "Yeah. I'm surprised."

"So, I take it you don't?"

"Like sex with Grant?" I felt the heaviness in my chest. "No, I don't. I never have. Not once."

"That has to be tough. Are you two very active in that way?"

"No, I suppose not. He wants us to be more but we aren't. Thankfully, he doesn't push it too much. School keeps us both pretty drained. Fatigue is a good excuse to go right to sleep."

"And this subject comes up today because of why?"

I pinched the bridge of my nose as I tried to remove the vision of him pressed up against me. "Well, I've been wanting to talk to you about it for a while now but he wanted to before he left and I just couldn't. The last time we did, I didn't think I'd ever stop crying. I just couldn't go through that again today."

"How will you the rest of your life?"

"I don't know."

"Mmmmmm," she moaned into the phone. "Then maybe that is telling you something, my friend."

I shook my head yes but didn't verbalize the sentiment.

"Sometimes the answers are there for us all along. It's the acceptance of the answers that holds us back."

"If you enjoyed being with Zach in that way, then why Violet?"

She chuckled. I had a way of making her do that. "It's not about sex. It never was with either one of them. It's the connection. I had an immediate connection with Vi. From the moment I met her, I knew she was the one and my life would never be the same."

Sam's face flashed into my head.

"You think a lot like Vi. It's part of the reason she and I can't talk about it. She knows I loved Zach. She knows I enjoyed our intimacy. It's hard for her because I think in the back of her mind she fears she doesn't truly understand why I made the choices I made. Somehow, she holds onto the fear that I will one day want to go back to the straight life since I had found a place in that world before I knew her."

"It's a reasonable fear, isn't it?"

"Not to me it's not. I love her. There's no going back to anything or anyone since her. She's it for me. I keep quiet about the things I know bother her most. Why spark her fears if I don't have to? Now I have a question for you."

"Shoot."

"Do you think the reason you felt the things you felt for Sam was because you didn't enjoy sex with Grant? Is it as simple as that?"

I tossed the pillow over toward the other end of the couch. "No, it wasn't that at all. It was her. It was the way she looked at me. It was the way she smelled. The way her hand felt in mine." I sighed. "It was everything about her. It was like she changed every single thing I knew to be true in the world when she touched me and kissed me. I'd never felt anything like it before and I'm terrified I'll never feel anything like it again."

"I get it. You feel like you had that one shot and now it's gone."

"Yes."

"Honey, I know you don't see it now, but you'll feel it again. It was Sam who opened up your world. Maybe that was her only purpose to be in your life. Maybe not. No one knows the future. It's what you do with your world now that truly matters."

Chapter 14

HE DAMNED RING slid up and down my finger as I struggled with the door lock at Jazlyn and Violet's loft. Lately, the only thing keeping it on my finger was the knuckle that hadn't seemed to decrease in size like the rest of me. I caught the scent of Jazlyn's SUV as I opened the door. I couldn't help smiling to myself. She sure loved her escapes to the beach. Thankfully, she and Violet had needed one this weekend. Jazlyn was right; I really didn't want to stay at Grant's apartment. So much so, I had even contemplated staying in an empty sleep room at the hospital while the repairs were done. Yet, that too brought back memories. It seemed there were few places I could go in Birmingham that weren't filled with memories of choices made.

The unexpected ruptured pipe was less than desired but walking into their apartment felt pretty darn good. Their place gave me the opportunity to be in a different environment. I didn't sit at a table that took me back to Memaw's cabin. I didn't fix my meals standing at a countertop with memories of Grant pressed against me. I didn't sit in a living room, envisioning Sam sitting in the chair across from me. I didn't sleep in a bed with a flood of memories of Sam's lips upon mine. No one but the two women who had become my friends followed me into this apartment. I dare say, not even Rayne followed me there.

With Grant away, I could find myself again or possibly even a new Rayne in my solitude. I was beginning to like the Rayne I was when I was around Jazlyn. In fact, I liked her more and more each day. And now I stood in a gorgeous downtown loft with nothing of the old Rayne carried as baggage with me. It was as if I was suddenly on an overseas vacation. I didn't even have call this weekend.

A piece of paper lying on the table next to a bottle of wine rustled as the air conditioning kicked on. It was a note from Jazlyn.

The place is yours. Make yourself at home. I put the number to the Thai restaurant below. EAT. You're wasting away on hospital food. Love Jazlyn.

Written below, close to the edge of the paper, the note continued.

By the way, you're getting a solid ass whooping if I ever hear of you needing anything at all and you not calling me right away! Just saying.

She had drawn a smiley face at the end.

Thai actually sounded pretty darn good. I placed my order, popped the cork on the bottle, and sat down to enjoy a rather large glass of wine. The crisp liquid continued to have a slight chill to it as I swirled the sip around in my mouth. Jazlyn must have waited until the last minute to set it out for me. I stretched my legs out in front of me and began to relax into the first night of my vacation.

"Look at me. I'm out of scrubs, kicked back, drinking a glass of wine with absolutely nothing to do." I rubbed my hand across my blue jeans and smiled.

The sound of a key in the lock jarred my head off the back of the couch. I ran to the door and watched as the key fought to unlock the door. *Were they back? Had something happened at the beach?* I stepped back quickly as the door opened all of a sudden.

"Mo?"

She seemed as startled as me. "Rayne? What are you doing here?" She stepped back away from the door.

I looked down at the duffle bag at her feet. "Looks like the same thing you are." I motioned to my bag in the middle of the floor.

A smile crept across her face. "This could get interesting." She picked up her bag and stepped fully inside the door. "I knew Jazlyn and Violet were out of town so I thought I could crash here."

"I had a plumbing problem at my apartment. They're having to replace a bunch of sheetrock stuff. Jazlyn said I could stay here instead of in a sleep room at the hospital. But I can go stay there so you can have the place." I looked down at her bag again. "If you want?"

"Why would I want that? Your company is icing. Unless you're uncomfortable being here alone with me?" She peered at me from under her raised eyebrows. "You know, without our tall chaperone around?"

"Ummm...no...no, not at all." I think I forced a believable smile.

"Excellent." Her smile expanded even more. "Now that we have that out of the way." She stretched her hand out to touch the hair along the side of my face. "Your hair looks great."

I ran my fingers through the recently cropped, thinned, straightened hair which now rested an inch below my ears. "Do you really like it? I'm still not sure what I think of it. I've not had it this short in a really long time."

"Well...I'm sure."

"And the color? It's not...I don't know...too much?" I had gotten it highlighted a caramel color throughout my hair but had my bangs and a few stray strands dyed a blondish color. It was definitely a new style for me. I didn't even have a picture as an example of what I wanted. I simply sat down in the chair of an unknown hairdresser and said that I wanted something different. The young man's face nearly burst with excitement as he described what he wanted to do with my cut and color. I didn't have the heart to chicken out. After he was done, he spun me around to look in the mirror. I didn't recognize the woman sitting in the chair. It was then I truly realized how different I was becoming. The physical me was beginning to catch up to the changes growing inside of me. My cheekbones had always been high and defined but the weight loss and this new hairdo accentuated them even more.

"Oh, I'm not saying it's not too much." She ran her fingers through the bangs. "It's too much alright." She let them slowly trace down the sides and around my neck. "But in a very good way." She winked.

"You're the first to see it."

I worried I had gotten carried away with the new Rayne when I left the beauty shop. Yet all of those worries fell to my feet with the reaction I was witnessing from Mo.

"I'm telling you, it's freakin' hot."

I felt the blush color my cheeks.

"Aw, and you blush so adorably."

The heat in my cheeks intensified a hundred-fold. "You know most people don't call it out when they make someone blush. It makes it a thousand times worse." I felt the coolness of my palms as I patted my cheeks to reduce the sting.

"At what point did you ever start to confuse me with most people?" She laughed and stepped to the side of me to walk further into the apartment.

"I'm beginning to see my error."

"Beginning?" She reached under the counter to pull out a wine glass. "Are you sharing?"

"Oh, sorry. Yes, please have some. Jazlyn left it out."

Mo poured herself a glass of wine, leaned against the counter, and gave me a quizzical look. She slowly sipped the wine as she watched me over the top of her glass.

Under her gaze, I felt the color return to my cheeks. I took more of a swallow than a sip of the white wine. "What brings you to Birmingham? Are you doing a…what's the word you use? A show or a gig?"

She smiled at me as if she found every expression I gave her and everything I said to her as something amusing. "I usually say gig but don't know that there is one term better than the other. And no. Not a planned…" She smiled. "Show."

"Oh."

Mo stepped closer to me. "Although, I try to always spin a few when I crash at Jazlyn's."

"I usually see postings when you're coming but I didn't see any."

"Ah. Keeping tabs on me, are you?"

Another blush. "Ummmm…no. Nothing like that."

She laughed and took a swallow of wine. "No, this is a stop on my way to another show. But like I said, I'll try to spin a bit to pay for my room and board."

"So, how will anyone know you're here? That you're playing?"

Mo held my eyes with hers. She didn't release me when she spoke. It was like she was reading every single thought I had. It made me very nervous. "I sent out a text to a few regulars earlier today. They'll get the word out."

"Oh."

She stepped even closer until she was nearly inches from me. Make that extremely nervous. I felt the wine glass slipping from my dampened palms but had no idea what to do with it. Mo stood so close to me that I would have had to slide my arm in between us to place the glass on the counter. I didn't dare let our skin touch with the way she continued to hold me within her emerald stare. Instead, I placed my other hand at the base of the glass to help support the stem.

"You say that a lot."

"What?"

"Oh." I was drawn to watch her mouth as she let the word draw out from her lips.

I felt the desire of my eyes not to leave the beauty of them. In barely a whisper, all I could think to say was, "Oh."

She watched my lips as I had done hers. I felt a rising heat not on my cheeks but one escalating between us as we both studied each other's lips.

Buzz. Buzz.

Mo and I jumped.

"Are you expecting someone?"

"No." I walked to the intercom and pressed the button. My legs were like Jell-O and took a great deal of will to get them to make it to the door without stumbling. "Hello?"

"Hey," a man's voice called back. "Got your delivery."

"Oh, yeah, that's right. Come on up." I looked back at Mo. "Sorry, I forgot I ordered Thai food to be delivered."

"Don't be sorry. Unless you didn't order enough for two. Then you can be sorry."

I laughed. "Well, I was starving when I ordered and they give really big portions so there's definitely plenty to share."

The smell of curry, lemongrass, and shallots escaped into the room as I opened the stapled paper bag. They swirled around my head like an aromatic tornado.

Mo walked from the kitchen carrying two plates. "Smells fantastic. What did you order?"

"Tom yum goong and green curry chicken."

"Nice. How about this? We eat, share another glass of wine, and then you bring that sexy new do downstairs with me while I do a set?"

I grimaced. "I don't know about that. I've never been when people are there."

"I'm sorry?" She dipped healthy portions of both dishes out onto her plate and filled both of our glasses back up with wine. "What do you mean? Jazlyn said she met you at the club."

"Well, yes. That's true. But I've never stayed late." I took the container she was handing me. "I come early before the crowd and leave before it fills up."

"Ah. Gotcha." She licked the spilled sauce from her finger. "Can I ask why?"

I dipped out slightly smaller portions than Mo's and sat across the table from her. "I live here. I work here. I'm not sure what would be said if I was seen in a lesbian bar."

"Darling, the only way people can see you there is if they are there as well."

"Yes, I know." I sipped my wine. Okay, I took another swallow instead of a sip. "I heard about The Pineapple Post when I overheard a conversation between a girl in my program and her friends. She's really out and *really* loud. I wouldn't put it past her to say something in front of everyone. I don't know it just makes me nervous."

Mo pointed her chopsticks at me. "Now, *that* I get. I've known some lezzes like that in my day."

I pushed a large shrimp and shallot stem around on my plate. Why did I let everyone else, especially someone like Kylie, control what I did?

"You know that's probably why you've lost so much weight."

"What is?"

"You have to actually put the food in your mouth to be considered as eating. It's a little-known fact."

"Oh, is it?"

"It is."

I knew she was joking but I also knew she was right. I'd been guilty of mostly pushing my food around on the plate since coming back from Atlanta. Yet I hadn't noticed the weight loss until the nurses began giving me a smaller size in my scrubs when I came into the OR. Then there was the hint of that damn ring fitting looser upon my finger. I hated the way it slid up and down along my skin as a constant reminder of things left undone. Grant hadn't necessarily noticed or rather hadn't commented on the weight loss but he had made acknowledgments to the ring easily slipping from my finger. He'd offered to have it sized. That was his comment, an offer to have the ring sized for fear of me losing it. I vehemently declined as I didn't want its tightness to return to my finger.

"So why is that?"

I looked up from my plate to see Mo staring at me. "Why is what?"

"The food is pretty damn good so why do you sit there pushing it around your plate?"

It did smell absolutely delicious when I first caught its scent. On my plate, the scent only made a wave of uneasiness in my stomach. A wave that had been there since I watched Sam walk away. The wave which crashed through me with the knowledge she was gone from my life. No words had made her stay. No expressions of an unchanging love kept her by my side. All that stayed was a deep pit of loneliness left by her retreating form. Food smelled. Sometimes it smelled heavenly but the taste was absent on my tongue.

I felt Mo's hand cover mine. I realized my cheeks were soiled with fresh tears.

"That's some seriously big hurt in your eyes, Rayne. It'll consume you if you let it stick with you."

Consume me. Take me. Conquer me.

I let her fingers slide over the top of mine before I squeezed them to hold onto her strength. "And how do you stop it?"

"You feel it fully. Absorb every fiber of it." She squeezed back. "Then, you let it go. Let it leave you without a mark showing it was ever there."

"You can do that?"

"Absolutely I can do it. I've done it. Hell, I even wrote a book about it."

"You've had your heart broken?"

She released my hand and returned to her chopsticks. "We all hurt. Have been hurt. Maybe not in the same way but still with pain. It's what you do with it that makes the difference." She filled both of our glasses equally until the bottle was empty. "I tell you what. You quit beating that food around the plate and actually have dinner with me. Then we'll go downstairs so you can get lost in my music. Jazlyn always leaves a small sitting stool up in the booth. She knows I never sit but it's there anyway. I'll position you where no one will see you. You'll be my little secret." She held up her glass until I raised mine. She tapped against it lightly. "Good. It's settled. Eat."

Mo was true to her word. We entered the deejay booth through the back of the club. She sat me on the stool in the corner. I could barely see anything as it was quite dark in the booth. The overhead lights were positioned to shine out onto the floor and not on the little corner tucked in the back. She wasn't wrong about the crowd either. The place was packed. From where I sat, I could see the dance floor and part of the entrance to the bar area. The unrecognizable faces were a mix of women below me. There didn't seem to be an empty spot on the floor as they huddled in together. The aura of their excitement filtered up onto the booth and caused me to anticipate Mo's appearance as much as they seemed to.

The crowd screamed out when the lights went dark. They shouted Mo's name. The music silenced.

Mo's low, sultry voice sounded out over the crowd. "I've a vision for us tonight." She spoke slowly, meticulously giving each word its own showcase. "Let the lights…the music…the vastness of the night's possibilities take you away from the day." The silent crowd in the pitch-black space held on to her words. "Trust me. Take my hand. Come with me into the night." A rhythmic beat slowly built in the background. "I'll not let you go." The thumping beat was joined by a higher pitched almost siren-type sound. "It's our night."

A loud boom sounded as the lights blew up blazingly. The crowd screamed and there she was. Standing right next to me. She stole my breath again just as she had done earlier in Jazlyn's apartment. When she went upstairs to change for her set, I had never imagined she would come down dressed as she was. Her body was swaying back and forth as she manipulated the board in front of her to create the sounds that had the women matching her motions below us.

Why wouldn't I be attracted to her? She was elegant in her natural beauty. Her lean form stood a couple of inches taller than me. Up until that moment, I'd only seen her with her hair either in a ponytail or stylishly messy and hanging off of her shoulders. The most makeup I had seen her wear was light-colored lip gloss. And in all of those times, she was still quite unbelievably beautiful.

That was not the Mo who walked down the staircase to greet me with a glowing smile. This woman was perhaps the most gorgeous woman I had seen outside of a runway or movie. She wore a form-fitting black dress that stopped below her hips to show off the legs I had seen sprawled across a catamaran but never had they looked like this. Maybe it was the black high-heeled shoes. Maybe it was the way she walked with a sway to her hips. I don't know what it was but I couldn't take my eyes off of her. She had stopped at the stairs and gave me a look which told me my ogling had not gone unnoticed. Now those legs stood within arm's reach of me. The effect they caused at this close distance was far more than the one they had triggered with a simple walk. Her hips and legs moved with the music. Her head bobbed in a harmonious flow with the cadence. I sat in my little black corner and soaked in every drop of her.

"Feed my craving, ladies." Mo put her hands up over her head and counted out the beat as she pointed out into the crowd. "Let me feel you," she sang out.

She shifted her weight and leaned over me. "Feel the music, Rayne. Let nothing else be in your mind." She tapped my forehead lightly with her finger. "Let this go and feel the music." She put a set of headphones over my ears. The music flowed through them uninhibited by any other sound or noise of the crowd.

Mo slowly mouthed. "Feel it."

With nothing but the metrical tempo sounding in my ears, I could watch her with unreserved eyes. No, I could feel her. I could feel the vibrations of the music. Everything about her was sensual. Her hips bumping against the board as her fingers turned dials and slid across the turntable to spin it in her desired direction. Each movement for a purpose. Turning, spinning, dancing in the air, adjusting her headphones. All with the beat of the music in my ears. I felt sweat bead at the small of my back as I gave in to her rhythm and the precision of her fingers manipulating the board to her whim. She wasn't touching me in any way. No skin upon my skin. Yet I *felt* her. Felt the warmth of her long slender arms and hands. The strength in her fingertips pressed against my body. The pressure of her hips against me. It was as real to me as the night she held me in a dance.

I caught the gleam of her eyes as she looked at me. She leaned over me and placed both hands on the sides of the stool by my legs. She pushed one side of the earphones off of my ear as her lips came to rest there. I could feel the softness of her hair across my cheek and chin. It tickled me.

"That's it. Now you're free."

THE MOONLIGHT BOUNCED off of the tinted shower wall to light the bedcovers I laid beneath. Nearly two hours ago, I had said goodnight to the verdant eyes which had held me entranced in the form that was Mo. I had stared into the eyes emphasized with black eyeliner and blue eyeshadow until the moment she blinked to break our contact.

Kiss me.

The words had sung in my head as I stared at the twitch in her lips. I let my fingertips run along the edge of the coolness of my own lips. The October night's breeze carried a chill into the apartment. My stomach rolled in a wave of mixed emotions. The chill in the air—the chill of my lips last truly kissed by Sam.

Sam.

Guilt came with the vision of her eyes of blue holding me once as Mo had held me tonight. My desires for Mo felt like a betrayal to the only form of true love I had felt for someone whose blood didn't flow in my veins. I felt the all too knowing ache in my heart with thoughts of Sam. I still loved her and feared I always would. But she had said goodbye. She was the one who walked away and left me questioning every single thing in my life. My head pounded with the pressure of it all.

"Let all of this go." Mo's voice rang out over the mottled emotions that clogged my brain. I felt the gentle tap of her fingertip on my forehead as it released the pressure underneath. "That's it. Now you're free."

I rolled over to bury my head into the empty pillow next to me. I breathed in the scent of clean linen. This was my weekend of escape. I'm in a distant world away from my daily struggles. This was my time.

Free to be. Free to let it go.

Different but the same.

Chapter 15

"Get up, sleepy head. I need coffee," Mo yelled from downstairs. "If I don't hear movement in two seconds flat, I'm coming up there and yanking you out of bed. Your call."

"I'm up. I'm up," I called out in my unflattering first-morning voice.

"Then come on. Let's go get coffee."

I walked to the railing and leaned over to see Mo standing below dressed in black yoga pants and a long sleeve loose-fitting white T-shirt. "We're going out for coffee?"

Her face was freshened as if she had rested much more peacefully than I had the night before. Either the pull-out sofa was more comfortable than the bed or she hadn't been tormented by rambling thoughts. I predicted it was the latter.

"Yes, we're going out. Get a move on."

"Isn't there coffee here?"

She put her hand on her side. "Why, yes, smarty pants, but the bakery down the block has blueberry scones. Unless you can whip one of those up for me, I suggest you get your butt down here before I leave you."

I held my hands up in submission. "Okay. Okay. I'm going." I stepped away from the railing and got a few steps out of sight before I heard her shouting.

154

"Hey, you got any hiking boots or something like it?"

"I need hiking boots to go a block down the road for blueberry scones? These must be some pretty darn special scones."

"The best." She laughed. "You better wear pants too. Jeans if you got them. Coolish today."

I walked down the stairs in jeans, a long-sleeve pullover, and tennis shoes. "Sorry, these will have to do."

She smiled. "They're perfect."

I looked down at her feet clad in ankle-high, old-style Vans with no socks. "Okay so why is it I have to wear jeans and tennis shoes as I have no boots while you look mighty comfy in your yoga pants and Vans?"

"That's a very good question."

"One I suppose you aren't going to answer."

Her smile beamed. "Not at the moment but eventually. Let's go."

Mo STRETCHED HER legs out to rest her crisscrossed feet on the chair across from her. "What do you have planned today?"

"For the first time in a long time, absolutely nothing. I know you said yesterday you were stopping over on your way to a gig. When are you set to leave?"

She picked off a corner of her scone and plopped it into her mouth. "This morning."

I felt disappointment creep in. Hadn't I hoped my plans for the day had involved her? "Oh."

"And again with your favorite word."

"I'll see if I can't find another one between now and the next time I see you." I took a swallow of my coffee and winced at its coolness.

"You could do that or you could just hold that thought and decide to spend your energy on something more productive." She bit off the other corner of her scone. "Like spending the day with me."

"But you said you were leaving this morning."

"You asked when I was set to leave, which was this morning, but spending the day with you sounds so much better. You up for it?"

If I could have kept the silly grin from my face, I would have. I felt like a school girl who had just been asked out to the homecoming dance. Yet if I had masked it, I doubt I would have seen her matching one in return.

"Excellent. We need to make a detour first." Mo cleaned the trash from the table. She lifted my coffee cup. "I'm guessing you're done with this. You didn't seem too thrilled with that last swallow."

I followed her around the corner to a self-storage warehouse. She was grinning the entire time. Not a smile but a grin. I felt it and joined her happily. She stopped in front of a large garage door, pulled a key from her front pocket, and bent down to unlock it.

The metal garage door creaked and shook as she raised it open. Two black tires separated by two long chrome bars came into view as the door rolled upon itself. The smile twitched at her lips. She flipped on the light. The hanging fluorescent lights flickered until they came on to reflect off of the glossy painted gas tank. I would have sworn we had been transported into the middle of a premiere motorcycle shop.

"Well...what do you think?" She walked to the motorcycle and ran her hand along the sloping leather seat. "Isn't she beautiful? She's a 2003 Harley Davidson Night Train."

I watched the light dance across the brilliant black paint and let my mind wander back to a simpler day in my life. The day my adult life was starting. On that night, I'd stared out into a parking lot and watched overhead lights shine on my new Jeep and Grant. I shook the thought of him from my head.

Not now—not today.

"She definitely is. So, this is what you wanted to show me?" I walked further into the self-storage transformed into a garage. I pointed to the picture of a string-bikini-clad woman lazily stretched across the seat of a larger style Harley. "Really?"

An impish smile replaced her grin. "Hey, I was young when I did this place."

I tilted my head and raised my eyebrows.

"Okay…youngish. How's that?"

"More truthful."

"Give me just a sec and I'll be ready."

"For?"

She reached into the metal drawers I assumed was filled with tools and pulled out jeans and a black T-shirt. "To go for a ride."

I put my hands up. "Oh no. I'm not getting on that thing."

"What? Why?"

"For one, I've treated I don't even know how many people in the ER from a spill on one of those damn things. And for two…" I shook my head. "Nah, one is a pretty good enough reason on its own. No thanks."

She closed the distance between us and stood close enough that I felt the tickle of the clothing she held in her hand as it brushed against my arm. "If I remember right, it's you who drives a Jeep that hardly sees a top on it. Or so you've told me."

"That's entirely different." I felt the nervous strain of my voice.

"Yes, it is. If you think you feel free riding in your Jeep, you can't imagine what riding on this will feel like. There's nothing like it. I promise." She looked down at my chest. It rose and fell quickly. Her lip twitched as she held me again with her eyes. "Besides, it'll give me a reason to have you hold me tightly in your arms."

A reason? I swallowed hard and choked on the words I wanted to say. I wanted to be suave. I wanted to have a comeback, something like, "Do you use that line often?" or "Does that line usually work for you?" But nothing came out. I cowered in my shyness to leave the words spoken only in my head. Besides, didn't I know the answer to both of those questions anyway?

She held me in her stare a moment longer. "Now would you mind rolling that door down so I can change clothes?"

"Here?" Geez, did my voice just crack? I sounded like a nervous teenage boy. I cleared my throat. "I mean, you're changing here?"

She chuckled. "Ummm…yep, that was the idea." She grabbed the hem of her shirt and pulled it over her head.

Oh shit. I turned quickly to roll the door down. A loud boom sounded as it slipped from my hand and slammed hard against the concrete.

"Safe to say the neighborhood is up," she said as she laughed.

I didn't turn around.

"You're good for my ego, Rayne. I don't know that I've ever changed in front of a woman who chose to stare at a metal door instead of looking at me."

I don't doubt that. *Idiot*. Yeah. Idiot sums it up nicely.

"You can turn around now. I'm dressed," she said as she sat on a black futon and laced up her leather boots.

"Do you stay here? I mean, the futon. Do you sleep here?"

She smiled and shook her head. "No. But I'll come here sometimes to escape the noise."

"Noise?"

"Close your eyes and listen."

I shut the vision of the room out and stood in the darkness of it.

"Do you hear anything?"

"Nothing."

"With that door shut…in here, just me and my bike…it's just me. It's not Mo. It's me. Sometimes I need to find her to not forget her."

I opened my eyes quickly to see her watching me. I blinked to the understanding of what she had shared and to the fact she had shared. She seemed to notice too because she stood up, brushed the wrinkles from her jeans, and tucked her T-shirt into the front of her waistband. She pulled her long hair into a ponytail before walking toward me to reopen the door.

She turned her head to look at me as we were nearly face to face.

"There. You have a piece of me. A piece no one else has." She gently shook her head. "Not sure why you have it but there it is anyway."

The blue streak in her hair was highlighted as she stepped out into the sunlight. "Why don't you stand out here while I wheel her out?" She disappeared into the shadows of the garage and returned a few moments later behind the brightness of the sun shining off of the chrome bars. Her smile was ear to ear as she steered the large front wheel out into the alley between the buildings.

"When we get on, just follow my movements. If I lean, you lean. The city will be miserable with the stink of exhaust from the cars but when we get this baby out onto the Red Mountain Expressway, you'll swear we're flying. Wait until I get her cranked and ready before you get on." She bent down and turned the key, turned a valve, and then pulled a knob. She straightened again, straddled the bike, and freed the kickstand. She gripped the bar with her left hand as she pushed a button on the right handlebar. The engine roared and rumbled below her. Her body vibrated with the hum of the engine. A few times, she reached down to slowly push the knob back in. The engine grew louder and louder as it warmed. I felt the excitement in my chest as she twisted the throttle. The roar was exhilarating and brought about a grin of anticipation. With my fear washing away, I was eager to climb on the seat behind her.

She handed me a helmet after she pushed the knob fully in. "We're ready." She extended her hand to me as her smile filled her face. "Let's do this," she said loudly over the roar of the engine.

I grabbed her hand without an ounce of hesitation. The bike's balance shifted but quickly returned when she steadied the weight of us. I realized I really didn't know what to do from here. I sat against the back rest and placed my feet on the bars off to the side of the bike. I looked around to see a grip or anything to hold onto but couldn't figure out where my hands went.

"You're going to have to sit a little closer if you want to stay on," Mo yelled.

I scooted on the seat to get closer to her. I tried to move easily so as not to shift the balance of the bike again. Gently, I let my hands rest against the material at her sides. I dared not place pressure there for fear of feeling the warmth of her skin burn through the clothing.

Idiot coward. Better summation.

Chapter 16

WE LEFT THE city behind us as we cruised along the Red Mountain Expressway. The Ridge-and-Valley region of the Appalachian Mountains had always been beautiful to me. Many days, I purposely drove down Twentieth Street past the Vulcan Statue just to admire the beauty of its rust-stained rock seamed with hematite iron ore. But those views couldn't hold a candle to this. Nothing like the ones unobstructed by a door frame or window. Out in the open with nothing between us and the rock, I could fully appreciate the red sparkle of the ore. I'm not sure what sparkled more, the ore or the green of the eyes I caught in the reflection of the rearview mirrors. She seemed to be looking for my reflection as many times as I sought hers. At times, she looked at me which such intensity that I would pretend to notice some distraction and break our stare.

She pulled off the highway onto a small dirt road before turning the bike off and motioning for me to dismount.

"There's something I want to show you. We walk from here."

The sun filtered through the narrowed trunks of the forest to give the road a striped appearance. Some of the smaller trees leaned into the hill cut for the dirt path. Their tops joined those of the opposite side as they stretched across the dirt to create a canopy above us. As we walked, the shade cooled the gentle wind and chilled the moistened skin at my neck. We had left most of the traffic behind us when we turned off of the main road so there was little noise to pollute the nature around us.

"What are you smiling about?"

I blinked at her. She had stopped walking and was gazing back at me.

"I guess this." I held my arms out by my side and turned in a circle. "All of this. The sounds. The smell. All of it." I brought my foot up and down to crunch the gravel under my feet. "This. I love the sound of this. It reminds me of a place back home." I took in a deep breath. "And that. Do you smell that? It's nature. It's the dirt, the grass, and the trees. If there was some water around, I'd be one happy girl."

"If only." She smiled. "So, you're a big hiker?"

"No, not really. I wouldn't say it was hiking that I am enjoying so much. It's being out here. Being outdoors away from the city and its congestion. I feel like sometimes I'm being suffocated. But here, out in the open, I feel alive," I said as I bent down to pick up a handful of dirt. I let it slowly slip from my hand to fall back onto the ground. The finer granules floated in the breeze and came to fall further down the path. I loved the way the leftover dirt stuck to the palm of my hand until I brushed it off on my jeans. "Out here I can breathe again. It's my oxygen."

"It's nice to see something besides sadness in those beautiful green eyes of yours."

The warmth previously at my neck jumped to my cheeks. I didn't know how to take her flirting. Generally, I found it to be playful banter and considered it part of her personality. Out here, alone in the woods, I questioned if her flirtations were real. If in fact, Mo of the lesbian deejay world…all women want to be with Mo…was seriously flirting with me. No, it was most likely a good friend who was trying to make me feel better by being complimentary. That was more like it.

"But, yes, I know exactly what you mean." She studied the rocks beneath her feet for a moment and then bent over to pick up a light brown stone.

"You do?"

"You sound surprised."

"Yeah, I guess I am. I wouldn't have figured you would've felt like that. You seem like a city kinda girl to me."

She laughed and let the smile stay upon her lips. "I get you would think that way. It's the only venue you've seen me in." She rolled the pebble in her hands and started walking back down the path.

"It's not just seeing you there, in that setting; it's watching you in the setting." I quickened my pace to try to catch up to her. "It's watching how you affect the women around you. You take them to another world. It's a world you create for them. The music and the lights. It's sort of amazing really."

She stopped and looked over her shoulder. I didn't understand the expression on her face. She wasn't really smiling. I felt my mouth go dry the longer she held her words.

"What?" I asked.

She gave her head a single side nod. "Thanks."

"You're welcome," I said, painfully aware I had great difficulty reading her thoughts.

She stretched her hand out for me to take it as she stepped up onto the first step of a set of stairs made from flat rocks dug into the dirt hill. "No, truly, thank you for saying that."

She wrapped her fingers around my hand the moment our skin touched. The callouses of her palm scratched against my hand. Surely, they had been freshly roughened from the grips of the motorcycle ride.

"Here, I want to take you to a place over this hill."

She carefully led me up the crooked staircase. I followed along the path of her footsteps to avoid stumbling on the rounded-rock border. She kept my hand firmly within hers as we walked single file. Even in her strong grasp, I slipped on one of the rocks covered in a mossy mold. The shade above the staircase provided a perfect environment for the slippery green coating.

She stopped to look back at me as I regained my footing.

"Sorry. I'm not one for grace."

"I see that. Are you okay?"

I nodded.

She laughed. "It's probably a good thing I didn't know that before you climbed on the back of my bike."

She smiled playfully and leaned against a birch tree. The trunk was split low to the ground so her body was hugged between the divisions of the tree. The paper-like bark rolled out over her shoulder. This type of tree would always be a mocking reminder of the night Grant proposed. The night I watched the tears of my doing fall from Sam's eyes. The pain of it threatened to squeeze at my heart until I shook it forcefully from my head. I studied the tree for what it would be for me today and not of what it was of old. Today, it would be shedding its old skin for the hopeful promise of new...just like me.

"Anything else you wish to share before we keep walking?"

"What?"

"Anything else. Like for instance, what's with the look you have right at this moment?" She lifted her arm away from her side and pointed it at my face.

"What look?"

"Um, the look that would be the result of whatever you just felt. It washed over you like a cloak. What were you thinking? Care to share the thoughts you just had?"

"Do we have to talk about it?" I couldn't. I didn't want to talk about it. I wanted to escape into Mo's world she was creating for me. The past pain didn't belong here today. At least not right now it didn't.

"Nope. We don't." She started to head back up the hill but turned before taking a full step. She wound her finger in the belt loop of my jeans and gave them a pull. "But if you keep losing weight, these things are going to fall off of you and then we probably will have something to talk about." Her smile showed me her gloriously white teeth. "Or, well, in the very least something to *do*."

What was it with women causing a rush of blood to my cheeks?

I noticed the changing of the leaves as we climbed further up the hill. Crimson and honey-colored leaves sprinkled the hillside of our hike. Our footsteps were announced to the woods as we crunched on the already fallen leaves. Over the sounds of leaves beneath our feet and the rustle of foliage blown in the light breeze, I heard the stirrings of flowing water.

"If only." Mo pushed through the thickened brush and pulled at the vines to loosen them as she made a clearing for us. "We're here."

She set her backpack on the ground and took in a deep breath. She turned quickly to look back at me and her foot slipped off the edge of the embankment. She grabbed onto an oak sapling to steady herself.

The water's edge was filled with tiny trees of all kinds. They hovered close to the ground while the larger ones took up the sky. Their brilliant green leafage formed an arbor for the running brook. I was thankful she had encouraged me to grab a couple of bottles of water when we stopped for gas. I took a long swig.

She dug in her backpack and pulled out a wad of material. "I warn you. I've never had company in this thing before. It may be tricky." She looked up at me. "Especially since we have admitted to your lack of grace."

"Hey, I'm not the one who slipped on the rocks a second ago."

"Caught that, did ya?"

I smiled. "Yep."

She wrapped a rope around two trees standing close to each other and stretched out a purple hammock. The brook flowed below it. Some of the moss which had grown over the rock bed was lifted free into the water of the gentle current.

She stretched the material out and shook her head. "Sure, hope this thing will fit two. We may have to snuggle in." She cocked her head to the side to look at me. "Wouldn't that be terrible?"

A deep breath filled my lungs as I studied the hammock and her reaction to it. It was very narrow. There was no way we would manage without a snug fit.

She played with the hammock a little more, getting in and out of it to find the best position. She sat in it like a lounger with the material riding high against her back before changing position to sit with her legs hanging off of the side.

"I think this will work best. Come on in." She patted the small open space beside her.

The hammock dangled uneasily as I tried to sit without tipping us over. I found myself enjoying the sound of her laughter as we nearly tumbled to the ground. Or in this case, water since the stream was below us. She wasn't Mo of the lesbian bar scene when she laughed like this. She was just a woman being tickled. I liked it. I may even have liked it too much as it made me happy the hammock kept me close to her body. I relaxed in the comfort of my arm and side lying against hers. The babbling brook carried my stresses away on its current. I let them wash over the rock to become cleansed as they fell and dispersed in the stream. Slender streaks of sunlight danced off the rippling water. I felt the warmth of it on my ankle as my feet dangled from the hammock.

"This is so beautiful."

"It is, isn't it?" Mo inhaled deeply. "Sometimes I make time for this layover just to come out here."

"I needed this."

"I thought you might."

I bit my lip. "Can I ask you something?"

"Sure."

"This doesn't add up to the Mo I've seen. I mean this place. You coming out here. I don't know. Out into nature. Wouldn't seem like your place."

"I do get you feel that way, but can you elaborate why you do?"

I shrugged. "It isn't exactly a night club filled with pounding music. And you've essentially told me music is what feeds your soul. I've seen your tattoos. There's no music out here."

"Are you kidding me? There's more music out here than anywhere else. You don't have to be in a smoke-filled, strobe-lit bar to hear music." She twisted onto her shoulder to face me. "Close your eyes."

"You're always telling me to close my eyes."

She laughed again which made me realize how much I liked the sound of it.

"It's because you keep so much in that brain of yours I have to do something to try to block it out. You see the world in front of you and build up this protective shell. So yeah, I'm going to need you to close your eyes. And besides, one day I may just surprise you when you do close them but not right now." She placed her fingertips lightly over my eyes. "Please close your eyes and listen."

In the beginning, I heard only the silence. Then the brook came into my ears with its lyrical cascade over the rocks. I smiled into its chorus.

I flinched at the breath of her speech on my ear. "You hear it." Her voice was low and sultry. "Now listen closer to the scratching of the squirrels' claws on the trees as they play."

Yes, it was there. I heard the crinkling sound of the bark as it was loosened from the strain of their claws as they scurried up its base.

"Listen to the harmony of the birds as they sing to one another." The warmth of her breath ran a tingle down my spine. "And the beat of that woodpecker further off in the distance."

I heard their serenade. It sounded like a song of whistled love to the sky, to the water below them, to the earth giving them life and to the beauty of the day. They sounded happy.

"Now." Her voice was closer. I feared the brush of her lip against the lobe of my ear. *Feared or desired?* "Listen to the thumping base that's getting louder."

Thumping base? Yes, thumping base. Its rhythm was growing faster and stronger. I began to feel it against my shoulder.

"Hear it? Feel it?" she asked in a whispered breath as her lip touched my ear lobe.

I shook my head and was nearly dizzy with the wave of impulses throughout my body.

"That's us. That's our song."

I felt her body shift its weight further onto me. Her lips were a feathered touch against mine. Soft. Too soft. I wanted more. I wanted to feel the pressure of them fully against mine. The sense of it all rapidly changed my equilibrium to make me feel as though I had suddenly begun floating or rather falling into the air and into her.

Son of a bitch that's cold!

The water flowed over my back and onto my chest as we fell into its current.

Her laughter was infectious as we both hollered in the sheer utter chill of the water coating our bodies. We laid flat on our backs against a muddy bottom floor staring wide-eyed at the leaves above us. Apparently, the playful squirrels found humor in us as well because they moved their romp to the branches over our heads. Their nails loosened tiny pieces of bark which floated softly in the air before falling upon our chests. I felt as free as those chips of wood as their fall was more of a slow drift along a curvaceous pattern in the air instead of a direct, straight path to the earth. I felt free and very cold.

Mo stood from the water and extended her hand. "Come on. I also know a sunny place."

"Thank goodness."

She took us back over the embankment to walk along a trail covered in kudzu. Beyond the brush was a clearing made years before. Within its center was an old, rusted structure nearly covered in the invading vegetation. Across from the building was a brick wall embedded in a dirt levee. It was stained with multiple colors and was probably once a very beautiful red. In the present, its clay was a mixture of white, red, and a moldy green.

"This spot should dry us out." She sat down on the ground and leaned her back against the brick wall.

The small trek up the hill had warmed my body some but it wasn't able to conquer the coldness of the wet clothing against my skin. I sat next to her and tried to convince myself I kept little distance between our bodies as a means of sharing heat. But I knew better. I wanted to be close to her.

Her eyes had grown from their usual bright green to an almost hunter appearance. Maybe that was what sent us on our tumble to the water. I had opened my eyes. The promise of her lips against mine was too much to take without seeing the woman who was dangerously close to deepening an innocent kiss. I'd felt the wave in my belly with the nervous anticipation I had once felt long ago with Sam's lips so close to mine. It felt good. It felt damn good to feel alive again.

My weekend vacation had come to find me wishing to burst from the shell that had encased me. Burst from its borders and tear down its walls to feel a woman's touch again. It was what I had begun to recognize and believe was the void I would not feel any other way. Yet this time it wasn't Sam's touch I yearned for so much but rather the woman whose shoulder rested against mine.

"I feel like that sometimes."

Mo kept her head braced against the wall. "I'm sorry." Her eyes were closed.

"That building over there. Half standing. Half falling apart. I feel like that sometimes." I breathed in deeply. "Most of the time actually."

She fixed one eye onto the shack across from us. I followed her gaze with my own. The kudzu vines had all but overtaken the structure as they grew up one side, over the porch, and onto the rusted tin roof. The right side of the porch and roofing had given to the weight of the dense compounded leaves. It sloped to that side which caused the wood planks to lay low to the ground. Somehow, the noxious weed had spared the small clearing between our feet and the building. Yet its coiling vine was virtually uncontrolled over the top of the brick wall as it trailed like a blanket across our shoulders.

"How so?"

"Like I'm smothering. Like there's this weight of everything smothering the air from me and growing over me so fast that I can hardly take in a breath. Life isn't much different than those leaves. I mean, look at it. Thick, velvety leaves like large clovers with these racemes of purple flowers shooting up all over the place. It's pretty, right? Beautiful even. Just like life. It can be beautiful, parts of it anyway. But in essence, it can still smother you. Shade you in the conformity of it all until you no longer grow. Until you wither and die. Not ever leaving its shadow."

I didn't dare look at her straight on but instead kept her in the corner of my eye as I waited to see how she would respond. I was taken back at how I had opened up to her to express something raw and previously hidden deep within me. I couldn't stand it if she made fun. She wasn't this emotional woman. She didn't open up to express anything. Why? Oh, why did I say all of that crap? What had I expected her to say?

She bit the corner of her lip, shut her eye, and raised her face to the let the sunlight bask over it. She sat still for what seemed several minutes. The rapid, raptor-like call of a woodpecker was almost deafening in the silence between us.

"Meredith." Her voice was soft. "Meredith Ohlen. That's where Mo comes from. It's my initials. I shortened it after I saw the not-so-pretty side of life. After I felt what you described." She shifted and rolled her shoulders as if trying to release the tension from them. "My father, the last of the Ohlens, was killed in an offshore accident when I was sixteen. It was their mistake. A work order had been removed when an inspection threatened to shut them down for a few days. A loss of three days was too much money to lose. So, they improvised." She kept her eyelids closed but I saw creases form in the corners as they tightened. "There were four men killed that day. The families of the other men filed a lawsuit. It never went to court. Let's just say it was a hefty settlement. One that allowed me to pay off a not-so-up-and-up lawyer to keep me out of the foster care system."

"Foster care? What about your mother?"

"My mother." She paused.

Her eyes remained shut. I heard her voice in my head when she told me to close my eyes. When she told me to close my eyes and block out the sight of the world so I could see the feelings within me. This must not only be what she tells me to do but also what she herself must do.

"My mother wasn't exactly what you would call a mom. The doctors told my dad it was postpartum depression. I couldn't give a flying fuck the medical term they wanted to give it. She left shortly after I was born. He tried to stay home and not work offshore but he could hardly pay the bills. So, when I was about five, he went back to drilling. I'd stay with whatever girlfriend he was dating at the time while he was gone."

"What about your grandparents or any other family?" I was anxiously trying not to sound shocked or give pity to my voice.

"My parents weren't what you'd call good children. They were both wild, always in trouble, and hard to handle. They split from their families before either one of them graduated from high school. He grew up eventually and got his GED. Apparently, she never did. He used to tell me the only thing right in this world she ever did was have me."

The creases at her eyes tightened even more. She rolled the back of her head across the brick wall.

"Anyway, Mr. Shifty Lawyer Man set me up in another state where no one knew me or my father. It wasn't hard pulling it off for two years. I kept my grades up, my nose down, and stayed out of trouble. No one was the wiser." She opened her eyes to look at me. "I've been on my own since I was sixteen. At eighteen, I chose to live like the other side of that building. Free. Nothing growing on me. Nothing weighing me down. Hence Mo. Short and sweet."

I was dumbfounded and held speechless as I reveled in what she had shared with me. I found myself wanting to touch her and hold her close to me in comfort. Something told me she probably wouldn't want to be held...not right now anyway. I could sense she was rebuilding her strength and a physical comfort would only hinder its progress. Yet beyond those last few words, I knew little of her or what her wishes would be.

I heard a series of woeful, hooting calls above the nature's chatter. No doubt a mournful dove was perched beyond our reach. Its song was sad as if yearning to feel something else, maybe anything else. The lyrics of it brought me to Sam—the times wasted with her. The underlining sadness I had not been able to escape. The loss of appetite and recognition of beauty in anything around me since she said her goodbye. The unspoken words I wish I had shared. The touches I never felt because of my insecurity and questioning of right versus wrong.

The dove held them all in its song. Mo sat there with her head against the wall and her eyes closed, seemingly unfazed by the lyrical call.

The touches I never felt.

I heard the tearing of roots being pulled from the soil as I slid my hand across the grass toward Mo's. Once our fingers touched, she immediately opened her palm to mine. I sat quietly, letting our fingers mold into one another's.

Different and not the same.

"I'm not sure what to say," I said softly. "I'm not sure if you want me to say anything."

"Yes, do that. Don't say anything. It was over ten years ago and not really something I want to talk about in detail. Not right now anyway. Not with this." I felt her hand squeeze my fingers tighter. She turned her head and looked at me. "It's a beautiful day, isn't it?"

I let the sun wash over my face, felt its warmth and the growing warmth of the palm held within mine. "Yes, it is."

"I say we live in that. Live in that one and only fact of the here and now."

I returned her gaze. "What do you mean?"

She ticked her head to the side. "I mean live in the beauty of today. You're not that building over there and I'm not Meredith or Mo. We have the rest of the weekend to be who we want to be with someone who pretty much knows nothing of who we really are. You don't have to be anybody but the Rayne sitting next to me. No past. No future. Just now. Free to do what you feel without wondering about the next day or week. Not having to wonder what it all means. We take this time and ask nothing of each other beyond this weekend. I'll be me without labels or history or pain and you'll be you in exactly the same way. How's that sound?"

I let her words marinate within me. A weekend to be no one I had previously been or designed my future to be. A time to be exactly what I felt without excuse or explanations. A couple of days I could spend not worrying about labels or the pain they may cause.

"You mean something like a total brain shutdown?"

"Yes, a total brain shutdown." She smiled and used her other hand to tap my forehead. "If you think it could even be possible with that brain of yours."

"I don't know about that but I'm sure for giving it a try."

"Done."

I reached over my shoulder to pluck a kudzu leaf from its vine. "How exactly do we do this?"

"There aren't rules or steps. We just do it."

Rubbing the velvety leaf between my fingers, I thought of what she was saying. Two days of not being me. Not think of home, Charlie Grace, Grant, or what the future holds for me. Not think of the one who still held me captive with thoughts of her sun-kissed blonde hair as it fell over her blue eyes. I thought of Mo's hand within mine and felt a flush of guilt wash over my stomach. Did I feel guilty for wanting her next to me or did I feel guilty for letting Sam enter my thoughts?

"You know it's okay."

I looked at her. "I'm sorry?"

"Whatever you thought of. Or I'm beginning to think, whoever you thought of just now. It's okay. You don't have to hide your feelings from me. I won't judge you or them."

"What makes you think I thought of anyone?"

"Come on. Give me some credit. Whatever you just thought about puts so much sadness in your eyes. I'd have to be blind to not see it."

She reached into the kudzu brush and dug out a small stalk of purple flowers. She held it between her fingers. "We can talk about it if you want. We can ignore what I just said about leaving it all behind us and you can tell me about that sadness. Whichever one you want to do. I'm a pretty good listener."

I forced a smile.

Mo pulled her hand from mine and placed her fingertips over a purple flower. "She wants to talk." She pulled the flower from its stalk. "She doesn't want to talk." She pulled another one. "She doesn't want to go on an escape with me." And another one. "She wants to go on an escape with me."

I put my hand over hers. "She does want to take an escape with you."

She smiled with a girlish expression. She tossed the stalk over her shoulder "Excellent." She rubbed the material of her shirt between her fingers. "I still need to dry. How about you?"

"Definitely. Plus..." I returned to relax my back against the wall. "I'm not ready to leave yet."

She slid her hand underneath mine to intertwine our fingers again. "Perfect. It's a gorgeous day."

Her bass clef tattoo caught my attention. I followed the trail of musical notes around the wrist of her arm with my fingertip. "Tell me about music and what it means to you."

She moved her finger in slow circles around my fingertip. "It's everything to me really. It's what feeds my soul...makes me feel alive. I can find a lyric or beat to match any mood I'm in. I can let it get me out of that mood or intensify it for me. What is the one thing you can turn to whatever mood you're in and it's automatically better in some way?"

I thought for a moment. "I actually had this conversation with Jazlyn. She told me to find my thing. That go-to I searched for no matter my mood."

She laughed. "Hers is architecture. That girl loves her some buildings."

"She totally does."

"And have you found it. Your thing?"

"Yeah, I have. Think I always knew it was water, but it clicked with Jazlyn talking to me about finding it and then going to the beach. Walking along the shore with the water running over my feet. Sailing with my hands trailing along the sides of the boat. Standing out in the waves with you. I got it then. It's water. My thing is water."

She smiled. "I can see that in you. Now why? What does it do for you?"

"It does like you said. I hear it. Like you hear music. I hear water. I can hear it washing against the wood of a dock, or the side of a boat or hear waves crashing against a shore and I feel calm. I can let my fingers dip into it and feel peace. I can watch it as it ripples and have not a worried thought in my mind. It makes me happy."

"And there's your rhythm. There's your music."

I FLOATED ALONG the stream and listened to the flow of the current as it cascaded off of the rock into the deeper pool below me. My fingers twirled in the water as they rested off the sides of the float. The sun filtered through the covering of the tree limbs and warmed my cheeks. I was at peace and happy as I stared into the sky above me. I watched a leaf carried among the wind's breeze. It fell to and fro along the wind until it came to tickle my lips. I brushed at it but the tickle continued. A giggle arose from my lips and seemed to be joined by another's. I opened my eyes to see Mo holding a blade of grass inches from my lips. She was laughing.

"Hey, sleepy head. I think we're dried out now."

Sleepy head? Wait. What?

"Did I fall asleep?"

"Oh yeah. You were out like a light."

I was mortified. "I'm so sorry. I can't believe I fell asleep on you."

"Why?"

"That's so rude."

"Please. You fell asleep. It's no biggie." She shrugged. "Now, the drool on my shoulder is something entirely different."

"What?"

"I'm joking." She touched her fingertip to the bridge of my nose. "Although I think you got a bit too much sun and that I'm not joking about." She stood and extended her hand. "I guess it's time to head back."

The walk back to her bike was quiet but not in an uncomfortable silence sort of way. I was relaxed with her. I didn't worry about having to watch my expressions or my words. I had no worries of hurting her feelings or saying the wrong thing. I simply followed her footsteps along the path, took her hand when she offered it, and a few times when she didn't. It was us. Two women enjoying a hike in the woods. The closest I felt to being completely free since floating on the bayou with Meems. No excuses. No explanations. I felt entirely comfortable to do anything I wanted without reservation.

The ride back was smoother without the tension in my body. I sat against her and let my legs cradle and hold her. Little to no distance was left between us. She had given me one end of an earplug with the other kept for herself. The music of her iPod filled our ears simultaneously. Trees flew past us in streams of green mixed with gold and red as the motorcycle cruised along the expressway. The road noise was only heard when there was a break in the music between songs. Strong piano keys followed by a deep seductive voice quickly drowned out the world around me. Her voice drew me in with the strength of the emotion in her lyrics. She sang of a time lost between soulful looks in the mirror. In that time, the lines of her face had become clearer, aging her into a new woman. Her voice was pained with the desire of re-introducing herself to a world that would judge and turn their heads to her. She knew they would chew her up and spit her out with the hint of who she really was. Mo's back fell deeper into me, and I felt the full weight of her against my chest. I studied the small hairs of her neck as they glistened from the sweat beading on her skin. That voice. The voice of the singer filled my ears. Her lyrics pulled at my heart. Pulled at the wall encasing it. She sang of the desire to let her finger rove along a map of her lover's skin. I stared at the colored skin in front of me. I too bore the same desire to trace the lines of the quarter moon and stars tattooed at the base of her neck. There was nothing else. No road. No paths. Just me. Just her. Piano keys and a voice calling out every feeling I was having with her body within mine. Just the words of knowing the taste of her skin. The saltiness I found there as my lips first touched her neck. The taste of the colored quarter moon at the base of her neck. I felt the deep intake of air as her back fell and rose sharply against me. She released one handlebar to cup my hand within hers and pull it tighter around her waist. The story of her bones and her was one I wanted to know. Her music had taken me there. I was a part of her thing.

Chapter 17

"So, I KNOW this great little Indian place. It's a hole in the wall but really good." Mo stripped her boots off and laid them beside the door as we entered Jazlyn and Violet's loft. "We can walk from here if you want?"

"Only if you order. I'm not up on Indian food." I set my shoes next to hers and thought there was no way I was ever getting the soil out of them after our dip in the muddy stream. "But first I've got to shower some of this mud off of me." My once soft T-shirt made a crinkling sound as I pulled the material away from my chest. "A pleasant dinner date I'll not make if I don't."

She laughed. "Okay, but I'm next." She walked into the kitchen. "I'll grab us a beer. Or would you rather a glass of wine?"

"Are you kidding me?" I stepped onto the first stair leading to the upstairs bedroom. "I spent the day riding bitch on the back of a Harley. It's a beer for me."

She laughed. "Well, alright then."

Ruffled bed sheets reminded me of Mo's morning interruption as she rushed me out of the apartment before I had time to straighten the covers. Did the bed not bring thought to the way I had felt with Mo throughout the day? The design created an optical illusion of floating a foot off of the floor. There was a small headboard but no foot board or sides. Several times, I had started to look under the floating mattress but stopped myself before discovering its secret. It was better to live in the fantasy of the weekend and not know the reality of its design.

The walls surrounding the bed were plain white sheetrock, except for the one on the right. It was a tinted glass. I had studied the glass the night before. The chrome of the dual shower heads had reflected in the track lighting which shined from the exposed wooden beam. It was a gorgeous room in the simplicity of its arrangement. The only color was a single purple flower in a clear glass vase. It sat atop a bedside nightstand. I wondered the sentimental meaning of it shared by the two women who slept next to its petals. I wondered if my happiness of lying next to the person I loved was merely an illusion as that which was held in the bed's frame.

Droplets of warm water rained from the shower head sprayed onto the tense muscles of my shoulders. I smiled with the sensation of soap suds lifting away the remnants of the creek's muddy bottom. Mo's laughter had lifted me above the worries that were tucked hidden in the baggage I carried on my vacation away from my world. So much of her seemed to lift me up. She reminded me of another carefree spirit who had briefly shown me a different way of life.

I lifted my head to the water and closed my eyes. As Mo had said, this was our weekend. Our time to let everything go. We could be two people who had only this moment. We didn't have past hurts or those who had been a part of them. I let the spray wash away the twinge of pain I felt with the fleeting vision of Sam. I wanted to stop hurting. I was so tired of hurting or feeling guilt for each and every action I had taken for myself. I wanted to feel something other than pain and numbness. I want to be more like Mo. The light in the shower dimmed as a shadow passed in front of the bedroom fixtures.

Mo.

She stood at the foot of the bed watching me. The tint obscured her features but I felt the intensity in her stare nonetheless. She walked toward the shower and raised one palm flat against the glass. A single palm of invitation. Neither shame nor embarrassment crept into me. No, that wasn't what I felt with her eyes upon the nudity of my body. It was more as if she stared upon the nudity of my soul. I didn't try to cover myself. I stood still as she watched me. I waited for her to tell me what step was next. Waiting for her instruction of what she wanted us to be, if only for this weekend of living in a non-existent world. When she disappeared, I knew my answer.

I felt the skip in my heart when her silhouette appeared around the shower door. The tinted glass gave an obscured light to show her body to me. The water splattered against her exposed skin as she moved into its stream. I turned toward the shower glass to look at the illusion of the bed. This time was my own illusion of another world that didn't hold questions needing answers or futures needing plans. I saw only the illusion of this moment so close to Mo.

Running from a woman's touch had once before left me scarred and yearning for that which I had not allowed myself to feel. I wouldn't run again. It wasn't Sam. It wasn't the woman I loved who I felt step closer behind me. It wasn't Sam's finger that softly traced a trail down my spine. No, this was a woman who held a comfort in her I had grown to crave. A woman who looked at me without judgment, questioning or inquisitions of answers I wasn't ready to give. She took me as I was and who I felt I was at that very moment. Even if that person was an enormous ball of the unresolved.

"I'll go if you want," she said.

My knees weakened when I felt her palm across the small of my back. I feared I wouldn't be able to continue standing under her touch.

"You didn't ask me to be here. This may not be what you want." She removed her hand.

I felt the absence of it immediately and reached behind me to grab for its touch again. Even in the heat of the shower, the glass felt cool against my forehead, so much cooler than the warmth shared of our hands.

"It is." Those two words were all I could voice. Though my body screamed more, only those two words came out. My body screamed to tell her to take me into her arms and show me the passion it so badly desired. I pulled her toward me and felt the frailty of the strength in my knees grow as I felt her breasts press against my back. I released her hand and tried to steady myself against the glass. My fingers tensed against the wall.

She traced her fingertips across my back, along the back of my arm toward my hand, and interlaced her fingers within mine. "It's a need, Rayne. I've wanted you but now after today," she said softly against my ear, "it's a need. I need to feel you against me. But I'll stop if you want."

I let my head fall back onto her shoulder. "I need this too." I sighed deeply. "I need this so much."

She gently tugged at my hand to turn me away from the glass. I watched her eyes as they held me. They caressed every curve of me in a way that I didn't feel naked or raw in front of her. I felt like a woman being held, not nude, not shy, not anything other than held in her eyes. She placed her hands against the sides of my neck before letting them roam down along my collarbones. She held my eyes as one of her fingers read my skin like braille. The slow trace of her fingertip was awakening the tortuous need I had carried for so long. She leaned into me and softly kissed where her hands had been. She let her lips trail along my neck and across my collarbone.

"You're so beautiful," she said as she looked at me again. She brought my hand up to flatten it on her chest. She held it there just below her neck as she stepped back under the water spray. She closed her eyes and tipped her head back to let the water wash over her. I started to lift my hand from her chest as she weaved her fingers into her hair. She didn't open her eyes but removed one of her hands and put my hand back where it had been. The water and shampoo streamed over her and onto my hand and arm. It was my private time to watch her. My chance to see her without the scrutiny of her stare. My opportunity to study a woman's body not under blinding hospital lights or eyes of a doctor's study but rather under the eyes of a woman exploring another woman's body to feed a craving she had not yet allowed herself to feed.

I watched the soap run off of her long hair and over her shoulder. It covered the inked musical notes and birds on her left collarbone. Softly, I traced the lettering with my finger. "When the pain penetrates the music resonates." I felt the music that was Mo as she allowed me to take her in. The soap coursed down her body, across her breasts, and over her stomach where another musical design was found to the inside of her right hip. The sudsy water slid across her lower belly, down her legs, and settled at the top of her feet.

She stepped closer to me and brought the palm of my hand against her lips. I watched her as she placed a kiss in its center. I bit the inside of my cheek when I felt the softness of her tongue trace a circle. With her hand holding the back of mine, she led me to read the braille of her story. My heart beat wildly against my chest as she brought my fingertips to trail down her neck and over the inked expression she carried with her. Her eyes held me intently as we ventured together over her breast. I studied its perfection. I marveled at the response it held against my skin as my hand flexed to hold it. I heard the moan escape her lips and found her to be lost behind closed eyelids when I traced my thumb over her nipple. I watched her lips twitch and quiver as I felt the softness of it. She inhaled sharply when I bent down to take it between my lips. I felt it harden against my tongue. Her grip tightened over my hand. I looked up to see her lightly shaking her head before opening her eyes again. In the emerald of them, I wasn't afraid. Even with our bodies so open and exposed to one another, I didn't feel vulnerable, afraid or nervous. Mo held no judgments for me. She wanted no explanation of meaning from me. She only wanted me to feel what I felt in that very moment. And in that moment, I felt nothing of the world beyond these steamed-covered walls.

She grabbed our towels, handed me one, and took my hand as she led us out of the bathroom. The shaking in my knees returned when the bed's illusion lay in front of us. I steadied myself by leaning against one of the wooden beams that stretched from floor to ceiling. Mo stopped and turned to me. She held our joined hands in front of her. She studied them as she released her grip to let our fingers trace up and down each other. Lips upon my neck brought a scurry of twinkling lights behind my eyelids. I gave myself to her and let my neck roll into her kisses. My breath quickened against her thumb as she traced my bottom lip. Slowly, the beam disappeared against my back. I could no longer feel the wooden pressure of it supporting me. I felt only her. I felt only her lips against my neck until they took my kiss from her thumb's touch. Her kiss was a thief to my equilibrium. Tenderly, her tongue found mine and swept me away in the music of their dance. I was dizzy in her arms and pulled her closer as I fell completely into her. The towel tickled my ankles as it loosened in our embrace.

Don't stop. Please don't stop.

My body screamed words it had only dared to say once before. I was hers completely as she lowered me to the bed and stretched out beside me. She brought my lips back to hers with a single finger under my chin. She hadn't been a woman of words. She hadn't been a woman who overly expressed her thoughts in words. But in her kiss, I felt all she wanted to say. Her words were slow and soft as they mixed with those of my own. I felt the softness of her tongue everywhere. I felt it tracing along my lips and against the side of my own. The feel of it coursed through my body to the small of my back and then much lower below my abdomen as the intensity of it deepened. I was lightheaded in her kiss and became nearly faint as her hands traveled across my chest and breasts. I knew what I had caused her to feel in the shower as my breath matched hers with the squeeze of her hand and the touch of her tracing my breast. I knew the sensations that had earlier elicited the sharp inhale of her breath when she bent her head to place her lips upon my breast. I ran my hand through her hair and reflexively squeezed when I felt her tongue outline my nipple. She arose back up to watch me as I had watched her. She focused on my lips and held me there as I felt her fingers travel over the ridges of my ribs. I felt my muscles tighten as her hand trailed further down my side.

"I want to feel all of you, Rayne," she whispered through heavy breath. "Can I touch you?"

I felt the skip in her pattern and a tingle soar through me as her hand found the inside of my thigh. I bit the corner of my lip but gave her a resounding yes with the motion of my head on the pillow. She brought her lips again to mine. The intensity of her kiss had grown exponentially to take me away into every part of her as her hand found me. In that moment, she was my bayou. She was a slow ripple against a dock. A ripple that grew stronger with the motions of her hand as it brought my body to move to her will. My hips reached for her. My hands gripped what they could—one in her hair at the base of her neck as the other held only a crumble of cotton sheet. Her fingers took my breath as they filled me full of her touch.

"Don't stop. Please don't stop." My entire body screamed the words my mouth whispered as it writhed within her touch.

My back arched as the back of my head searched the pillow to understand the feelings she was causing in me. The way I felt nothing yet everything with her inside of me. The bayou had become an ocean. She was a race of building waves as they beat against my shore. I felt them crashing over me to take every single doubt of who I was out into the endless sea. I opened my eyes to reach for her and let the desire I found there hold me to completion. I let myself go in her touch. Let myself wash away onto her shore as I screamed against her neck. A moan that rose from inside and released for the first time under a woman's control. Not only had she given me my release sexually but she had also given me a release to be who I was. In her arms, within her touch, I had found a peace I had never felt.

The night kept the room darkened with all but a sliver of moonlight reflecting off of the glass shower. A twinge of guilt threatened my deepest thoughts. A guilt of infidelity as another woman had given me a pleasure my body had never known. I had found a release in her arms that I didn't know existed for me. It wasn't a guilt of cheating on Grant. No, it was Sam that filled my thoughts. I'd cheated on Sam and my love for her. It should have been under the touch of her hands to give me this night. But she had moved on. She had been the one to walk away from me. That is what I reminded myself. She had moved on and most surely had already found pleasure in the arms of another. After all, sex was sex to her. Right? I swallowed the guilt of my betrayal and yet again told my heart to tell her goodbye.

I reached down and pulled Mo's hand up to my chest. I cradled it in my arms for all it had given me. Her slumbering breath filled my ears as she slept soundly pressed against my back. I kissed her fingertips as I held onto the memory of the night in her arms. I felt her squirm as she molded her body closer to me and tucked her legs behind mine.

She let out a soft moan in my ear. "It's not time to get up yet." She kissed the lobe of my ear. "Sleep." She tightened her arms briefly as if hugging me into her. "I've got you."

She's got me. The cotton pillowcase indented against my smile as I drifted off to sleep.

"GET UP, SLEEPY head." Mo shook my shoulder. "Come on. Let's go up to the rooftop and drink coffee."

I opened one eye and peeked through. "It's still dark out."

"Yeah, but not because it's late. There's a rain shower coming in and it's super cloudy."

"But the bed is so nice and cozy." I tried to pull her on top of me but she stood firmly next to the bed. "I want to lie next to you some more."

"Then get up and let's go."

I twirled my finger around the material of her boxer shorts. "Yes, but in here you won't need these."

"I won't need them up there either."

I sat up to let my legs hang off the side of the bed and pulled her body into me. I lifted up her shirt. "But in here, I can do this," I mumbled against the skin of her lower belly.

She ran her fingers through my hair. "You can do that up there too." She knelt down in front of me and took my breath with her kiss. "Come on. Trust me already." Her words tickled my lips. "I want to show you this."

She stood up, held her hands out for me to take them, and pulled me up off of the bed. The morning air was cold against my bare legs as we stepped out onto the fire escape.

"Oh yeah, this is very private." I pulled at the bottom of my shirt tail in a failed attempt to cover the skimpy pajama shorts I was wearing.

"Oh, ye of little faith." She stepped onto the staircase, reached behind her back for my hand, and led me up toward the rooftop.

"I never knew this was up here," I said as I climbed the small steps that led over the brick wall of the rooftop.

"Jaz had it renovated a few years ago. We sneak up here at least once when I come over."

The décor of the home extension carried the same flow as that downstairs—clear glass, walnut-colored wood, and dark metal.

Mo walked to the kitchen area and poured two cups of coffee. "Black, right?"

"Uh, yeah. Black." I gave the enlarged swing a push. "This thing is pretty awesome."

"See. I told you." She ran her hand along the thick pillows that were propped against the wooden backboard. "I've slept many nights up here."

"I can see why. It's more like a bed than a swing." The oversized swing reminded me of the porch swings I loved to sit on back home except the bench on this one was wider and longer than the ones I was used to.

"Totally. Jaz had hell when she was first thinking of making it. She was scared it wouldn't be stable enough but it's not too bad." She walked around the swing to open the three sliding glass doors. A breeze poured through them and brought with it the smell of an impending rain.

"Climb in and I'll hand you your coffee." She steadied one of four thick metal chains fastened to the corner of the bed-type swing with her hand so that I could climb onto it.

"The breeze feels nice." I leaned against the tall backboard and stretched my legs out in front of me. The bench was long enough that my feet didn't come near touching the end of the cushion.

"See I told you." She shook her head. "When are you ever going to start trusting me?"

"Oh, I trust you alright."

"Is that so?" She climbed in next to me.

"That is so." I kissed her lips as she brought them closer to me.

"Maybe we'll test that theory one day." She winked at me as she took a sip of her coffee.

We settled our backs against the softness of the pillows. She swept her leg over mine and we stared out into the sky as we quietly drank our coffee. The width of the swing did afford her room to not have to sit so close to me but I was surely happy she had chosen not to use the extra space. I was enjoying the feeling of her body nestled up against mine.

Clouds swollen and grayed with the threatening rain hovered right above the skyline. Slowly, they moved closer to us to kick up the breeze to blow Mo's hair across her face. She tucked the freed strands behind her ear. Distant thunder rumbled in the quiet.

A smile twitched at her lips. "I love weather like this."

I felt a heat rush my neck as I pictured her head lying against the pillow with the same type of smile playing at her lips. Last night, I had pushed the thought of her sharing her body with the many women I knew had seen her beauty before me. I pretended my touch was the first she had felt. Otherwise, I doubt I would have been able to overcome the hesitation in my timid, inexperienced hands as they explored her. She had lain in front of me and welcomed anything I wanted to give her.

She brought her cup back to her lips. I studied the tattoo on her wrist and remembered the night before when I had kissed the musical note found there. Her pulse underneath the ink had quickened with the trace of my tongue. It raced even more when I kissed her neck. Her breath became more labored with each sweep of my tongue upon her neck. I watched her take another swallow of coffee. Her lips parted to take in the sip. They had parted in much the same way last night when I first touched her. She had taken in a sharp inhalation as I first went inside of her. Raindrops tapped on the roof in a rhythm much like the pulse of her neck that I had watched while I explored her. Rolling thunder broke through the patter of rain as her moans had broken through the depths of her breaths. The wind strengthened and brushed the scent of her hair across my nose. The scent I had inhaled as her body moved against me under the light sheet. She brushed the fallen strands again behind her ear but my mind took me to the night before when her hand was swiftly brought into the side of her hair as she lifted her body into me. A flash of lightning buried deep in the clouds gave light to the sky and my daydream of the desire in her eyes as she tightened the grip of her hand in her hair. I had been entranced with her every response to me as I made love to her. I watched her teeth as they bit into her bottom lip. My body molded into hers when her back arched into me.

The raindrops beat faster and trickled down the glass. I felt her in my hands again. The way I knew who I truly was from the moment I was inside of her. Thunder rose and rolled through the clouds just as her body had risen into me and rolled into my life. An impending storm that would not be denied. Lightning flashed. As dark as the room was the night before, it didn't have enough strength to keep the light from me when Mo gave herself to me. Her release within my touch unshackled my darkness. Lightning flashed again and gave light to the darkness that had been forever changed by the feel of our bodies held tightly together.

"What are you thinking about?"

I took the cup from her hands, set mine beside hers next to the bed, tucked my finger under the collar of her shirt, and pulled her toward me.

"This," I whispered against her lips. I took her in my arms and relived the awakening of my own storm the night before as the rain pattered against the roof. The swing flowed in the breeze of us.

Chapter 18

"Hat's next? I mean, I've never done this before."

"This?" Mo looked up over her menu. "Generally, you look at the menu and pick out something that looks good to you."

"You know that isn't what I mean." I leaned across the table to whisper, "A one-night stand."

She met me as she leaned forward too. "A one-night stand, you say?" she whispered and then began to lightly laugh. "By my count, it was one night, one morning, and one very long afternoon."

Somehow, I foolishly thought maybe my ability to blush would be lessened after the night she and I had experienced. I was wrong. I felt it take over my cheeks yet again. Carefully, I leaned back away from her before she noticed. Although, I couldn't go back too far as the small padded stools didn't give much leeway in leaning back too far. At least they were only about a foot off of the floor so it wouldn't be a high fall.

"You are so adorable." She poured us a glass of white wine that she had ordered for dinner. "Here, sip on this. It'll calm some of those nerves you seem to have found now that you've got clothes on."

The blush returned full fold and Mo laughed. I glanced around to see if anyone was eavesdropping on our conversation to notice two women who had spent the last day wrapped passionately in one another's arms. Quickly, I became angry with myself and the inbred fear of wondering what those around me thought of my actions. What the hell did it matter anyway if complete strangers had any inclination of the experience I had just had?

She held her glass up. "To our weekend of new experiences." She clinked it against mine. "For both of us."

The taste of the riesling caught me off guard. It wasn't as sweet as I remembered and I was quite sure I flinched or made a face as I swallowed it.

Mo chuckled. "What? You don't like it?"

"No. It isn't that. I wasn't expecting it. I thought this wine was sweeter than this."

"Not all rieslings are sweet."

I brought the glass up to my nose. There was a weird scent of petrol. "It sort of smells like diesel fuel. Maybe it's bad. Like spoiled or something?"

Mo laughed loudly. "I'm sorry I shouldn't have laughed. You're just so damn cute. I remember what it was like when Jaz and I first started drinking wine. Let's try it again and if you don't like it, we'll order another bottle or a beer. Deal?"

"Deal." Although I would have agreed to anything at that moment. She could have said, "Hey, let's go rob a bank after dinner," and I most likely would have nodded my head in agreement. She was absolutely stunning. The restaurant's backdrop brought out the green of her eyes brilliantly. They nearly sparkled as she looked at me.

Her expression turned serious. Perhaps she read something in mine as I watched her. She slowly brought her hand to her mouth and bit at her thumbnail. She took in a deep breath.

"Has anyone ever told you how dangerous those eyes of yours are?" she asked around the thumb resting against her bottom lip.

I couldn't speak so I simply shook my head.

"Well, they are. I swear I can read them sometimes. I can tell what you're thinking." She looked around the restaurant before fixating on the stone pillar at the end of our table. "If this had given us four walls instead of this one lonely column, I fear I would have to take you right here…right now. No wonder we haven't eaten. All I want to do is take you back to bed."

Butterflies swarmed my belly and refused to let go. "We could get it to go." My voice was shaky and soft.

"Or we could eat the fabulous meal I've ordered. Finish off a bottle of wine. All the while your eyes will continue to drive me crazy so that the moment we step into Jaz's apartment, all I will be able to do is rip your clothes off and hold you until the sun comes up."

"Or, yes. There's always that option."

Mo shifted on the stool and watched me in silence for a few moments before clearing her throat. "Now, let's see what we can do with this wine," she said softly. She brought her glass up to her nose and inhaled. "Try to smell past the diesel fuel. What do you smell beyond that?"

I brought the glass to my nose and breathed in its scent. I blocked the thought of petrol from my senses and inhaled deeper. "Hmmmm… citrus? Sort of smells like citrus." I smelled the wine again. "Oh, and honey. I smell honey."

A smile spread across her face. "Perfect. Okay, so this time after you breathe in to get the aroma past the noxious, I want you to take a sip. Swish it in your mouth until you can no longer detect the smell and then swallow."

I did as she instructed.

She followed my movements. "Now, what do you taste?"

"Mostly pineapple but with a hint of lime and apricot."

"Perfect." She smiled even broader. "That's why it's such a good choice with Indian food. It's the interaction you go for. The wine must complement the food, not take away from it. This wine won't take away from the complexities of spices in the dishes I ordered." She stopped and leaned back away from the table. "What? What's that look for?"

"I don't know. It's just sometimes you surprise me with things you say."

"Like what? Why?"

"Well, you're a Harley-riding, leather-wearing deejay who just taught me how to appreciate the combination of wine and food pairings. Doesn't actually add up, you know?"

"Don't we all have layers, Rayne? Don't we all have sides to ourselves that we don't share with everyone? Sides we only share with a few?"

I thought of the past day in her arms. I thought of Sam. She was the first outside of Meems that I had shown myself to. Yet hadn't I hidden some from her as well? Wasn't it true, I felt I couldn't share everything with her? I didn't share my insecurities of what being a lesbian would mean for fear I would hurt her or push her away. I didn't share my fears of what a life with her would do to my future. Well, I didn't until the end on the night I tried to see her through the tears blinding my eyes. The night I broke as I watched the mascara smear down her face. And then there was Meems. Hadn't I hidden from her, too? The one woman I felt loved me above and beyond every single wrong or right I could have ever done. Yet, I hid even from her.

The waiter brought our food to the table and broke my memories before the pain crept in. I finally noticed the colors surrounding me. My focus on Mo had prevented me from appreciating the pop of red in the restaurant's light fixtures, cloth table coverings, and wall decorations. Other than those key elements, the majority of the setting was made up of different tones of brown from a light beige of the stone walls to a rich dark chocolate in the molding and decorative clay pottery.

"I know we said we wouldn't, but do you want to talk about her?" Mo picked up my plate and filled it with the chickpea dish the waiter had set down alongside the Tandoori chicken. The smell of curry took over my senses as she spooned the chickpeas onto my plate.

"Which her?"

Mo raised her head up and gazed at me. "There's more than one her? And that's why, folks, you don't assume anything." She filled her plate and rested the spoon along the lip of the bowl. "I'm sorry, I guess I always thought there had only been one woman in your life."

"There was only one like you're thinking."

"I don't get it."

"What you see…what you sometimes see when you look at me.

The sadness? It's because of two women in my life." I reached for my wine and watched the liquid swirl up against the sides of the glass as I swirled it. I took a swallow to squash the tears I did not want to fall tonight. "I get sad when I think of my grandmother and a woman named Sam."

"Ah." She reached into the basket on the far side of the table. "Here, try this with it. It's called naan. It's a type of bread." She handed me a round, brown-spotted white bread. "Do you want to talk about them?"

"Is that what you want?"

"To get to know you better? For you to let me in? Yes, that's what I want. If it's what you want." She held up her fork to stop me from answering. "But if you do, then you have to eat while you talk. We've not had food since yesterday. I don't want you passing out on me." She smiled and pointed her fork at my plate before taking a bite herself.

I felt the heat again rush to my cheeks with the flashback of pulling Mo's body against mine as tight as I could. I hadn't seemed to be able to pull her close enough to me. A part of me already feared the next day. The day we would say goodbye. I knew I would see her again but in what capacity I had no idea. I wondered what it would feel like to see her again with all we have shared plus the exposure of opening up to her. Yet in the same breath, I had grown so tired of always fearing or planning for the future of what could happen instead of living in the moment of now. In the here and now, I had this gorgeous woman sitting across from me, sharing an experience of new food and wishing to know more about me. A woman whose attention was desired by so many lesbians and yet here she sat with me. Smiling at me. Wanting to know all of me. It was a freedom I didn't have with Sam. No matter what I told Mo, she wouldn't change the way she felt about me or about what she wanted from me. She didn't want the whole pie like Sam did. She didn't want the sunset. She wanted the moment.

"The first part of eating is to actually pick up a utensil."

I blinked several times and looked down at the plate she had put in front of me. "I'm sorry. My mind wandered away for a minute."

"Yeah, I see that. I think my head is going to spin right off of me if you ever start taking me on the journeys in your mind. Damn, girl, does that brain of yours ever stop?"

"Not too often, no."

"We're going to have to see what we can do to slow it down one day." She motioned her fork at me before taking another bite of food. "It's a little spicy but I think a Cajun girl like you can take it." She winked as she took a healthy swallow of the white wine.

I grinned. "Let's see what you call spicy." The curry and cayenne seasoning of the chickpeas warmed my tongue but didn't send the sometimes-searing hurried need for cooling after I tasted foods back home. Nonetheless, I took a swallow of the wine Mo had selected to pair with dinner. She had done well. "You're right. The wine does complement the spices of the food. It's like it enhances it."

Her smile was wide as she popped a piece of naan into her mouth. "Thank you. It's much like the company sitting across from me."

I let the matching smile reach my heart and calm my nerves of opening up to her and remembering. "I would say there are two women who've changed my life. One I've always known and one I knew for only a short while. Both of them are gone now."

"Gone?"

"Yes. Memaw passed away last November."

She covered my hand with her own. "I'm so sorry."

I didn't flinch away from her touch even with all eyes to see. In fact, I rolled my hand over and basked in the comfort of it.

"Thank you." I squeezed her hand. I liked the feeling of it within mine. Especially, as I continued to talk. "I'd never really considered life without her. It wasn't factored into my plans. For as long as I can remember, I was going to go to medical school and go back home to live. She and I were going to set up my practice. I'd spend my days working and my weekends with her. I'd finally do what I wanted to do. Live under my own roof. Not have to answer to Charlie Grace. But now she's gone and I feel utterly lost."

"Charlie Grace?"

"My mother."

"Ah, you call her by her first name?"

"It's become a habit. One I have to watch when I'm around her. She's another story altogether."

"Sounds like it. And do you still want to go back home?"

I took in a deep breath to let her question filter in. I tucked my bangs behind my ear but they fell back over my eye. "I do. I truly do. It's my home. The people there. The culture. It's like a bond I still have with Memaw." I took a sip of wine to let the hint of pineapple cool the heat I was sensing on my tongue. "But I know it'll never be the same without her there." I looked up at the overhanging light fixture in an attempt to control the looming tears before they fell.

"And the other?"

"Sam?" The pang in my heart returned with a vengeance. The night in Mo's arms had surely intensified the feeling of loss and searching when I thought of Sam. It had solidified her loss to me. What do I say about the woman I considered to be the love of my life? How do I describe her to a woman who had been my first real experience at physical love? One had opened my heart to new experiences and one had opened my body to them. I searched her eyes and focused on the tiny brown circles mixed among the green of her pupil. The pupil that was now dilated as she studied my face.

She reached behind her neck to pull her long hair over her shoulder. "You know you can tell me anything. I've told you before and I mean it. I'm not one to judge. You won't hurt me. I see what you feel for her in your eyes. If it'll help you to speak them, then do. If not, then don't. Nothing you say will change what I feel for you." I watched her earring dangle against her neck.

Her eyes held the truth of her words. They held safety to say anything my heart wished. I closed mine briefly to find the words in the darkness. Without my sight clouding my senses, I caught the scent of her perfume. It gifted my nose, reminded me of the scent from the pillow we had shared and calmed my hesitation.

"You're safe," she whispered as she leaned over the table.

Safe.

"Her name is Samantha LeJeune but she went by Sam. I met her in medical school."

Mo sat back in her chair and pulled her wine glass in front of her as if she was focusing completely on my words.

"I was instantly attracted to her. Although initially I couldn't or wouldn't acknowledge it for exactly what it was or meant. Everything about her excited me. Everything about her made me nervous. I tried to deny it because deep down I knew what accepting it would mean for my life." I shook my head as I thought of the denial of the truth that rested right at my fingertips.

She took a slow, small sip of her wine. "Rayne, we all did. I did. Jaz did. We all did. What? It was supposed to be easy to identify something about yourself that you weren't raised to know as a possibility? Give yourself a break."

"But I should've known. I should've known before I lost her. I questioned it too much. I was stronger before Memaw passed but then I let these fears of God and religion overwhelm me. I think I know it wasn't my fault she died. I tell myself it wasn't." I grew angry at the lump building in my throat.

"How on earth could anything you did cause your grandmother's death? What burden are you carrying?" She slid my glass of wine in front of me.

I took her hint and brought it to my lips for a swallow…not a sip, a swallow. "The night she passed. The very night she passed, I had let myself feel free. I had let go of all of the fears and went to her. I stopped fighting my attraction to her. My love for her."

"You two slept together?"

"No, not fully."

"Not fully?"

"My pager went off."

Mo chocked on the sip of wine she had just taken in. "What?"

"I guess you could say we were in the middle of it when my pager went off. I was on call that night and had an emergency car wreck patient come in. I couldn't stay with her."

"Did you two ever finish what you started?"

"No. We didn't. I got the call about Memaw when I was operating on that patient. Everything went dark from there." I swirled my wine glass and studied it again for a moment. "When I kissed Sam…when I touched her, I felt home. I don't know. That probably sounds stupid, but I did."

"It doesn't sound stupid at all."

"It felt right for the first time ever. For the first time in my life, intimacy felt right. Never with anyone else. Never with…" I looked down at the ring still on my finger.

Her eyes followed mine. "Rayne?"

I looked up at her.

"Don't look at that ring. Keep telling me about the woman who felt something for the first time. I doubt you're going to find the answers in that ring. I only care about you. I only care about knowing the woman you are. The woman I've kissed and touched. The woman I've connected with. She's who I want to hear about right now."

"I never felt right with him. I've heard about sin, sermon after sermon. The guilt of sin. I've only been with three people my whole life. You, Sam, and him. And the only time it ever felt right up until this weekend with you was that one night with Sam. But then I was wrong because that's when she was taken away. The very night I was with Sam, Meems died." I swallowed hard. "I couldn't forgive myself for what I had done. For letting go. It all fell apart with Sam after that. Do you know I was literally skipping on my way to the OR that night? Skipping." I shook my head. "I was so happy. Felt so alive and then the pager went off again. I didn't know how to be or what to feel after that."

She wiped away a tear from my cheek with her thumb. "And now? How do you feel now?"

"Apprehensive?"

"Apprehensive about what?"

"I guess a part of me is waiting for the pager to go off again. But I really don't have anything else to lose."

"I don't know what things you were taught as a child. What

religious threats you heard. So, I don't know exactly what you are basing these beliefs on. What I can tell you is how I believe. I listen to what is being spoken. You can read verses in the Bible. You can listen to people spout their beliefs about what those verses mean. Or..." She dipped her head until I looked up into her eyes. "Or you can listen to the whispers in your ears. You can listen to the spiritual voices telling you the direction of your path. Whether you want to believe that voice is God's, an angel's, Buddha's, or just the universe itself, it's up to you. The most important thing is to listen. Being spiritual and following a higher power is everyone's right to find on their own. It's their own relationship between them and their whispers. It's not just some inflated man yelling from a podium."

The pineapple and apricot sweetened my tongue as the wine trickled down my throat. I watched the woman behind the expression. I watched the softening of her eyebrows as she returned my gaze. A woman who I once thought kept her feelings either ultimately controlled or didn't feel at all sat across from me with an expression which told me the falseness of all of my previous beliefs. She had become a woman who held the ability to ease both my body and my mind's struggle.

"Can I ask how you feel after being with me?"

"You mean beyond incredible?"

"Who's the lady charmer now?" She shook her finger at me. "Yes, beyond that. How do you feel as far as the right and wrong of what we shared?"

I hesitated for a moment to consider my thoughts. A part of me believed maybe the guilt wasn't there with Sam because I already loved her when we shared our intimacy together. Maybe it was the love which kept the guilt at bay?

"Hmmmm, maybe I shouldn't have asked. You're hesitating awfully long. We can forget I asked."

"No, wait. I'm thinking. I want to give you an honest answer." There wasn't any guilt in the way she was thinking. But I wasn't in love with her. I was in love with the moment in time she gave me and for right now, that was enough. I extended my arm across the table to grasp her hand. "It feels incredible because it feels all kinds of right."

Chapter 19

"God, I missed you so much." Grant reached across the gear shift to grab my hand. "And then I hardly got to see you when I got back. Who would've thought plastic surgery would be so demanding?"

I didn't acknowledge the condescending statement to my specialty. It was fair as he had not commented on the flinch of my hand with his touch. He also didn't speak of the tightened thigh muscles which lay beneath our joined hands.

Technically, I could have seen him more over the last couple of weeks since his return from New York. The extra hours he spoke of were volunteered hours. Some could say even begged volunteer hours as I had taken nearly all call others would trade with me. I wasn't ready to answer Grant's questions nor be alone with him in the same room. As I sat staring out his car window, I realized it was more that I didn't want to be alone with him in the same room. After the weekend with Mo, I knew in my heart there were things with Grant that I could never do again. Those things seemed to find their way to possibility when we were alone. There was safety in riding with him home for Thanksgiving because we had no time for a detour or stopover. Both of us had difficulty getting off earlier than the Wednesday before the holiday.

"Rayne, you would've loved New York. I didn't spend a lot of time outside of the hospital. But, man, when we did get out, it was freaking amazing. There was so much to do."

Man?

"There was always something open. We could leave the OR at four in the morning and go anywhere we wanted. If we wanted a drink… yep, there was somewhere to go. If we wanted breakfast or dinner, there was a place for that too. It was crazy."

"Yeah. Sounds great." My tone was flat as I hardly had any interest in the conversation much less the desire to participate.

He, however, was full of excitement. He stared out through the windshield and I wondered if he even saw the road in front of him. His eyes looked out into the two-lane highway as if he saw only the lights of New York. Its worn white-and-yellow lines were hardly visible under the overcast sky. It wasn't necessarily a cloud-filled sky but rather one with a uniform grayish color.

"It was. The hospitals. Did they ever have their shit together? They had one whole wing for vascular patients. The whole OR team was specialized. Not once did I have to explain to a scrub what I needed."

"Sounds great."

"It was. You would really love it there. I was thinking maybe we could run up there before Christmas. Take a weekend trip, you know? Maybe do a little shopping. Take a look around."

Christmas already. I was barely hopeful to get through Thanksgiving much less let my thoughts venture on to the next holiday. "I don't know. We'll see. Maybe after the first of the year."

He reached behind the steering wheel to turn on the windshield wipers. They screeched across the mist-covered glass and thudded back into their place above the hood. "Okay, but soon after the first. Like maybe the first week in January?"

"Maybe. We have plenty of time to plan a weekend trip."

He turned the temperature knob to add a touch of heat to the circulating air. "Yeah, but they need to know my timeframe shortly after the first of the year."

I snapped my head toward him. "They? Timeframe?"

"Yeah. New York-Presbyterian Hospital." He looked at me as if I was somehow to know what he was talking about. As if I had forgotten something he had already discussed with me. "They offered me a residency position at their Vascular Institute."

"I was wondering when you were going to tell me about that."

He looked away from the road toward me. "What do you mean?"

"Tyler told me you and Paxton were going for a year residency there. That this little stint up there was just a stepping stone to see who they wanted. *You* didn't tell me anything about it."

He turned away from me shamefully. "I know," he said as he sighed. "Truth is, I didn't think it would be a thing to discuss. They've been considering people from all over the world to join them. I didn't think I had a snowballs chance. Hell, I was surprised I made it as far as I did. But that's not even the best news." He was smiling when he glanced back over into the passenger seat. "I could finish out there with the likelihood of a staff position once I'm done. Can you imagine, Rayne?"

Could I imagine? What was he telling me? "No, actually I can't. What do you mean a staff position?"

"Meaning they want me to stay on after I'm done. I would be part of countless studies and have who knows how many opportunities to publish."

"But what about home?" I turned down the heat I found stifling. "What about your family? I thought you wanted to move back home to open a practice."

"Well, yeah." His knuckles whitened as he gripped the steering wheel tighter. "I mean, I did. But you and I both know I'm going to get few if any real good cases there. And I sure as hell won't get to be a part of any major studies or grant opportunities. Rayne, this is my chance to be more. This is my shot."

"Real good cases. Is that what the people we grew up with mean to you? They're cases? What happened to wanting to come back home and make a difference in the lives of the people we grew up with? What happened to the man who dreamed of that?"

"He grew up."

"Ah. I see. He grew up, huh?" I turned to look out the window. The scenery I recognized but the man in the car next to me, I no longer did.

Truthfully, if he could see all of my thoughts of the future like the ones he was sharing with me, he wouldn't recognize me either.

"You know what I mean."

"I do know what you mean." He was right. We had grown up. We had grown from the kids that once left Brennin.

"And just think of the opportunities you'll have."

The muscles along the back of my neck twitched as I wrenched my head to look at him. "I'm sorry. What did you say?"

"You'll be able to do any type of plastics you want. Burns. Reconstructions. Cosmetics." He counted them off as if he had practiced this conversation multiple times. "Think of the clientele base you'll have if you go for cosmetic surgery."

"What makes you think I'll be going there and when did I ever insinuate at any point in time that I wanted a cosmetic-based practice?"

"Well, if I am," he said as he turned to look at me, "then aren't you?" He sounded surprised.

"No. I *absolutely* am not."

The wind felt stronger against the car as I watched the speedometer needle move clockwise. "No. Just no? You wouldn't even consider coming with me? I thought we wanted to live our dreams together."

"That was when our dreams were on the same path. Why would you even think I would all of a sudden want to move to New York?"

"Maybe because we're engaged. Maybe because we're going to be husband and wife soon. I sort of thought couples did that sort of thing for one another."

"Soon? And couples did what? Changed the game plan to fit their wants and then just expected the other to follow."

"Don't you do that?"

"Don't I do what?"

"Make changes I'm supposed to follow? Like your friends, for instance. First there was Sam. You meet her and bam I'm like an annoyance to you. Like it's a chore for you to spend time with me. And now you've made more. These I haven't even met yet but I could hardly get you on the phone when I was away. I knew it was because of you being with them. So, tell me again about changing the dynamics of the relationship and expecting the other to follow. Because that's a conversation I've been waiting to have."

"Grant, I don't want to fight. Can we just change the subject?"

"Yeah, that's what I thought you'd say." His knuckles turned white again as he gripped the steering wheel tighter. "We have both made changes. I have accepted and gone along with yours and now I'm asking you to do the same for me."

I felt myself growing angry at him, yet I knew the fact he was right in what he was saying was the real reason for my anger. I wasn't ready for this particular conversation so I held my tongue from saying anything and sincerely hoped he would change the subject.

In the distance, I noticed a fast-approaching small oak tree. Its branches were covered with brilliant yellowish-green leaves. They were a stark contrast against the dark green needles of pine branches around it. The tree glowed with life as it held on to the last of its remaining color before the cold temperatures stole it in the night. It seemed to stand in defiance of the overpowering pines and gray skies. Its light would not be dampened. It would not be shadowed.

After we passed the tree, I focused on Grant. I watched the stiffness in his jaw as he twitched his muscles. He was angry too. He was upset with my response as if I would have gladly changed my future dreams because somehow it was expected of a dutiful wife. He had accepted my changes without even commenting on the fact he noticed them. Now he expected the same from me. It was painfully obvious we had both made choices with the end result of us seeing a future that did not find us as husband and wife.

"Listen to the whispers." I heard Mo's voice in my head.

Maybe this was a way out. Maybe his choices gave me an out to live the future I wanted? Yet should I really cower behind the simplicity of location as a reason to cancel our nuptials? Would I betray the small oak's strength if I were to succumb to using another reason behind my choices other than being strong in the truth of who I was?

THE SOUND OF the car's tires was louder than I remembered as Grant drove along the drive lined by pecan trees. The trees had once provided a staple and source of income for the large plantation home but now they served only as a decoration.

Crunch. Crack. Crunch. Crack.

Quietly, I stretched my neck to look out the window at the ground. Hundreds of pecan shells, some freed from the black outer covering while others were naked of their shells, lay across the road and ground. The house came into view.

"What are you guys like the fucking Kennedys of Mayberry or something?" Sam's comment had once brought a laugh. Today, it left me with a feeling fitting of the gray sky.

Charlie Grace walked out of the large French doors of the house. Her movements were slow as she stepped down the brick steps. She looked radiantly put together. She looked elegant. She looked…older.

"I had nearly put my mind to y'all missing dinner this evening." Her dramatic flair was as much a memory as Sam's voice. She opened the passenger door as Grant rolled to a stop. "Well, it's about time you two got here. Oh, dear Gawd, what did you do to your hair?" She flipped the short strands of hair that fell below my ear. "At least we have time to let it grow out before the wedding." She frowned. "But those blonde highlights will take forever to grow out."

And there she is, Charlie Grace.

"Hi, Mother. So nice to see you too." I stood from the car and gave her our standard brief hug.

She ran her finger across my bangs and cringed as if they stung her hand. "Really, Rayne. What were you thinking?"

"I don't know. I suppose I was thinking 'Hey, I'd like to get a new hairstyle.' You know, something crazy like that. Kids these days."

"Such sass." She looked over my shoulder. "Well, at least you shaved that crap off so I can see your handsome face again."

I looked over the hood to see Grant's cleanly shaven face. *Wait? He shaved his beard?* The look on his face was as quizzical and questioning as the thoughts in my head.

"You two have seen each other, yes?" Charlie Grace looked back and forth between us. "I mean, you did just spend hours with each other in the car or am I wrong about that? Good Lord, you two look like you're seeing each other for the first time."

"I don't know about that but, Charlie Grace, you're a sight for sore eyes." Grant stepped around the hood of the car to lift her up in his arms.

She laughed. She literally laughed before patting his face with her hands. They looked smaller. I wasn't sure if it was the actual size of them or maybe it was a new shirt. She usually didn't wear her shirts this loose with the sleeves opening out over her wrists. Or is she smaller?

"Hey, look at you two!" Jacques took the brick steps more rapidly than Charlie Grace had. He took me fully in his arms and hugged me with a tight grip that held me close to him. "Rayne, you look beautiful. Something's changed." He leaned back away from me to look at me. "What is it? Hmmmm."

"Well." I ran my hand through my cropped hair. "I got a new haircut."

He smiled. "Yeah, maybe that's it. But damn if you don't look absolutely radiant. Whatever it is, I love it."

I wrapped my arm around his waist as he pulled away from the hug. He kept his arm around my shoulder and squeezed it slightly as he spoke.

"Grant, thanks for bringing our girl home to us." He looked down into my eyes. "We've missed you."

"I've missed you too."

He dropped his hand from my shoulder. "Come on, son. Let's get you unloaded."

I looked past Jacques as I waited for the others to come out of the house. "Where's Glenn? Are they still in the woods?"

Jacques looked over his shoulder toward Charlie Grace who hung her head as she retreated back into the house. The door closed softly behind her.

"Not this time, honey. They didn't come up this year." He patted me softly on my shoulder. His and Charlie Grace's actions spoke volumes beyond words. This was not a topic to be further discussed.

Grant and I followed Jacques into the house. If not for the smell of basil and peppers warming my nose, I would have been uncomfortable with the chill in the foyer of the house. I shoved my hands into the pockets of my jacket. Yet it wasn't a temperature that chilled my body. It was the house. The sense of the house. Nothing was as I remembered of Thanksgivings past. I peered into the den where Charlie Grace sat quietly staring at a fireplace filled with burning candles. The rich fall colors were absent from the drapery. The purples and golds found during the beginning of football season still remained the focus of the room's decorations.

"Are you making pasta tonight?" I sat down on the couch beside her.

"No. Pizza."

"Pizza?"

"Yes, this one here got a wild hair to learn to make pizza. A few thousand dollars later, we have a renovated kitchen with a brick pizza oven," Jacques said as he and Grant walked into the room. "If she keeps trying new things, I won't be a bit surprised if she says she's going parachuting next."

"Oh, please. I hardly think a brick oven is the same as jumping out a perfectly good airplane. I find the comparison to be utterly ridiculous."

"You're right. I would've spent a helluva lot less money on the parachute jump." He and Grant chuckled.

I could tell Charlie Grace was anything but amused. She stood from the couch and disappeared into the kitchen.

"You're in the doghouse tonight, old buddy," Grant said as he sat in the loveseat closest to where I was.

"It's okay. I've been out there so much lately it's like a second home to me."

"Where are all of the decorations, Jacques?" I placed a sofa pillow over my arms.

Jacques looked around the room. "Yeah. She said she didn't feel much like putting them out this year."

"Is she not feeling well? She looks like she's lost weight."

"She's not eating the best." Jacques winked at me. "She's gonna be okay."

Charlie Grace cleared her throat. "She's absolutely fine and happens to be back in the same room. She also doesn't appreciate being talked about behind her back." She sipped on the fresh martini in her hand as she sat back on the couch.

"What? No Irish Coffees?" The chill hovering over the room grew.

"I'll make you one if you want." Charlie Grace pulled a shawl from the back of the couch and wrapped it around her shoulders.

I shook my head. "No, that's okay."

Everything was off. I recognized the look in Charlie Grace's eyes as she stared into the burning candles. I saw the familiarity in the gray version of my own. The eyes which stared back at me when I thought of Memaw. When I felt the pain of her loss. Did I really see the same in hers? The signs of lines at her eyes drew her lids down into a frown. I caught the faint lines of clumped makeup around the sides of her mouth. When did she age so?

"Come on, Grant. Let's go ice down some beer to go with this delicious smelling pizza. Who needs Irish Coffee with pizza?" Jacques said while he walked toward the door.

After the men left the room, Charlie Grace and I watched the flickering candles in silence.

Chapter 20

"I DON'T KNOW, JAZLYN. It's just so weird here." I sat on the porch along the back of the house as I hardly wanted to be inside a moment longer.

"What? Being back home after so long or is there more to it?"

"More. Way more. The whole place feels off. Charlie Grace. The house. The traditions. They're all off." I rocked the chair and leaned my head against the back of it. The chair squeaked in the too-long silence.

"Is this the first Thanksgiving?" Jazlyn's voice held a tenderness.

"Yes."

"And it was this time of year?"

"Yes."

I heard Jazlyn's deep intake of air. "Oh, my friend. This time will be tough on everyone."

"Not Charlie Grace. That woman is made of stone."

"But she lost her mother."

"You didn't see her at the funeral." My voice cracked.

"I'm here for whatever you need. If you want to cry, I'm here. If you would rather not right now, then we can make that happen too."

"I could use for a change of subject."

"Well, alright then. Let's do this." I could hear her smile within her words. The smile that was so wide and open I swear I could see her molars. It brightened her whole face when she smiled. It brightened mine. She was truly a best friend. "They have a new dish at the Thai place and it's freaking unbelievable."

I laughed. "I thought I heard you chewing when I first called."

"Sorry, dude. I was trying to hide it." She was not, however, trying to hide it now as I could tell she was talking around a mouth full. "It's just so freaking good and I'm a starving' Marvin over here. The club is crazy tonight. Damn lesbians are trying to dance their asses off before the big turkey day."

"Hey, you gotta do something to make room for that extra piece of sweet potato pie."

"Yuck. You can keep your little potatoes of the sweet. I'll take this chicken with coconut and tarragon."

I heard her take a sip of liquid. "What are you drinking?"

She laughed. "Damn, you're on your investigative skills tonight."

"That I am."

"We thought a new meal deserved a new wine choice."

"We? Violent home tonight."

"Nah. She's on call. This is her holiday. Mo's here."

Mo's there? The thumping of my heartbeat drowned out the creak of the rocking chair.

"She came in to spend Turkey Day with me. We are grabbing a bite in between her sets."

My mouth was too dry to speak. My throat was tight with visions of Mo's eyes as she watched my lips. The eyes that watched me as her body lay on top of me. Her face obscured by the hair which fell as she rested above me. The smile that crept across her face as she tucked the loose strands behind her ear.

"Hey? Did I lose you?"

I swallowed.

"Damn cell phones."

"No, I'm here. Sorry. So, Mo's there?" Geez, was that as pathetic as I heard in my own head?

"Yeah, she's here. Just walking in from her set." Jazlyn's voice became muffled and I wondered if she had moved the phone away from her mouth. It didn't keep me from hearing her words. "Damn, girl. Do I need to put a fan up there with you? You're drenched."

When I heard Mo's laughter and voice, my stomach flipped like an ocean wave had crossed my belly.

"Talking to Rayne. Want me to tell her anything for you?"

"Ah," I heard Mo say. "Sure. Tell her I said hi."

"Mo says hi."

The wave suddenly turned to nausea. "I heard. Thanks. Tell her I said hi back." I started the chair rocking again to take my mind off of the feeling in my stomach. "I'll let you two go enjoy your new fab dinner." I hoped my voice sounded chipper than I felt. I hoped it sounded anything other than the disappointment I felt knowing Mo was back in town and hadn't contacted me.

"Are you sure? We can keep talking if you want? Mo can entertain herself. You know that."

"Ha. Yeah. She's a woman of many talents." I forced a laugh. I was sure Jazlyn would hear it, but maybe she would think it for reasons besides the pain of knowing the truth of our one-night stand. "But, yeah. I'm good. Getting ready for bed actually. Y'all have fun tonight."

THE SOUND OF a trickling rain beat lightly across the roof of the balcony outside my bedroom. The pattering of its drops was comforting and just loud enough to attempt to deafen my thoughts. I massaged my forehead to try to rub away the aching throb between my eyebrows.

What was it about life these days? Could nothing be simple anymore? I had gone from a life of worrying of nothing more than when I would go fishing with Memaw again to why a woman I had shared the most intimate parts of my body with had never called me afterward. In between those thoughts were the facts: I was engaged to a man I knew I could never marry; I had a mother who seemed to be slipping into a depression—which was unlike anything I had seen of her before; I had fallen in love and loss with a woman I believed was truly the love of my life; and I was filled with the eternal blackness left the night Memaw passed in my arms. How? How did it all go so wrong in such a short amount of time?

I looked up when my phone vibrated on the small wooden night-stand. It startled me. I managed to catch it before it fell off the table.

"Hello," I answered.

"Hey, you."

Mo.

"Hi."

"Did I wake you?" Mo's voice was hoarse. It got that way after a night's show.

"No. I'm in bed but not sleeping."

"Oh."

I became acutely aware of the high-pitched drip of water as it fell through the guttering. I counted the drops as they hit against the metal.

Mo took in a deep breath and let it out slowly. "I wish I were there with you."

"Where?"

"In your bed. Lying next to you."

I bit into my bottom lip.

"Rayne?"

"Yes."

"I wish I were there with you now. Or you here with me. Or anywhere for the matter. Anywhere that found your body against mine again."

"You didn't call."

"Neither did you."

"I'm not the one that sleeps with random women."

"Is that what you think you are to me? Is that what you think it was?"

"You tell me." I didn't want to argue. I didn't. All I wanted to do was fall into her voice. All I wanted to do was envision her as she had described with her body lying behind me and her arms wrapped around me while we listened to the rain. Yet I feared the pain of letting my thoughts go there. She hadn't called. In the days since I kissed her goodbye at Jazlyn's loft, I had thought of her. I wondered if she had moved on to another woman. A distant roll of thunder shook me from that train of thought.

"Is that thunder?"

"Yes. It's still far off but yeah."

"I love thunderstorms."

"I remember."

"Rayne?"

"Yes."

"If you want to talk about who didn't call who, we can do that. Or, if given my choice we can accept that either one of us could've called the other but for whatever reason we didn't and let it go right there." She let out another deep sigh. "I want to be there with you," she whispered. A whisper that set my body on fire. "Lying behind you. Holding you in my arms. Listening to the storm."

Just like that, with the sound of her whisper in my ear, I was there again. Listening to the rain on the rooftop of Jazlyn's loft. I felt the warmth of her body. The touch of her fingertips. The yearning ache in the pit of my stomach. "I don't want."

"Hmmmmm. Okay then."

"No. I mean, I don't want to discuss who didn't call who." I followed her whisper and hoped it had the same effect on her as hers did me. "I want you here or me there. I want that so badly."

"That's better." Her words were drawn out.

The thunder was closer this time and vibrated the glass of the balcony door.

"Sounds like it's getting close?"

"Yeah, I think it is."

"Wish you could see the moon tonight. I'm up on the rooftop and it's a gorgeous night here."

"I remember that rooftop."

"As do I." I heard rustling. "I remember how your body felt under these sheets."

"Oooh. You're on the bed." Another butterfly.

"I am."

My throat closed again to the words I wanted to say.

"I've thought of you. Hell, thought about nothing but you. You've sort of captivated me, Rayne Storm. Fitting we are talking while one is happening."

She thought of me? I tucked the pillows in behind my back to sit up against the headboard.

"I was waiting for you to call. A part of me was afraid you may have been freaked out after our weekend. It's not like you're completely available. You're engaged and your heart belongs to someone else. I also didn't know if you were comfortable with the time we shared. Was it an experience to get out of your system or were you thinking it may in fact be a part of you? Every time I picked up my phone to call you, I had those thoughts run through my head. So, I waited."

"And I never called."

"You didn't but it's okay. I only said it to tell you where I am with all of this."

"It's more than a part."

"Is it?"

"Yes. It's more than a part of me. It is me."

She paused for several seconds. "Because you feel that way or because of something I said and you think it's the way you should respond."

"Because I feel it. Because I know it." I straightened the covers across my lap. "Because I accept it now. I'm a lesbian. Have always been."

"You know you don't have to tell me that. It doesn't change how I feel about you."

"I know, but it's the truth."

I could hear her breaths over the storm outside. They were steady and I was beginning to wonder if she had fallen asleep.

"I'm really into you," she said. "More than I thought I would be. Can't stop thinking about you actually."

I let her words sink in like a slideshow played in my head. It was a collection of all of the thoughts I had been having of her. I had hidden them pretty well until then. I'd also hidden the fact I too thought of her endlessly. Hadn't I awoken several times to reach for her across an empty bed? I let the feeling of all of it in. Let it truly in and let out a releasing breath.

"I've not stopped thinking of you and I don't want that to change," I said.

"Do you want to try to see what happens here? Talk a little more? Call? Maybe make plans to see each other the next time I'm in town?"

I let my head fall back against the wooden frame. I smiled for the first time since I returned back home. "Yeah. I think we should do that."

"Excellent. Until then, I suppose." I heard the smile behind her voice too. "Good night."

"Good night."

I nestled into the bed and suddenly felt the calmness of a night's sleep calling me.

Chapter 21

"LAWD, CHILD', IF you ain't a sight for sore eyes."

I hardly rubbed the fatigue from my eyes or expressed a good yawn before Flossie had me in her arms.

Brown sugar and honey. Wait! Brown sugar and honey?

I pulled back quickly from her. The look of surprise on her face matched the surprise I felt.

"What you got that look for, sis?"

"Flossie…you…you smell just like Meems." The heaviness of the black hole opened across my heart. Its weight changed the beat and caused a flutter in my chest.

She dropped her head slightly and tugged at the dishrag she held in her hands before throwing it over her shoulder. "Yeah. Dat heifer gave me her damn recipe for the soap she'd been using all the time. I found it a piece back." She shrugged and turned her back to me as she walked to the coffee pot. "Sorry, sis. I done forgot I was using the stuff. You want some coffee?"

I took her arm and pulled her tightly against me. I breathed in all of the scent that reminded me of the last time a hug felt like being held. "No apologies. It's nice. I didn't think I would ever smell this again." I held her hand in mine and gave it a gentle squeeze. "It's a nice reminder, Flossie."

"So is laying eyes on you. If'n you ain't the spitting image of her, I don't know what is."

"Eeeeek." The ear-splitting squeal was followed by clapping hands. "Rayne Amber Storm, you done slipped in on us ol' gals."

I turned toward Cora's voice and stared shocked at the stiff-styled coif upon her head. It was of the same style but this time the usual blue-to-gray color was dyed a coal black. I recoiled as I looked back at Flossie for support. She merely rolled her eyes, shook her head, and turned away from me.

Cora ran, well…waddled over to me. She swooped me up in an embrace that squeezed every bit of the wind out of me with her well-endowed chest. She rocked me back and forth in her arms. "I was thinkin' you weren't ever gonna get here. We been waitin' pert near an eternity for you to come home." She pushed me away from her with nearly the same force as she had pulled me into her. She looked me sternly in my eyes. "Yo' momma been needin' you, baby girl. She been needin' you something fierce I tell ya'."

"I hardly doubt that, Cora. Charlie Grace needs no one but Charlie Grace."

Cora slapped my arm hard. "You hush that talk around me, young lady. I'll not have it." She stomped her chubby foot against the tile floor and brushed my shoulder as she walked past me. The force of her hip knocked me into the kitchen island. "Now you sit and I'll gets us some coffee."

Flossie was already pouring the cups. She turned around to hand two to Cora before sitting at the bar.

I took a sip. "Now this is coffee." I took another long sip. "I can't get good hot strong coffee like this in Birmingham." Not that I had been out for coffee much lately. "And you definitely can't get it anywhere in the hospital which is where I spend most of my time. I sure miss it. Doesn't taste near this good there."

Flossie smiled over her cup. "Ain't nothin' as good as it is back home." Her voice was flat.

Cora spooned the fourth teaspoon of sugar into her cup. "And you best be listening to her on that one, Missy. It's time you be gettin' that fanny of yours back home. How much more you got up there in that big fancy school?"

"Not long now."

"Lawd Jesus in Heaven." Cora threw her arms up and brought them forward as if praying. "Please let my Charlie Grace make it 'til her baby girl comes home." She looked at Flossie who sat quietly drinking her coffee.

Wait. Flossie is sitting drinking coffee?

I looked around the kitchen. There were no pots on the stove. No iron skillets on the counter. No anything. "Hey, wait a minute. Isn't it like a quarter past time for you both to be in frantic cooking crazy mode?"

They looked at each other with eyes that told the sadness between them both. Cora shook her head and sipped her coffee. She patted her hand over her chest above her cleavage line. She looked back at Flossie as if asking her to speak for the both of them.

"Flossie?" I put my cup on the counter to focus on her.

"We ain't cooking this year."

"What?"

Cora's thump against her chest became stronger and more rapid. "She's catering the whole thang. That chef from N'awlins is cooking our Thanksgiving dinner. Can you believe that?" She put her cup in the sink. "The menu's so uppity I can't near pronounce half of it. It ain't right, I tell you. It ain't right." She pulled a tissue from her cleavage and wiped at her nose. "If'n it weren't for yo' wedding to plan, I think that woman would done dried up to nothin'."

The wedding. I failed to catch the sigh before it escaped my lips.

"It seems I'm quite the topic of conversation since you've come home, Rayne Amber."

Startled, we turned to the door. Charlie Grace walked by us with barely an acknowledgment, as we were between her and the coffee pot.

She filled her cup, blew a breath out onto the coffee, and took a sip. "Oh, please don't let me interrupt. It sounds like a thrilling conversation." She walked out without another word.

Flossie and Cora caught each other's eyes again before they looked at me as if to say, "See?"

216

Cora slung her large bag imitating a purse over her shoulder. "Guess I'll be goin' too."

In a kitchen which would have normally been filled with clanking spoons against metal pans, the chop of a knife against a wooden cutting block, the whirl of spinning mixers, and the shouts of needed ingredients, there was nothing but silence. There were no smells of cornbread browning in the oven nor onions and peppers sautéing on the stove. There was only the smell of burning coffee as the practically empty pot still sat on a heating plate.

"What the hell's going on around here?"

Flossie drained the last of her cup. "So much, baby girl. Just so much. Wanna come help me out at the turkey fryer in a few hours?"

"You're still frying a turkey?"

Flossie winked. "Come on out den."

A FEW HOURS later, I found her sitting alone next to a large metal pot that rested over an unlit gas burner. She sat perfectly still while she stared out into the woods. Leaves and pine cones were scattered about the clearing. I couldn't tell if they had been present there for some time or if they had been scattered about from last night's storm.

The crunch of them under my feet startled Flossie. She turned her head to me. "Well, hey, sis. I didn't hear ya come up."

"Ummm…yeah. You were studying those trees over there pretty hard."

She laughed. Well, she sort of laughed.

"You know that grease isn't going to get too hot without that flame lit." I pointed to the gas burner as I sat down in the chair next to her.

She stood, raised the metal lid off of the pot, and reached into the depths of it. Instead of a hand dripping with oil, she pulled out a beer. "I didn't say I was frying a turkey. I said I was at the turkey fryer."

I peeped into the pot. The tops of several bottles of beer stuck out of the crushed ice. "Well, now that's my kind of turkey."

Flossie popped the top and handed me the beer. She grabbed her one before sitting back down next to me. "Didn't seem right not being out here." She took a long swallow. "Don't feel much better this way none either."

"It's different here, Flossie. So much has changed." The cold beer felt good sliding down my throat. It'd been too long since I had a cold one on my lips as I sat outside my Louisiana home.

"Yep, sis. It sho is dat." She took another swallow of hers. I watched the liquid fall from its neck back into the bottle and realized she had already downed a hefty amount in two swallows. "It ain't the same without her. She done been the glue for us. For all of us." She rubbed her palm on her jeans. "She was da glue."

The lawn chair fabric gave to my weight as I leaned back against it. All this time I had forgotten what she meant to my family—to the town of her family. I'd been as guilty of what I accused Charlie Grace of being. I had lost sight beyond myself to see the others affected. The hurt I felt in my heart, the black hole of loss, it was in the eyes of those around me. It was in Flossie's eyes.

"It been hard here without you." She kept her head down but looked at me from the corner of her eye. "Been missing ya more since I been'a missing her so hard. We all been needing you home."

Charlie Grace's face flashed in my head. "All of you except Mother."

"What? She'd da one been missing you'd the mosts."

I rolled my eyes and took a drink of beer.

"What? You not see her dis morning? You not see'd her a'toll? A good damn gust of wind pass'n her by and she gone be carried off with it. I'ma bettin' she ain't ninety pounds soaking wet."

"Yeah, I noticed she had lost weight. Is she not feeling well? Has she been sick?"

"She heartbroken."

"Over?"

"Addie. Time. You." Flossie drained her beer. She stood, opened the metal lid, turned the empty bottle upside down in the ice, and grabbed another one. She pointed it at me. "You ready?"

I looked at the half-empty bottle. "No thanks. Not yet."

She sat down hard in the lawn chair as if it took all of her strength to stand up to get another drink. "Time passed her up, baby girl. She done thought she'd had all the time to make things right. Now dat time gone by. She gone have to accept it and let it go."

"What time? She needed time for what?"

"To make things right with Addie. To forgive Addie in the time Addie was here for her to forgive. Now she gone have to wrestle dem demons all by herself." She tipped her bottle up to her lips. "Den she gone have to wrestle dem with you." She looked at me. "And you gone have to do the same."

"I don't know what you're talking about, Flossie." I finished the beer and stood. "What demons? What on earth did she have to forgive Meems about? Meems never did anything to deserve the way Mother treated her. Were you not at her funeral?" I felt my voice escalating as I pulled another bottle from the pot. "So why the hell should I help fight her demons with her?" I rubbed away the ice from the bottle and sat back down.

"I was dere."

"Memaw didn't deserve that. She was the best mother I had."

"She was for you. Charlie Grace done growed up with a different Addie. She didn't have that same Addie you had."

What was she saying? Why? Why would she talk about Meems like this?

"Don't you be giving me dat look. Sis, we all growed up in this life we get. Addie was dipped in gold fo sho but she tweren't always like dat. Yo' momma knew'd a different Addie. She held onto dat Addie for so long she couldn't see the Addie you done know'd." She turned to me. "And now she got to live with it. She ain't ever gonna get the chance to make it right with her. She ain't ever gonna be able to say she see'd the true Addie. I ain't wanting to see dat same hurt in yo' eyes."

I understood the depth of her swallows and took in the same amount of beer.

"Did I ever tell you how'd I met Addie?"

I shook my head. Words were trapped within the thoughts she had started of Meems being a different person and mother to Charlie Grace.

"Lawd, child. Me and my old man had been in the moonshine something fierce dat day when we came up on Addie and yo pa. Drunks ain't got no business being around drunks. Throw in a couple of pistols and we sho nuff got trouble. Throw in yo pa's temper and my old man's in da mix and you end up spending the night locked up to sleep it off."

"What? Y'all went to jail?"

"Sho did. Spent the whole damn night dere. Dat's when Addie and me made friends. After we done sobered up, that is. Dat Addie she was filled with piss and vinegar I tell ya. Piss and vinegar. When my old man cursed yo pa for crawfishing on his bet, she plum near jumped on his back to beat the cotton pickin' stew outta him. I'd always say'd it was because she missed that bottle on her last shot. 'Course she'd never agree to dat. Our old men thought it be fun to see who was'n the better shot between us. They threw'd up beer bottles in the air and we'd shoot 'em with our pistols. Lawd knows he'd was watching over us drunks with dem guns." She shook her head and took a smaller swallow of beer. A smile crept across her face. "Yep, she was full of piss and vinegar."

"That's funny. Picturing y'all all lit up like that."

"Tweren't too funny for yo' momma. She had to spend the night with the sheriff and his wife. Ain't nobody else around to watch her overnight. Yo' momma always did talk about the night her friends at school saw her riding in the back of dat police car. Yo' momma got dem scars just like you carry 'round. They gone fester in time if'n you don't let dem go."

"Yeah, well. I don't see her growing much. She's the same she's always been."

"Give her time. She a good mom now but she gone get better for you. Just like Addie did for her. I'ma just hoping you see it before it's too late. You gone have to come back home to see'd it tho'."

"I know." I turned the bottle up and realized I'd already taken the last swallow. I don't think I had ever given thought to Meems being anyone different in her younger years. I had never given thought that maybe Charlie Grace had a reason for her distance with Meems. The nice little package of Charlie Grace's actions as a part of her personality seemed to fit the best in my mind. Anything else clouded the negative I felt for her. This made her more human. I didn't like the confusion it stirred inside of me. I wanted the subject changed. "Where was Cora headed off to and what's up with that hairdo?"

"Oh, Lawd. Don't get me'a startin' on dat. That crazy ole mule done lost her mind, I tell ya'."

"It must be the toxicity from the hair dye."

"I dunno know about no toxicosity but she had lost her fool mind fo sho. That heifer got on one of dem dating computer things. They done put dat whatever it is on dem computers at the home where you can talk to people but not talk to people. I plum near don't get it. She be telling me she talked to some man but I ain't once seen her on the phone. She just'n pecking away on dem keys. Peck. Peck. Peck." Flossie put her beer between her legs and moved her middle fingers in the air as if she was searching for keys on a computer. "Giggle. Peck. Giggle. Peck. She sounded like some fool school girl over there giggling. Hell, the first time I saw dem ole mules circled all around that thinking box, I thought they's were lookin' at nudie pictures. Nope, it tweren't nothing but words."

"Cora started online dating?" I laughed. A laugh that felt really good. "And she met someone?"

She nodded her head a vigorous yes. "Sho did. I swear she be thinkin' dat man gonna fart and she ain't gone be there to smell it."

I spit the swallow of beer down my shirt and wiped at the mess I made. "Good gracious, Flossie. Give a woman a little warning before you say something like that."

"I only tellin' the truth. It's Harold dis and Harold dat." She turned her voice into a high-pitched sound. "I gotta go get dis for Harold. I can't tonight. I'ma goin with Harold."

"Wow. Cora's got her a boyfriend. I'm a little shocked."

"Oh, I got me a word for it and it ain't dat one."

Text message from Mo at 2:25pm: "Thinking of you"

Text message from Mo at 2:30pm: "Still want to be in that bed with U"

"Awww, now there's a smile. Was that your friend Sam? Don't see much of her no more. Ain't been hearing much about her from you either."

"No. It wasn't Sam." My smile faded but damn did that beer taste good. "She moved." My words threatened to open the door to the feelings of Sam I was learning to keep locked away. "We don't talk anymore."

"That's a damn shame, sis. I really liked her. So, did Addie. But you just'n got a smile I once saw on your face when dat Sam was around."

The thought of Mo's text brought the smile back. "She's a new friend."

"Ah." Flossie took a swallow of her beer. "Maybe I'll get to meet her one day."

"Maybe." Suddenly, the patch of woods which had held Flossie's attention called upon mine.

Mo wouldn't be the type of woman I would bring home. She's said many times over she wasn't a girlfriend type. That is what helped me to be myself around her. She never asked for more. In the here and now, it was that part I needed most from her. But I did wonder if in the future I would wish she were different in that way.

"Sis, it been eating at me. Somethin' been playing on my mind pretty hard."

I turned from the woods to face her. "What is it? Are you okay?"

"I'm going to be okay. Dis ain't 'bout me. It 'bout you. Addie and I had talked 'bout dem eyes of yours. Dem you had a when you looked at yo' phone and then dem you had a second ago. They be filled with so much happiness and den in a blink of an eye so much sadness. Tore us up to see dem on you when they flashed like'n dat. Damn near broke Addie's heart every time." She raised her bottle and inspected the last little bit of liquid in the bottom. She stood. Her knees wobbled for a second until she steadied herself with the arm of the chair. Its opposite side raised off of the ground against the weight of it. She took a step toward the fryer. "She done fell to the same time dat yo' momma fell into. She left'n something unsaid to you." She raised the metal lid but kept her back to me. "You ready?"

Ready for what? Another beer or what it is Meems left unsaid to me? Yes. Yes to both.

"Yeah. I'll take another." I put my empty in the hand she offered behind her back.

I watched her shoulders rise and fall with the depth of the breath she took. Another came and went before she turned to me. Her eyes showed the many thoughts behind them. Slowly, she handed me a beer. She didn't let it go after I had gripped it but instead held onto the neck. I looked into her eyes until I felt the full weight of the bottle in my hand. She held my stare a moment longer before she spoke again.

"Addie really liked dat friend of yours. She told me so. She told me in secret." She looked up at the sky before stepping away from me to sit in the chair. "I'm not betraying her you know. If'n she was here, she'd want me to say dis. I know'd it in my heart. I feel like she's telling me to tell you. Like her hands are on my shoulders right dis minute. Pushing me to tell you." She swiped hard at her cheeks. She took a long swig of her beer. "She done told me the way dat girl looked at you. She know'd you were loved."

I felt a sudden spin from the alcohol or the words she was saying, I wasn't sure which was the reason. I couldn't move. I couldn't swallow. I couldn't blink.

Flossie rubbed her thumb over the lip of the bottle. "She know'd you two loved each other in a way she had found with'n yo pa."

My heart raced in my chest.

She looked at me and placed her hand on my knee. She held me in her eyes. I've no doubt she saw the fear mine held. "She saw the way you looked at her too. She saw love, baby girl. I saw'd it." She squeezed my leg. "It yo' life to do what you want. What dis old lady saying don't mean a hill of beans. It yo' life to make it. But I'ma figurin' you need to know how Addie felt before you puttin' down the roots you talkin' 'bout with dat boy. We saw'd the love you girls held in dem eyes and we thought...she thought...it was a beautiful thing. She gone up in Heaven, knowing her baby girl was loved."

I felt my head shake in disbelief. *No. No. She didn't know.* "No, Flossie. No. She didn't know. Tell me she didn't know." My hand hurt with the tension of my grip on the bottle.

"Aw hell, sis. She know'd you." She squeezed my leg again and followed it with a pat. "She was proud of you. It done her heart some kind'a good to know'd you found love. She wouldn't want to see dis hurt back in yo' eyes. I don't know what happened between you two but if'n it can be fixed, I wanted you to know Addie was so damn proud of you and would want you to be fixin' it. She loved you more than anything on dis earth. Ain't nothin' ever gonna change dat."

The chair could no longer hold me as I slid to the ground on my knees. She met me there. My jeans became wet with the beer as it spilled from the overturned bottle. Her arms engulfed me and held me tight against her.

Brown sugar and honey.

Chapter 22

"I DO DECLARE, CHARLIE Grace, these here shrimp things are to die for." Nadine Thibodeaux had apparently found the pounds Charlie Grace had lost. Seemingly, she wasn't done with her additional poundage as she shoved the coconut shrimp beignets in her mouth as fast as the server added them to her plate. A drop of red pepper jelly hung to her bottom lip.

I looked around to see if anyone had taken notice. Grant was texting on his phone. Charlie Grace stared blankly at the food in front of her. Jacques and Ned swirled their scotch and sodas as they whispered to each other.

"I'm glad you like them, dear." Charlie Grace finally took notice. She used her napkin to dab at the corner of her own mouth.

Nadine brushed her fingers across her lip until the jelly fell into her lap. "We need to write the name of these things down. They'd be good horse whatever you call them for the wedding."

I'm pretty sure I rolled my eyes. I caught Flossie's snicker. Yeah, I had rolled them.

As if to deliberately have the meal unlike anything we had done in the past, Charlie Grace held it in the formal dining room instead of the sun porch. The walls were a fresh coat of a deep merlot wine color not unlike that within my glass. A wave of indigestion rolled across my stomach with the thought of mixing the red wine with the several beers Flossie and I had shared earlier in the day.

Charlie Grace gave the smile I had known for most of my life. Yet this time, I caught the shadow of the creases in her cheeks. "Yes, they would be a good addition to the menu. We'll need to try to finalize all of that before too long. I'll want to make sure I can reserve my chef."

Ned downed his remaining scotch as the servers came to pick up his and Jacques's glasses. "Can't let old scotch like that go to waste." He looked down at the bowl of butternut squash soup the server had placed in front of him. "This is a fine spread you folks have invited us to." He elbowed Grant. "Ain't it, son?"

Grant looked up quickly and nearly dropped his phone. "Oh yes, Dad. It sure is. Thanks so much for inviting us to share Thanksgiving dinner with you."

"Nonsense, my boy." Jacques blew on the hot soup as he brought a spoonful to his mouth. "You're practically family now." He smiled at Charlie Grace who nodded in return.

I looked away before I rolled my eyes again. Cora sat next to Flossie with her two guests—her mile-high black volcano of hair and Harold Whitehead. I was thankful the motif of the room had not included any type of flamed candle. Harold sat upright with a stiffened spine. He was bald except for the thickened beard and a ring of hair over his ears. His hair was starch white, excluding his mustache and eyebrows which were quite similar to that of Cora's hair. Flossie was right. Cora was a ball of giggling nerves as she sat next to the man she couldn't seem to take her eyes from. Seemed the rolling of the eyes was an epidemic in the room as I caught Flossie roll hers when Cora placed Harold's napkin in his lap. I let the knowing smile drag across my face as Flossie glanced at me. She gave a guilty smile back.

The conversation over the next course of duck-stuffed turkey breast, braised greens, and oyster cornbread stuffing was muted with the enjoyment of the meal. Small topics varying from school to the wedding filtered in the air between us. I watched the controlled look on Grant's face. He didn't give a hint to his plans of moving to New York. He conversed with them of the town, of graduation, and of the future. Never did his poker face change to let on he wasn't returning to the life they believed he would be coming back to.

"I've found a grand location as you leave downtown going into the Garden District." Charlie Grace sipped the light red wine from the crystal stemware she held in her hand. "It would be perfect for a dual practice. The grounds are divine. There's sufficient room for a decent parking area without the need to lose the curb appeal of the property."

Grant piled a bite of braised greens onto a small piece of turkey. "It would be ideal if it were close to the hospital for on-call days."

Charlie Grace nodded her head. "Oh yes. It's a short walk through the trees lining the back property. The trees provide a coverage to show the façade of distance between the hospital. It was one of the appealing factors that separated this property from the others I looked at."

"Sounds like you've done your homework." Grant shoved the prepared bite into this mouth.

I watched him construct another bite onto his fork. It was the perfect blend of greens, turkey, and stuffing. A combination of each dish offered on his plate. I felt the nausea swirling in my gut. The perfect blend of his own design. Had I become not much more to him than that bite? We were a carefully constructed plan. Was he going to leave his family, my family, and the town oblivious to his true post-graduate ideas until we too had been carefully designed? It was a side of him I had not seen before but one I surely couldn't deny since our car ride over.

"Well, son." Ned stretched his back and slid down in the chair. For a moment, I wondered if he had unbuttoned his pants to accommodate the swelling in his belly. He had stopped the caterers twice already as they walked by with the entrée dishes. "Since Charlie Grace opened the can of worms, I'm going to put my two cents worth in. Me and your momma weren't going to say anything until it was closer to your hitching date but we've started clearing the land out behind that field your grandpa used to farm. It's right nice back there. A piece away from us but close enough Nadine can watch them babies of yours."

Nadine squealed and clapped her hands which squeezed her large bosoms together. "I sure can. You doctors can just drop them beautiful babies off every single day. I'll spoil 'em some kind of rotten before you take them home."

Babies?

Jacques chuckled and tried not to choke on the scotch he had sipped from his fresh drink. "Between all of us, those kids are going to be so rotten they'll smell."

Nadine saw the dessert being brought into the room and pushed her plate to the side. "Y'all aren't going to want for a sitter. And just think of all the weekends you'll get to work on more babies when they stay over at our house."

Grant laughed. "They have surgeries for that now, Mom. But we can still practice, eh, Rayne?"

Are you fucking kidding me right now?

The nausea turned into a sickening taste in my mouth. I couldn't believe I was sitting here listening to this. Flossie across from me fidgeted with something in her lap. Jacques kept eating at the remaining piece of turkey on his plate. Cora was practically spoon-feeding Harold. And here I sat wondering what in the hell was going on with this conversation. I looked at Charlie Grace. Why, I have no idea, but I did. The smile on her face was the smirk I was accustom to. It was what I saw most. She sipped her wine and tipped it toward me. What? What is she saying? I felt Grant's hand on the top of my thigh and my knee hit the underside of the table.

His look was controlling. His eyes were on the verge of stern. "Isn't that right, honey? But we've got a couple of years before we start popping out kids." His grip tightened and I looked up at him.

Honey? Popping out kids? Had some medical miracle occurred to where he was going to start popping out kids? This would surely be news to me.

"Ned, I didn't know you and Nadine were planning on the kids building out on your land." Charlie Grace used her fork to cut a bite off of the pecan praline semifreddo. She spread the bite across the bourbon caramel that had pooled around the bottom of the dessert but left the fork resting across the plate.

"Yep, me and the Mrs. been racking our brain, trying to figure out what to get these lovebirds for their wedding present. Figured this would be graduation and wedding all wrapped up."

Not much one for dessert, Jacques folded his napkin onto the plate. "I say we all take a drive out to the land tomorrow to take a look around."

"That's an excellent idea, Jacques." Grant shoved a loaded fork into his mouth and wiped at the caramel dripping off of his lip.

My head snapped up. I could take no more of this. These lies of omission Grant obviously found to be okay to leave on the table. *Lies of omission.* The words stuck a chord and held heavy in my mind. I searched the table again before landing on Flossie's eyes as they held me. A simple nod was all she gave me. It was all I needed. A simple nod from one who knew the tumult soul beneath my shell.

Listen to the voices. Different but the same.

The table kept with its conversation. The voices became an unconscious understanding of mumbled words. The massage of my fingertips against my temple didn't quiet nor add comprehension to the growing agitation of words around me. Words of lies of omission grated on me like sandpaper on raw skin. Pain. Omission—I was no better than the voice of Grant's that was causing a cringe in my soul. Under the table, I felt the edge of the diamond dig into my finger as I held it with a tightened pinch. I was no better than Grant. I had fallen in love with a woman. I had given my body all the pleasures I had for so long denied it in the arms of another woman. Lies of omission that I could ever go back to a man's arms.

"She know'd you. She loved you more than anything." I heard Flossie's voice in my head.

Mo's face appeared so perfectly in my mind I thought for a moment I could reach out to trace the bottom lip of the smile I was being given. Sam's tear-streaked face was a vision right behind hers. Then, with all the strength I needed, Meems with her blue eyes smiling at me and loving me for who I was came into my sight.

I pulled at the band of gold and stone until my finger was free of it. Among the intermingling voices, I slowly brought my hand from under the tablecloth. The gold snapped against the cloth-covered wood as I placed the ring on the table.

"I can't do this anymore." I heard the flatness in my voice. I heard the tone to its words.

No one stopped chattering.

A smile played at Flossie's lips as she gave me another supportive nod. "I'm right here. You can do this," she mouthed.

I cleared my throat. "I said I can't do this anymore."

Charlie Grace blinked at me. "Can't do what?"

Shit. I had their attention. *Can't do what? Can't marry Grant? Can't pretend I'm someone I'm not? Can't do what, Rayne?*

I lifted my hand from the table to reveal the jewelry hidden under my palm. "I can't pretend anymore."

Grant stared at the ring on the table.

I caught his eyes as he looked away from the gold. "I can't pretend we want the same things anymore, Grant."

His eyes closed for longer than a blink. He opened them and was no longer looking at me.

I gently placed my hand on his arm. The rest of the room was silent. "We've grown to want other things." The rest of the truth could stay private until the time we both saw fit to reveal it. This was not the time for me. Yet I knew its time was closer than I had once thought. "We've grown to see a different direction in our lives and I can't pretend that isn't there. I can't keep going down a path that sees us married when we both know in our hearts we've grown to want different futures."

He shook his head silently but didn't look up.

"What on earth are you talking about, Rayne Amber?" Charlie Grace asked. Her voice was laced with irritation.

"Mother, this is between Grant and me."

"It would seem we could argue that point as you are saying this in front of all of us."

"Charlie Grace." Grant looked up at her. "It's okay." He held his hand up as if to tell her he had the understanding to all of this.

"What?" Cora had awakened from her ogling over Harold. "It most certainly is not okay. You can't do this to yo' poor momma. She needs this wedding."

Flossie turned to Cora. "Then you be giving her a wedding to plan. Dis Rayne's life, not yo's or her momma's."

"Wait a minute here. Let's just wait a minute." Nadine put her fork down next to her plate. "What's happening here?"

"I believe our boy is getting dumped." Ned reached over, grabbed Jacque's scotch, and slammed the rest of its contents back.

"Mom…Dad…it's nothing like that." Grant's voice was calm if not emotionless. "Rayne and I have some things to be discussed. I don't think she is trying to say we are splitting up. We just have some things we need to talk about." He looked at me. "Right?"

Not the place. Not the time.

"We have many things we need to talk about. Yes."

"Well, at least you haven't lost your sense of drama." Charlie Grace crumbled her napkin into a ball and tossed it across her plate. "Must the attention always center on you that we can't have a decent meal with friends and family without it being about you?"

"Drama?" Had she just called me dramatic? "I'm dramatic. I'm the one demanding attention? You walk around here snapping at everyone. Changing every single tradition about our Thanksgiving all on your own and I'm the one who is ruining our holiday?"

"Well, pardon me for not living up to your standards." Charlie Grace stood from the table.

I followed. "Are you kidding me right now? As if you've ever shown me I lived up to yours?"

Jacques stood up and waved his hands between us. "Now…now… let's take a breather." He put his hand on Charlie Grace's shoulder. "Honey, sit down. Let's not do this right now. It's Thanksgiving."

Her stare didn't falter. Her gaze burned through me. "I'm fine and will not be man-handled thank you very much," she said through gritted teeth as she shrugged his hand from her shoulder. "Let's have it. Let's all hear about how I've wronged you as a mother. How you're breaking this man's heart, throwing all of the hard work we have put into establishing a future for you here in our faces because of me being a failure as a mother. Let's hear it, Rayne. You think you could hurt me anymore at this point?"

"Hurt you? How have I hurt *you*?"

I felt the caress of a hand within mine and realized Flossie had come to stand by me. "Come on, baby girl. Let's let dis breathe for a minute." She led me from the table.

"Oh sure, Flossie. Take over where Mom left off."

"Not like dis, Charlie Grace." Flossie's voice was as tender as the eyes that held Charlie Grace. "Not here. Not like dis." She softly shook her head as she led me into the kitchen.

I heard chair legs scrape across the hardwood floor as Charlie Grace said, "Happy Thanksgiving, everyone."

"What just happened?" Nadine's was the last voice I heard before Flossie had me outside on the back porch.

"That was a complete disaster."

"Come on, sis. I gots something to sho' you." Flossie's hand was soft with the thinness of her skin over the prominent bones in her hand. "Thinkin' this may make you feel better."

She led me around the corner of the house to the circle drive. A full moon's light reflected off of the faded yellow paint of Memaw's Silverado pickup truck. My knees buckled with surprise and sadness. Meems.

"Flossie? How?"

"Old fart left'n for me." Her smile was edged with grief. "Dat lawyer, you know the one dat read her will, gave me the keys and a note in her scribble. All'n she put on dat paper was 'get outta dat damn home'. I do it too. I drive dis piece a junk 'round for her."

She walked to the driver's door and opened it for me. In the stillness of the night, the horrendous screech sounded for miles. A light-hearted laugh tickled my heart before it escaped my mouth. I let the smile play upon my lips as I traced the vinyl bench seat with my hand.

"I didn't think I would see this truck again. I've wondered what happened to it but I was scared to know the answer. I guess I thought Mother had it taken to the wrecking yard to be sold for scrap."

Flossie dropped the keys in my hand and I swear she skipped around the front of the truck to climb into the passenger seat. I sat in the seat and ran my hand along the narrow steering wheel. I let my fingers slide over the notches along the back. The cold vinyl seat quickly cooled the back of my legs as my blue jeans were little barrier for the November chill that had dropped the temperature twenty degrees earlier in the day. The sound of the engine caused another ripple of happiness to course through me. I pushed the levers of the thermostat to the right which released the smell of heat into the cab. I pulled the knob on the bottom left of the dashboard and smiled at the headlights shining across the yard. Meems was here. The thought of her spirit surrounding us lifted my soul and my spirits. She was here. I let my forehead rest against the wheel once held in her hands. Deep breaths filled my lungs.

"Let's take her for a spin," Flossie said as she rubbed my back.

Chapter 23

"Hi."

"Hi, yourself."

"We've got to stop meeting like this."

"Are you sure you want that?" Mo said as she straddled across my waist. She leaned her back against my legs when I bent them behind her. "I mean, I sort of thought you liked meeting like this." She raised up off of my legs and let her fingers travel down my bare stomach. "Or so it seemed early this morning."

My tongue ran across the sore spot at the corner of my lower lip as I remembered her surprise knock at the door. She had hardly waited for the taxi to pull away before taking my breath with a kiss filled with passionate need. We had not made it further than the couch before she had me undressed and totally surrendered to her control.

She touched the break in the skin my tongue had roamed over. She made a face of remorse. "I'm sorry about that."

"Don't be."

"I am. I didn't mean to bite you." She placed a small kiss at the corner of my lip and whispered, "I just needed those clothes off so bad but I couldn't stop kissing you."

Butterflies swarmed across my belly when I remembered her teeth biting into my lip. "I'm serious. Don't be. It was ummmmm…"

She gave me a mischievous smile. "It was ummmmm what?"

"I'll show you what." I pulled her lips to mine and kissed her with the matching intensity she had given me the night before.

"Oh, that?"

"Yes. That." I unzipped the leather at the wrist of her jacket. "I like this outfit you've got going on here."

"Well, I had to put something on to call and order the pizza."

"I'm not sure if a leather jacket and," I slipped my finger underneath the waistband of her black boy-cut briefs, "these constitutes putting something on."

"Would you like for me to put something else on?"

I kissed the tattoo at her wrist and traced my tongue over ink. "Oh, I didn't say that."

She started to slip her arm from the jacket. "Would you like for me to take some of this off?"

I put my hand on her arm. "Oh, I didn't say that either." I dropped my hand to rove the exposed skin between her breasts and down her belly to her right hip. "How about you stay just like that."

The muscles of her belly tightened as I trailed my fingertip along the musical notes leading over the side of her hip. "How much time do we have until the pizza gets here?"

Her breath was shallow and rapid through parted lips. Her eyes were filled with desire as she guided my hand to where she needed it most. "Enough."

I couldn't take my eyes off of her as she gave herself to me. I watched what my touch did to her body. It was open, exposed, and raw to let me see all she felt. My heart beat wildly against my chest. I didn't need her to touch me as I couldn't have felt more had her hands been on me. We held our stares as my fingertips explored her. Her body rocked as it remained straddled over me. I lost sight of her eyes when her head fell back with release. She collapsed next to me and struggled to catch her breath.

"Holy cow." She labored to slow her breaths. "That…was… incredible." She bent her arm over her forehead. "Give…me…a… second…to…catch…my…breath."

The knock on the door was loud and we both jumped.

I laughed. "That is what I would call perfect timing." I stood up and put on my robe.

She attempted to reach for my body but her hand plopped down on the bed. "Yes, I need sustenance."

I skipped down the hallway and called over my shoulder, "I'll be back and then you really are in trouble."

"Someone call an ambulance."

Thankfully, both a twenty and a five-dollar bill lay on the table next to the door which would save the need for change or further delay from climbing back into bed with Mo. "Here you go. Keep the change," I said as I slung the door open.

"It's two o'clock in the afternoon. Why on earth are you still in your robe?" Charlie Grace stood at the door.

"Mother?"

"Why are you still in bed this late in the afternoon? Were you on call last night?" She started to step inside the door but stopped when I hadn't moved away for her entrance. She gripped the leather strap of her purse that hung over her shoulder. "Aren't you going to let me in?"

"Mother? What are you doing here? And no, I wasn't on call last night."

She stepped back on her heels. "Our phone calls have been sparse, short, and tense since Thanksgiving. I was hoping we could talk face to face. Perhaps over a day of Christmas shopping. Grant told me when I talked with him that you weren't on call so I was hoping my timing would be good."

"This isn't a good time."

There's a half-dressed woman in my bed. This really isn't a good time.

"Let me get dressed and I'll come pick you up. Where are you staying?"

Charlie Grace took a side step to reveal a small suitcase that had been hidden behind her.

"Oh?"

Shit.

"I can go find a hotel if you don't want me staying here."

Double shit.

"No, I didn't say that. It's just you've never stayed here before so I assumed this was no different."

"I think we could use the time. Don't you?"

"No." I shook my head. "I mean, yes. Just let me think for a second." I held my hand in the air in a failed attempt to hold onto anything that would steady my jerking knees.

"Think?"

"I'm starving over here. Wear a girl out and then hold food from her. So wrong."

NO!

Charlie Grace's eyes widened and her mouth fell open.

I winced at the sight flashing before my eyes of Mo dressed in leather and cotton briefs. Surely that was the sight causing the look on Charlie Grace's face.

"Er…" A young man carrying a pizza box walked up behind Charlie Grace. His face was flushed and his neck was reddening. "I've got a pizza delivery here." He reached around the stone statue that was my mother.

I placed the palms of my hands firmly against my eyes and pushed in with force in the hopes of blocking out the scene that was playing out in front of me. Nope. Everyone still stood in place. My only assumption was Mo was as frozen behind me as the two in front of me.

I took the box from the boy and handed him the folded bills. "Keep the change."

He scurried away without another word.

Charlie Grace blinked before she looked back and forth between my face and the one that must have been over my right shoulder. "Rayne, there's a half-dressed woman standing behind you." She looked back at me. "And you're hardly dressed yourself."

All I could do was step aside to allow her in and hopefully close the door before my neighbors saw the chaos unfold. "I suppose you should come inside, Mother."

"I'm not sure I want to do that now." Her fingers whitened as her fist tightened on the purse strap.

"You're not one for scenes, Mother. Please let's not change that now."

She pursed her lips as she stepped past me. She left the overnight bag at the door. I wheeled the bag inside, closed the door, and turned. Mo's outfit, which had caused a much different reaction in the pit of my stomach, was now the highlight of the scene that could very well be the collapse of my life as a known straight woman. I leaned the bag against the wall and came to stand between Charlie Grace and Mo as they gazed at each other.

"I'm going to go get dressed." Mo's voice cracked.

"Yes, I think that would be a novel idea, young lady."

"Mother," I said sternly and then looked back at Mo. "I've got this. Why don't you go back to the bedroom?"

"Back to the bedroom? What the hell's going on here, Rayne?" Charlie Grace let her purse fall with a thud to the floor.

Mo looked between us before retreating down the hallway into the back room.

"Mother, please calm down. Let's talk."

"Talk? You want to talk?"

"Yes, I would like to talk. Can we go sit down?" I pointed to the sofa in the living area.

"No, we cannot sit down. There is a half-naked woman in your apartment. A half-naked woman that obviously knows her way to your bedroom. And more importantly, it seems you're just as naked as she is."

"Can we get off the subject of our clothing and onto why you pop in on me since we've barely talked in the last couple of weeks?"

"I don't see that as being the topic at hand. So, no we cannot."

"This is my home. I'm a grown woman. I can live and do in my own home as I wish. You came unannounced."

"Oh, please excuse my ill manners. I didn't know I had to call and ask my daughter permission to come see her." She put her hand over her chest as if she was appalled I had made such an accusation.

"Don't get dramatic."

"Me? Me get dramatic? Look at your hair." She flipped my bangs between her fingers before I could move my head out of her reach.

"Don't do that."

"Well, look at it. You cut it so short and then bleach these ridiculous looking highlights. Is that her? Is that her influence?" She pointed down the hallway to the closed bedroom door.

"I can wear my hair however I want." I tightened the loosening robe around my waist. It was that or slam my hand down on the table in front of us, which would have given her a real reason to call me the dramatic one. I would not give her that pleasure. This was my house—my life.

"Is Miss I-don't-wear-clothes the reason you called off your engagement? Does Grant know about her?"

"No, she isn't actually, and no, he doesn't. Couldn't you give me a little credit that maybe he isn't being completely honest here? That maybe he isn't an innocent victim? That maybe all of this is not entirely my fault? Every time I called you, all you could do was say how I hurt him. How this was all of my fault. Have you ever considered maybe there is more to this story?"

"Oh yes, I'm beginning to see that now. You're sleeping with a woman, Rayne Amber Storm. Please tell me how you can twist this around to be anything but a result of your own actions and therefore entirely your fault."

"Whatever, Mother."

"I'm sorry, this is somehow Grant's fault? Or hey, better yet, maybe you can turn this around to being a result of my bad mothering."

I let my back fall against the wall. "I didn't say that. I never said that. This is me. This is who I am and who I've always been."

"Who you are? So, you're gay all of a sudden?"

"Not all of a sudden."

"So little Miss Hot-to-trot is going to be my son-in-law? Is that what you're saying? You hear that little Miss Hot-to-trot." She raised her voice. "Are you going to be my son-in-law now?" She started to walk down the hallway toward the bedroom.

I grabbed her arm above her elbow to stop her. "Leave her alone, Mother. She has nothing to do with me and you or even Grant. She never tried to come between us or ask me to make any changes where he was concerned."

"Oh, she just fucked you."

I felt my eyes widen to the callous tone of her foul language. I couldn't remember a time I had heard her ever use that word before. Much less did I ever imagine she would use it in such a way toward me.

"Well, that makes it all the better, doesn't it?" Just as quickly as the vulgarity had flown, she returned to the southern belle accent and tone.

"I think you need to go."

She picked up her purse and gave me the hardest look I have received from her eyes. "Yes, I think I should."

SEVERAL MINUTES PASSED before I could walk into the bedroom. I hated the fact Mo had not only been a witness to Charlie Grace's worse side but she had also had a portion of it directed at her.

"You're not staying?"

Mo looked up from her duffle bag. "I think it would be best if I didn't. Don't you?" She turned back to the bag and shoved a pair of folded jeans into it.

"Actually, no. I don't." I leaned against the doorjamb. "I was hoping you would stay."

Mo stopped her packing and sat hard on the edge of the bed. "Rayne, that was a bit much, you know?"

"Yeah."

"I don't think I want to be here when she gets back."

"She won't come back."

"Ha. I somehow don't think all of that is over yet."

"Oh no. It's not." The crumbled white linen behind her was a sore reminder of the time we had lost with Charlie Grace's surprise visit. Even without her consciously knowing, she was playing a hand in the demise of Mo and me. "She'll wait for me to come to her. She won't come back here." She won't have to.

Mo bent over to put on a sock. "I've never really had to deal with the whole parent issue." She put the other sock on over her toes. "Mine were gone before my being a lesbian was an issue and well…" She ran her thumb underneath the band of the sock and patted the side of her leg.

"You've never been the girlfriend type to have to deal with it before either."

Mo sat straight up but looked at the wall instead of me. "No, I haven't."

I sat next to her on the bed. "I'm not asking you to be my girlfriend or do any of what you just saw because of me. You know that, right?"

"I know." She traced her fingers down the finger recently bare of the white gold engagement ring. "This never bothered me. I mean, it didn't change us."

"I know." I kicked at her duffle bag with my big toe. "And it doesn't have to change us now."

"Did you do it for me? Break off your engagement because of me? Because of what you wanted or hoped would become of us?"

"Well." I leaned back on my elbows. "Not because of you, per se, but in a sense because of this." I motioned between us. "A part of the reason is because of the feelings I have when I'm with you. I knew with S… I knew before that I was a lesbian. Knew but didn't accept." I slid my hand across the comforter to rest on top of hers. "With you, I accepted."

She sat motionless.

I brought my hand tighter over the top of hers and let her fingers fill my palm. "Mo?"

Motionless.

"I don't want you to go." I squeezed her hand with each word to emphasize my deepest desire for her not to leave in this moment or in the ones to follow.

The painful tug at my heart was beyond evident with the way her hand didn't turn to hold mine. It was in that moment I knew definitively she meant more to me than a physical answer to a long sought-out question. She had gotten in. Not to the degree Sam had found her way to my heart, but in nonetheless. I dared not tell her it was more than sex to me. I dare not tell her I had grown deep feelings for her. Not now.

Instead, I continued to plead with her. "Mo? Please. Please stay."

Mo's expression said everything. It was more than her leaving the moment. She was leaving the situation. She was leaving me.

"You're not just leaving today, are you? You're leaving…leaving."

She stood from the bed and turned her back to me. "Rayne. I…" She walked across the room to sit on the floor next to her boots. She slipped on a boot, pulled the laces tight but left them untied. "I'm not girlfriend material. It's not who I am. I never asked you to be anyone other than who you were. You can't. It's not right for you to ask that of me."

"Did I say that's what I wanted from you?"

"No, but look at everything. You cancelled your engagement. And now you have to deal with your mother. Just think about what is down the pike for you. This is the tip of the iceberg." She tugged tightly at the laces again and then tied them in a bow. She pulled her jeans leg back over the boot and played with the hem. "You'll look to me for support. You'll want me to be here. You know I never stay long in one place."

I knelt in front of her feet. "Mo, I'm a big girl who can take care of herself. I'm not asking you to do anything but keep us like we are."

She said nothing nor looked up at me. She pulled at her other pants leg to slide the other boot on.

I placed my hands on her bent knees as she worked with the laces of the boot. "I'm not asking for us to grow into anything. I'm not asking us to change at all. You go and come as you do. We get together when you're in town. That's all. I'm not asking you to be anything other than what you want to be."

"You'll want more," she said under her breath. "They always want more."

Her words were a stinging reminder of the women who had shared her time before me. I swallowed hard. "Then shame on me if I do, but we'll cross that bridge when we get to it."

She rested her chin and cheek on her hand as she propped her elbow on her knee. I was lost in the whirl of emotions in her eyes. She cared more than she wanted. I saw it there.

"Mo?" I traced her chin with my finger. "Meredith? Please. I'm begging you."

She raised her eyes and focused over my shoulder instead of keeping our eyes connected.

"I'm here. I'm right here telling you I want from you no more than you're wanting to give me. I won't push. I won't pull you into anything you don't want." I leaned my head to the side and tried to force her eyes to meet mine. "You have never, not once, asked anything of me. Never asked me to change or be more than I was ready for. That made me comfortable to be around you. It gave me ease to be myself. All I am asking for is a chance to be that for you."

She stretched her hand up to brush the bangs from my eyebrows. "That's all I ever wanted you to be."

"And that's all I want you to be with me. Don't you see?"

"You may not ask me to but what if I care too much for you that I will want to? What if I'll be pulled to be with you? And then I fail you miserably about the time you start to depend on me? I don't think I could take it. You're more than sex to me, Rayne. That alone was something I was having a hard time dealing with, but this? This with your mom and your whole life change? With this, I know I'm in over my head. I'll only disappoint you."

"You won't. I promise you won't. I'll take whatever you can give me. Just like you did of me."

She brought our lips together and softly took my bottom lip between hers. Her tongue was timid against mine. Her kiss was gentle. The passion it once held was gone from her lips. It was goodbye.

"I'm sorry," she said softly against my lips. "I can't."

I followed her to the door but knew I couldn't kiss her again. I couldn't feel her lips upon mine while knowing they were to be the last of our kisses. She didn't try either. I watched her shoulders rise and fall in a deep sigh before she stepped fully out of the door. She kept her back to me as she walked down the driveway carrying her large duffle bag across her shoulder. She didn't look back when she climbed into the cab nor did she look out of the window as it drove away.

Crack.

Chapter 24

THE QUINTESSENTIAL CHARLIE Grace had not answered calls nor texts after she left the apartment. I suppose my own stubbornness prevented me from leaving a voicemail. I dared not leave a message that she could play over and over as a way of holding something over my head. I could only hope time away from me and the truth of me was giving her the clarity she sought. Or perhaps it was the calm after the storm she yearned to master. No matter which it was, she was not responding. Which was why I knew it wasn't her knock at the door hours later. She would never take the first step. Not Charlie Grace. The knock became persistent.

Mo?

I almost tripped over the back of the couch on my way to the door. She had come back. She didn't want to see our end any more than I wanted it. I knew there was more behind her eyes than what her words were telling me.

I pulled open the door. "Mo, I'm so glad you came back. I know we can work this out." With my hand still on the knob, I stared frozen.

Grant stood in the doorway. He was solemn and had quite visible tear-stained cheeks. They shimmered under the glow of the porch light. His shoulders were taut as if he was desperately trying to hide the sobbing. He looked as if inward sobs were threatening his body to collapse at the doorway. Yet he left his feet firmly planted on the doormat. They were the cement to keep his statue preserved.

"Is it true?" He lowered his head. He made no attempt to come in.

Damn you, Charlie Grace!

"Grant, please come in."

"Rayne! I asked you if it was fucking true!" His eyelids were lowered over his eyes as he squared his look at me.

With a shaky hand, I reached for him. "Please come in. Let's talk inside. *Please.*"

He followed the pull of my hand but let his feet drag across the door frame as he stepped inside. The door closed behind him. He collapsed against it and wept. The back of his head rested against the wood.

"Rayne, please tell me it isn't true," he said in a rough, broken voice. "Please, God. Tell me you love me. Tell me it isn't what she saw."

I had never seen him cry like this. In fact, I couldn't remember a time I had seen a man give in to the emotions that would cause tears such as these. My reserve, my strength was mangled right along with him. I let my own tears flow. I cried for all of the things building inside of me: the stress of finally accepting who I was, the look of disgust on Charlie Grace's face when she saw who I was, the ending of a chance to be with the woman who had helped me not only accept being a lesbian but also made me feel okay with it, and now standing across from a man who would be, at least in the short term, destroyed by the realization of what I had hidden for so long. The tears, strong as they might be, weren't enough to blur the vision of the man hurting at my own doings. A man I did truly love. There was a distinct difference between being in love and loving. I loved him and knew I always would. Yet I also knew I would never love him the way he wish I did.

"I do love you, Grant. I do." My voice matched his. "I'm so, so sorry. I never wanted to hurt you."

"So, you fuck her behind my back?" He slid down the door onto the floor. "What, Rayne? What? Are you like gay with her or something? Or was this like some college sewing wild oats thing?" The anger of betrayal was evident in his tone. Anger that was surely spurred by his hurt. "What did I do wrong?" he said barely above a whisper.

I knelt down in front of him. "Grant, please, let's not do this…not like this. You didn't do anything wrong. It's not you, don't you see? It's me. This is all me."

He didn't look up to meet my eyes. "What does it mean? Is it over? I know you cancelled the engagement but I thought that was because of New York. I thought New York was what you meant when you were saying we wanted different lives. I thought it was only about New York."

I slid around him to sit next to him against the door. "I've always felt something inside. Something that I couldn't explain to anyone, even myself." I rested my head against the hard wood of the door. "I had no idea what that meant until I met her." I knew he would think the woman Charlie Grace had reported to him and that was fine by me. "I never meant for it to happen like this. I swear to you. I was looking for answers without truly knowing I had questions."

"Is any part of it because of New York? Because you were mad at me for wanting to go there instead of home."

"What? No."

"Because I don't have to go, Rayne." He looked at me with hurt behind his eyes. The tears were building again. "I won't go. We won't go. If it means losing you, I'll go back to Louisiana with you. I'll do anything. Just tell me what to do."

"No." I put my hand on his forearm but felt his muscle twitch to my touch. I let my hand fall back in my lap. "It's not that. It's not New York. And why? Why would you do that to keep us together? A couple…a loving couple…would want each other to live their dreams." I rubbed my moistened palm against my jeans as I tried to carefully choose my words. "We grew, Grant. We grew into different people. We weren't expecting to find the directions we found but they are here and we can't deny it. Now that we see the paths in front of us, we can't look away to pretend they aren't there."

We sat in silence that was only broken by sniffing as we let our tears fall.

"Then this is it. We're over?" He sniffled again. "Is this it or are you still trying to figure things out? Do I even have a chance anymore?" He turned and rested his side against the door. "Are you sure you're gay?" His eyes searched my face. He lifted his hands off of his lap but quickly let them fall again. "We could have such a good life together. You and me, we could have it all. Careers. Family. Life." He looked down. "What if," he said softly, "what if we still stayed together? What if I overlooked your, you know, when you wanted to be with a woman? What if we just didn't talk about it?" He kept his face down and stared into his lap.

"Grant." He didn't look back at me and I wasn't going to force it. "No, Grant. No. We can't do that. We shouldn't do that. It wouldn't be fair to either one of us."

"And this is?" The hurt and anger built in his voice again. "How is this fair?"

"I didn't mean to hurt you. I didn't. I hate it happened this way. I tried so hard to not let this be who I am that I pretended to be someone else."

"Why can't you just keep pretending?"

"Because I can't."

"Why? You can have your time with your friends. It doesn't have to ruin us. You can have your time. You know, to do what it is you need to do and we can still have us." He turned to bury his head against my chest. I felt the dampness of his tears as they soaked through my shirt. "Rayne, I love you so much. You have to love me too. You just have to." He wrapped his arms around me tightly.

"I do love you, Grant. I do love you very much and I'll always love you." I ran my fingers through his hair. "But I don't love you the way you deserve. You deserve more."

He pulled away from me abruptly. "I just don't see why we can't keep going the way we have been. I didn't force you to be with me. You know like that. I didn't force sex on you. Why can't we forget all of this happened?"

"You don't mean that. You don't. I want more. I want more for me and for you." I took in a deep breath and hoped he would start to understand the depth of what he was asking. "And you should want more too."

He closed his eyes. He opened and closed his mouth several times before he spoke again. "I just..." He lifted his head. "I just want to be happy again." His head fell back against the door. "I want to feel like everything is going to be alright again and that I actually know what the hell is going on in my life."

"Grant?"

He blinked but kept staring straight ahead.

I put my hand on his leg. "You can have all of that. You have a great opportunity in New York. You were really excited about it before all of this. Why not feel that again? Why not follow your dream?"

"I thought we would do it together."

"But it was never my dream."

He stood and straightened out the legs of his blue jeans off. He stared down at me for several seconds. "Did I ever know you? Did I ever really know you?" He pointed at my chest.

"Yes." I stood up next to him as he put his hand on the doorknob. "Yes, you did and still do. We've grown in different directions is all. I'm holding on to that. We can still find a relationship between us that fits the people we are now."

He turned away from me. "You've destroyed me," he said as he walked out of the apartment.

Fissure.

Chapter 25

"HEY, YOU." JAZLYN's voice was muffled by something in her mouth. "I was just thinking about you." A rather loud crunch followed. "What's up?"

"Besides a shattered eardrum, you mean?"

She laughed. "Sorry. I'm starving. The club is crazy tonight. Mo surprised us tonight and the place is packed."

I don't know why I thought she would go anywhere else but the club. I felt my heart sink at the sound of her name. I had realized my feelings for Mo were growing the more time I spent with her but I didn't fully appreciate the depth of them until I watched her walk away. If I had thought it would have done any good, I would have chased after her. I would have grabbed a hold of that damn duffle bag and pulled her back into my apartment. But the look in her eyes had told me she was leaving no matter my words or my actions. My thoughts had not been consumed by her with all of the other happenings going on. That is until the moment I heard Jazlyn say her name.

Another loud crunch followed. "I kept waiting for her to take a break after her first set but she's like a machine tonight. She went right into another one without a break." This time, the crunch was somewhat subdued by the sound of paper ruffling in the background. "Do you winna come over? I'll buy you a drink?"

"No." I pulled my knees up against my chest as I sat against the headboard of the bed. "I'm actually not in town tonight."

"Oh, yeah? Where are you?"

"Louisiana."

"Ah. Going home?"

"Yes." I was a basket case filled with anger, sadness, and confusion. I was heartbroken by the pain I continued to cause those in my life. A basket case that needed to talk out my feelings with my friend—the one constant in my life. Yet, here I sat on the other end of the phone not knowing how to even begin to open up to her. How could I, without exposing Mo and me? I had overheard Jazlyn ask Mo not to start anything with me. Had Mo kept us a secret from her and if so, was it my right at all to betray her?

"So...Mo's there?" Well, that sounded completely idiotic.

"Yeah. I didn't know she was coming into town this weekend. She showed up on my door this afternoon."

"Oh." I pulled the pillow next to me across my chest and hugged it tightly. "How is she?"

"Mo?"

"Yes."

The pause seemed like an eternity as I waited for her to finish swallowing her drink. "She's okay." She took another drink. "She's worried about you but otherwise okay. Now she's lost in that damn booth."

"She's worried about me?"

"Mmmmm hmmmm. Are we going to keep pretending I don't know what's going on?"

"You know?"

"I do."

"Oh Jazlyn, I need to talk to you so bad but didn't know if I could. If Mo had told you...told you about..." I hesitated when I realized I didn't know what all she knew.

"About you and Mo?"

"Yes, that."

I heard another crunch and momentarily wondered what in the

hell she was eating. If it was an apple then surely, she must almost be done. But if it was carrot sticks or celery, I was done for.

"What has happened between you and Mo is between you two. You're both my very best friends and two of the most incredible women I know. I'll respect you both and let you work it out while I don't get in the middle. How's that sound?"

"Sounds good."

"Now tell me about your mom. Mo said it was a very compromising position that she walked in on."

"You could say that again."

"Are you okay?" An apple. It must've been an apple because the loud crunching had finally ceased.

"Honestly, I have no idea." I pulled at the corners of the pillow as I told Jazlyn the whole story. The parts Mo had missed. It felt good to be able to tell someone all of my fears without feeling judgment on the other end of the line. Jazlyn truly was my best friend.

"I don't get why she would do that." Jazlyn's voice was muffled by more paper rattling. "I think I'm in shock."

"You don't know Charlie Grace. Nothing shocks me anymore."

"It's one thing for her to come into your home and act that way but it's something else altogether to tell Grant. I mean, dude, she completely outed you. It was up to you to tell Grant or anyone. Not her."

"Again, you don't know Charlie Grace. I wouldn't be surprised if everyone knows by now. I'm sure her phone has been hot in her hand on her drive back home. She'll need to rally the troops to support her in her heartbreak."

"Is that why you're home?"

"I'm not there yet. Stopped over at a hotel for the night. I didn't want to face this in the middle of the night. But, yeah, that and I need to face her. I need to get this talked out. I can't function in anything with this looming over us. Not at the hospital…not studying…not anything."

"I get that. And Grant? What will he do?" I could tell she was talking around another bite in her mouth. She really must have been hungry.

"I have no idea. I imagine not much of anything as far as telling people. He isn't really one to discuss his feelings. He hardly talked to me about any of his thoughts before all of this. I think I always wondered if he didn't have any or if he just didn't want to talk about them. But I doubt he'll be too anxious for everyone to know. He'll most likely think it will be taken as a reflection on him. Gawd, Jazlyn, I hurt him so bad. I just can't even let myself feel that part."

"Then don't. Baby steps, my friend. Baby steps. You've got to take one step at a time. First your mother. Then you'll decide where to go from there."

A thought flashed. "Oh, dear Lord, Nadine."

"I'm sorry. What?"

"Nadine. Grant's mother." A wave of anxiety washed over me. "I had completely forgotten about her. I was only thinking about the wrath of Charlie Grace. Hell, if she doesn't tell the whole town, Nadine sure will. She'll want to have a good reason to take the blame off of Grant for our break-up. I'm not looking forward to talking to her at all."

"The pros and cons of family, I suppose. Geez, it's not like it's hard enough to come out but damn, girl, you've got to come out to the world within days of coming out to yourself."

"Feels much like that."

"Hey, you know what?"

"What?"

"You've got this." Her mouth was full again. "You know that? You've got this," she said with a strength that seemed to carry across the distance between us. "I've got all of the faith in the world in you, my friend. You're one of those women I admire. You've got this incredible strength in you. A strength in you that you don't even realize. Once you tap into it, you're going to be a force let me tell you."

"Thank you." I felt a hint of what she described and let myself collapse into it. "You're my best friend. Don't know what I'd do without you."

"Lucky for you," she said as she took another bite, "you'll never have to find out."

"Good God woman, what are you eating? The whole refrigerator?"

She laughed. "Pretty much. I told you I was starving."

"I believe you." I set the pillow I had been clutching next to me and slipped my body down into the comfort of the bed. I had to try to find some form of sleep before I faced the fury which awaited me a short two hours' drive away. "Hey, Jazlyn?"

"Mmmmm hmmmm."

"Is Mo really okay? Charlie Grace was a real bitch to her."

"She's fine and trust me, she's had worse in her life."

"Maybe so, but not in front of me and not by my mother's hands."

"She's okay. I'll tell her you asked about her and that we talked."

"I didn't want her to leave, Jazlyn. I really didn't."

She was quiet for a minute. The sigh I heard her express seemed to tell me more than her words did because all she said was, "I know."

Was she sighing for me? For Mo? Or maybe for both of us?

Chapter 26

"WELCOME TO BRENNIN, Louisiana. The friendly city." The letters were written in a semi-circle over the picture of a fleur-de-lis. The hum of my jeep engine was the only sound I heard in the silence of the morning. I hadn't intended to get out of the jeep when I pulled off of the road but I felt my strength wavering when I saw the sign. It marked the entrance into the place I had once found to be a breath of air into my lungs. It represented a happiness of home which filtered into my nasal passages as pure oxygen gifted solely to me. Now it was tainted by a sourness tinged with bitterness as to the wonder of what would be in the place I called home. Not just the home I had grown up in but the home in the town. The town itself was as much my home as the one where Charlie Grace awaited me. The brick-laid streets of downtown were like my playground. The eclectic shops were like my bedroom. The bayou and the outskirts of town were my toys. And the people…the people…all of them were my family. How much of this would change today? How much if any would stay the same? Would it continue to be the friendly city to me? A lump formed in my throat as I let my forehead fall to rest against the cold metal of the road sign.

"I wondered when you'd be here." Jacques was sitting alone in a rocking chair on the expansive front porch. A coffee cup rested on the rocker's arm. Steam floated from the cup's rim into the crisp December air.

I sat in the chair next to him. "You knew I was coming."

"Figured but didn't know."

"Does she?"

He blew into the cup before taking a swallow. "I'm not sure but probably."

"Jacques?"

"Yeah, kiddo?"

"Do you hate me?"

He stopped the rocker firmly in place and looked at me. "What? No. Why on earth would I hate you?"

"Disgusted by me then?"

He bent over the arm of the chair to put his cup on the concrete and stood in front of me with his arms spread wide. "Sweet girl, I could never hold anything but love for you and never, ever disgust."

I rose quickly to be consumed by his arms. I cried into his chest as he held me tightly against him.

"You're my daughter, Rayne. There's nothing you could ever do to change that. There's nothing you could ever do that would lessen the love I feel for you." He slowly rocked me in his arms and didn't lessen his hold until my tears slowed.

I pulled away to look him in the eyes but remained in the comfort of his arms. "So how bad is it going to be in there?"

"On a scale of one to ten?"

"Sure."

"Oh about..." He pretended to think. "A hundred and ten." He smiled and returned to his rocker. "Might as well bite the bullet."

I found her in the kitchen. Her back was to me as she stared out the window. Her breaths were rhythmic and steady. Her arms were relaxed across the kitchen sink. I watched her for several minutes before I let my presence be known. There was an absence in the air. One I had not come to recognize in Mother's kitchen. I'd recognized silence before. The eerie silence where there wasn't a sound carried in the air. The calm of a day or night when not a sound was heard…not a breeze rustling leaves, nor an insect's call or a bird's song. I'd heard that silence before.

This was a silence of scent in a kitchen known for its smells of cooking, baking, or simply brewed coffee. There was nothing in the air. Nothing tickled the nasal passages.

"Hello, Mother."

Her back stiffened yet she remained facing the window.

"Mother, we need to talk."

"About what?"

"Well for starters about yesterday. About me. About Grant. Why did you do that? Why did you tell him?"

"Did you not think he deserved to know?" Her voice was calm, flat, and without emotion. I wondered if she had always been calloused like this. It didn't seem genetic as I had not been equipped with such a talent. Neither did I remember Memaw having such a measured insensitive composure as what Charlie Grace exhibited. Surely this was a talent acquired over years of practice.

"Of course, he deserved to know. But in my time, not yours."

"And exactly when was your time, Rayne Amber?"

"I don't know, Mother. But it was my choice to make, not yours."

"Well, it seems you've been making many choices lately." She turned to me. The strength in my legs buckled. "And not one single one of them is any good."

Never had I seen her look this way. It wasn't simply the fact that I could count on one hand the times I had seen her wear such little makeup as she wore today but rather something in the eyes. It wasn't just the redness and puffiness of eyes changed by a night of tears. It was the way she held me with those eyes. The way she looked at me.

I had asked Jacques if he was disgusted or if his love for me had changed after he found out about what Charlie Grace had seen of me. I had asked because I didn't see the evidence in his eyes and wondered if they hid his true feelings. There was no need to ask her as she held me in the grayness of them. Fittingly ironic, the color of her eyes. Gray. But the look was pure black and white without any doubt to the emotion behind them. I wouldn't want to admit it was hated. But perhaps disgust would fit nicely? Yes, I could say that easily. One could even go with contempt. I found the words I had practiced in the brightness of my headlights as they reflected the passing miles to be absent. The speech made in preparation of our imminent debate was gone. The arguments I had devised in defense of who I had learned or accepted myself to be were also gone. All of them, vanished. Lost in the abyss of the gray eyes before me.

"Tell me, what is it you drove all this way to say?" She leaned her back against the kitchen sink and folded her arms.

"I don't know so much as to say something versus talking. I would like to talk about this."

"Talk about what?"

"Yesterday, Mother. Don't be like this. It's hard enough without all of this."

"Talk about yesterday. You want to talk about yesterday." She walked around the kitchen island and sat at the breakfast table. "I'm not sure there is much to talk about."

"Oh, isn't there?" I started to walk toward her but she turned to the window as if hoping I wouldn't come any closer. Not that I minded her taking those eyes away from me to look out into the backyard.

"I suppose there is one question I have to ask."

"Yes, and what's that?" Slowly, I took a step closer to her. I hoped she wouldn't hear my footsteps on the tile floor.

She kept her attention fixated on the willow tree outside the large bay window for what seemed like forever. "Was that my son-in-law?"

I stopped my steps. "I'm sorry. What?"

She turned in her chair to face me. Her eyes still held the same emotion as the one earlier yet this time my knees didn't threaten to give way. She propped her arm on the back of the chair. "I said." She looked directly at me as if daring me to not answer her question. "Did I meet my son-in-law yesterday?"

I was horrified. The contempt I felt with her words and her accusation caused a rancid taste in my mouth. I suppose it was in that moment of feeling protection for Mo I realized I loved her. I wouldn't allow Charlie Grace to compare her to a man or insinuate she to be like a son-in-law. I had the sickening thought of Charlie Grace's actions causing Mo to leave me—to end whatever it was we had or were trying to develop. Not that Mo was even thinking of anything developing. She had made that all too obvious. Which bothered me the most was difficult to answer.

"I find that question to be completely crass and uncalled for."

"Oh, did I offend you? Did you not like the way I referred to the nearly nude woman I found in your home yesterday? The nude woman who obviously has such high morals that she had sex with an engaged woman."

"I'm not engaged."

"Don't remind me. I was there. Remember? The night you made a spectacle of the entire evening. Did you break off your engagement because of her?"

"Not because of her." I walked to stand in between her and the window she tried to look around me to see. "Let's forget her for a moment."

"I'd like to forget her for more than a moment if it suits you just fine."

"Mother, please. I'm trying here." I sat down in the chair across from her. "It's not about her. It's not really about Grant. Even though he and I grew to want other things in our lives. This has nothing to do with him either." I pointed my finger at my chest and tapped my sternum. "This is about me. Only me. No one else. This is who I am."

"Don't be absurd, Rayne. You don't just turn gay overnight."

"No." I shook my head in agreement. "No, you don't. I've been this way for as long as I can remember. I never had the strength to accept it until recently."

"Don't be ridiculous."

"I'm not." I reached for her hand but she pulled it away and dropped it under the table.

"What?" She looked down at her lap. "What did I do wrong? Are you so angry with me that you would do this to me? Do you have such ill feeling toward me that this was a way to get back at me?"

I continued to shake my head "No" to all of the things she kept saying. "No. No. That's not it at all. This isn't a choice I made to get back at you or to punish you. It's not a choice at all."

"Don't fool yourself, young lady." She lifted her head. "This most certainly is a choice."

"How? How do you figure this is a choice?"

"Because it is. You are choosing the path to sin. You are choosing a path against God…a direct abomination against him. You are to repent and pray for forgiveness. Choose to have faith in the word and not let yourself be tempted. You can choose to not be this way. To not act on those urges and live the life you are supposed to live."

"Supposed to live by whose design?"

"By God's. There is no gray line here, Rayne. You are choosing a life of sin and fornication."

"I committed fornication with Grant but I don't seem to remember you getting all up in arms about it."

She pushed her chair away from the table and stood up. "I'll not sit here and continue this any further."

I stood to meet her. "Mother, wait." I reached for her arm and this time made contact before she could pull away. I felt the muscles of her forearm tighten as she tried to pull her arm free. "Please just wait. Let's not be like this."

"Are you going to continue to live this way?"

"I'm going to continue to live the way I feel is for me. I'm going to continue to follow what I feel…yes."

Her chin gave a small quiver. "Then I can't love you this way."

I fell back into the chair and was thankful for its support. "You're my mother." I wished the wooden seat could magically transport me to another time or another place. One that didn't have the words she had spoken hanging in the air with such sharpness and need to cut. "You're my mother. You're supposed to love me no matter what."

She started to turn away but shifted her shoulder to look at me again. There was no hesitation in her voice nor was there doubt behind her eyes. "I can't love you like this." She turned on her heels and walked to the door. Her back stiffened as she stopped just inside of the doorway. "I can't love a daughter I know in my heart I'll not see in eternal Heaven. You're an abomination to all that I believe in. I'm sorry I ever gave birth to you."

Crack.

Fissure.

Break.

Two steps later, she was gone. I sat in the quiet for several minutes, I was unsure if I was waiting for her return or if I merely lacked the power to stand on my own two feet. Of course, I knew this would not be easy for her to accept. Hell, it was damn hard for me to. much less her. Yet I had never entertained the thought her reaction would be this strong. Who could look their own daughter directly in the eyes and tell them they were no longer or could no longer be loved because of who they fundamentally were? How could a mother feel, much less say, she hated her child to the point she longed for the day they had not been born?

Had I been cursed with such a woman for a mother or did she feel as the majority of those felt? Flossie had given me a glimpse into a very different response. Was hers and Memaw an example of how others in the town would feel or would they be closer to Charlie Grace? The better question was, could I handle it if they were?

Chapter 27

I HAD BEEN TO the cabin this time of year. Not many times, but enough to where I wasn't expecting it to feel as differently as it felt today. I suppose December in the south was different than many other states. Our December most likely felt like their fall season. The leaves had browned and dried but many still remained attached to their branches. The sound from them was coarse when the breeze rustled them.

The sun's light was bright with enough warmth to keep my body comfortable as I sat out on the dock. The drive here had reminded me of those long before I had left for medical school. The days when I drove with Memaw to our place on the bayou. The days when I tried wholeheartedly to soak up every ounce of the feel of my home. I felt the pull of losing the one place that centered me in this world. The one comfort I had when all else was lost.

Today, I drove here again with the same looming need to once again absorb every facet of Brennin. It wouldn't be something taking me away this time but something pushing me away. I lay back against the wood and stared at the cloudless sky. The blue called me to remember the other comfort I once had. There had been two sets of blue eyes that had held me with the tenderness I had grown up to know. Two sets I would undoubtedly never see again. Two sets that would hold the key to shaking the pit of loneliness I felt myself falling into.

My whole body was startled with the shadowed darkness of the sun no longer being cast upon my face. I opened my eyes to see a larger-than-life-looking Flossie standing over me.

"Hey, baby girl. I knew'd you'd be out here." She shifted her weight and I squinted to the brightness of the light no longer shielded by her body. "Mind if'n I take a seat?"

"Not at all." I sat up to scoot over so she would have enough room on the edge of the dock.

"How you doing?"

"I've been better."

"Yep, I imagine dat's 'bout right."

"How did you know I was here? Did Charlie Grace call you?"

"Nope. I hadn't heard a peep outta her until I went over there dis morning." She wiggled her feet as they hung off the edge of the dock. "And truth be told, it tweren't her dat told me a thing. It was Jacques. He's mighty upset with'n her. Mighty upset. In fact, dat man left right behind me. Said he had to get away before he done said words he can't take back." She looked at me. "Dat man worried about you. He just 'bout bust with love for you. Plum near broke dis old lady down to see dat much hurtin' in his eyes. He asked me to find you. I didn't think you'd a wantin' me to bring him out here tho."

"No. You're right. I like this place being my own and I don't think he could keep it from Charlie Grace. I wouldn't want to ask him to keep a secret from her. That wouldn't be right." I pulled at a piece of splintered wood underneath my finger. "So, you didn't see her or talk to her?"

"Nope."

I felt a tightness in my throat. I was unsure as to how much Flossie knew. How much anyone or everyone knew. "What all do you know?"

"From what I can piece together, it done sound like you got caught with'n yo' hand in the cookie jar."

"Something like that." I pulled the splintered wood completely free and played with it in my hands. "It was horrible, Flossie. If ever there was a wrong way to come out, that was it."

"Ah hell, sis. None of us gone have life figured out and 'bout the time we done think we do something gonna slap us in the face. You can plan all you be wanting, don't mean it gonna happen dat way."

"This would definitely fall into that category. Do you know she told Grant?"

She turned from gazing at the water and squinted at me. "Yep. Dat little piece right der part of the reason old Jacques fit to be tied. He done tired of her sticking her nose in yo business." She put her hand over the top of mine. "It look like to me with these here old eyes dat it all in place fo you now."

"What do you mean?"

"It all out now. Maybe not the way you were a'wanting but it all out. You free to do what you want. Free to live the way you be wanting."

"Yeah. Free to be alone. Free to not have a home to come back to anymore."

"What you spouting off?"

I threw the piece of wood out into the water. "I'm not welcome here anymore, Flossie. Charlie Grace told me she couldn't love me like this. That she couldn't love a daughter who was going to hell." I covered my eyes with my hands and rubbed the tears away.

Flossie straightened the slump in her back. "She said dat to you? She said dem words to you?"

"Well, she didn't say the word 'hell' but, yeah, pretty much everything else. She said she couldn't love me if I was like this. Said she wouldn't see me in eternal life. Didn't leave much to the imagination that she was basically telling me I was going straight to Hell. She said she wished she had never given birth to me."

The paper-thin skin of Flossie's hand tightened across her knuckles as she balled her fingers into a fist. "Oooooh. Dat woman gone bring a hurtin' on herself she speak dem words around me. Addie done turning over in her grave right 'bout now. Charlie Grace done said dem words gone make me face her." Her voice was elevated and shook with emotion.

I placed a reassuring hand on her arm. "Don't get worked up about it. You know she probably feels like most will feel when all of this comes out. They aren't going to think like you and Meems."

She turned her body to face me. "How you know'd dat? You ever talked to any of dem 'bout dis? You ever given any of dem a chance? Yo momma ain't speakin' for dis town, sweet girl. She ain't the voice of dis town. I'd say many a folk gone be might pissed off they ever know dem words she done said to you."

"Flossie, I have to face facts. Face the truth. I can't pretend it'll all be okay and I can just move back here as if nothing has changed."

"And what done changed?"

"I'm a lesbian!" I didn't mean to yell.

"What? You tweren't no lesbian when you were home for Thanksgiving? What, you all of a sudden dis woman? You gone tell me you not have these same feelings…been dis same woman last Thanksgiving when Addie and I done watched you with your friend? Dat you not been dis same women that growed up in this town?"

"No." I ran my finger over the roughened wood I had pulled the piece from. "I'm not saying that."

"We all done loved you den. We all gone love you now. You ain't no different den the girl we done watched grow up into a fine young woman."

I looked up into her eyes. They weren't blue like the ones I had thought of a few minutes ago but they were tender. "Do you really believe that?"

"With all my heart." She shook her head with emphasis and pulled me in tightly for a hug.

Brown sugar and honey.

"You gotta give us a chance," she whispered. "Give yo' people a chance. Dis town a chance."

The vibration of my phone interrupted her hug. My heart leapt into my throat for fear it was Charlie Grace's name on the screen. I doubted I could handle anymore of her words.

Flossie's eyes followed mine to the phone in my lap. "Dat one of your new friends?"

Mo's name flashed on the screen and I felt a smile try to take over the hurt. "Yes, it is."

She smiled back at me. "Den why don't you answer dat while I go call Jacques and get these groceries cooked up." She pointed to the pickup truck pulled up next to the house.

"You're staying with me?"

"Always." She stood up. "Now you best be gettin dat phone."

"I think I will." I pushed the button to accept the call while I let the happiness of seeing her name, the excitement of hearing her voice soar through me. It was quickly followed by a nervousness as to why she was calling.

"Hi."

"Hi. Jaz told me you went home." She sounded nervous too. "How are you doing?"

"I'm hanging in. How are you?"

"I'm hanging in too." She paused. "So, how bad is it?"

"Probably as bad as you could imagine."

"Are you coming back to Birmingham?"

A large oak leaf drained of its color floated in the breeze that blew high in the trees. I watched its stem hold firmly onto the branch as the wind lifted it up within its current. "Not right now. I'm drained. Physically. Emotionally. I'm just drained. I honestly don't think I could make the drive until I can get a little bit of rest."

"Do you have friends there you can stay with or are you staying with your mother?"

"Oh no. I'm not welcome there. If I have any doubts or confusion in all of this, that's one thing I can hold certain. I'm not welcome in my home." I watched Flossie carry grocery bags from the truck into the cabin. She caught me looking at her and waved. "But I'm not alone. I'm staying with a friend." I paused. "No, I'm staying with family at my cabin."

She was quiet except for her breathing. "Hey, Rayne?"

"Yes?"

"Do you have doubts and confusion?"

"Well, yeah, of course I do."

"About being a lesbian?"

I watched the leaf take another ride in the force of the wind. "Not about being who I am. Not about that. I have my doubts as to what the road ahead will be but not about who I am."

"And what are your thoughts about me? Do you have doubts and confusion about me?" Her voice was even more nervous than it was before.

"Well, to be honest, I'm a little confused. I'm surprised you called."

"Can't say I blame you there. And doubts?"

"No. I can't say I have those. In fact, I've actually never been surer of what I want from you."

"Oh yeah?"

"Yeah."

"This that you want, would it be the same you asked me for in your apartment?"

"The very same."

She took in a deep breath. "What if I disappoint you?"

"And what if I disappoint you, Mo? We don't know what each other will need in the future. We don't. How can we possibly know if we are going to be all they need when those times come? But what I do know is, you're here. You called me. You're here now. That's what's important to me. For once, I want to live in today and not my carefully planned out future."

"Well, alright then." I heard the smile in her words. "So, what are you doing tomorrow?"

The breeze was becoming cooler as it lowered closer to the water. I drew my legs up against me to try to overcome the damp chill of it. "Tomorrow? I'm not sure. Why? What do you have in mind?"

"I was thinking maybe you could drive over to Baton Rouge and pick me up at the airport."

"You're flying into Louisiana tomorrow?"

"I thought maybe you could use some company driving back." She hesitated for a moment. "And besides, I miss you. I need to see you."

The smile I had felt when I saw her name as the caller was nothing compared to the smile I was wearing now. "Watch out, Mo. You're getting dangerously close to acting like a girlfriend."

She laughed. "I know. It's pretty scary, huh?"

"Not to me, but how are you handling it?"

"I think it might look good on me."

I caught sight of the leaf as its stem gave away from the branch to be carried gently in the air until it landed on the surface of the bayou. Its ripple altered the mirrored reflection of the trees lining the water's edge. It floated away until it was lost in the brilliance of the sun on the water. It was free to drift into parts unknown. There wasn't a way to know what was beyond the future immediately in front of me. There wasn't a way to see past the sun's light. Yet I was free of the branch that held my stem. Free to set my own path as I drifted into the next phase of my life.

I held the phone against my chin and thought of the woman whose voice had brought me happiness and security at the height of the next phase of my life. I thought of the woman in the cabin who had come to make sure I wasn't alone in the first steps of this new life. I thought of Jazlyn's calm, friendly voice of comfort in my ear at a time when I felt my world spinning out of control. Then I looked up into the sky and thought of the woman who had loved me unconditionally.

It was these things I would hold on to. It was these women who would give me strength. And it would be these women that would walk this next path with me. I wasn't afraid. I wasn't alone. I turned from the sun as it dipped lower in the sky and let the heat warm my back as I walked toward the cabin. Tomorrow was a new day.

My phone vibrated yet again in my hand. I chuckled at the thought of Mo calling me back so quickly.

"Wow. You really do miss me." I didn't even look at the screen before answering.

"Rayne."

"Sam?"

"Yeah." There was a long pause. "Can you talk?"

After the Storm

HE WEIGHT OF her heels carried on her fingertips grew exponentially with each step Samantha LeJeune took walking away from the only woman she ever loved. She wanted to turn back, take Rayne Storm into her arms and run away from everything that would keep them apart. The problem was Rayne wasn't ready to give her what she needed to make a life with her. If she couldn't run away with her, she would at least run away from her and all of the memories of Alabama. Without a clue as to her destination, she hit the road with nothing on her mind but healing her broken heart strong enough to never fall in love again.

Gentry Bell didn't really have a home like others would describe. For her, home was a small town filled with suffocating memories of painful abuse and betrayal by those who were supposed to love her. There were only two woman who kept her from moving as far away as possible. The sudden passing of one of those women and a new job with the National Park Service, were her signs that it's time for her to move on. She's never feared being on her own or venturing out into the unknown. Actually, it has always been her breath of life. But this time, she isn't alone. Maybe the silence of the wilderness will have the answer she needs to decide what to do about the baby she is carrying.

An immediate connection develops when these two broken women meet on the road that carries them away from the life they were living. But will it be enough to open their hearts to trust again? And if so, will they be strong enough to hold onto that connection when an unborn child seems to be pointing them to return back to a home where memories of trauma and a first love are still ever so present in each of their hearts?

About the Author

CD CAIN GREW up in Louisiana fishing the bayou cutoff with her papaw, gardening vegetables with her mamaw and riding her three-wheeler in the woods when given a full tank of gas. These childhood memories are the essence of her Louisiana roots. A woman torn between medicine and creative writing, she eventually decided to do both. When she's not trying to find precious bits of time around her clinic practice to write, she's somewhere out and about enjoying nature. This may be paddling on the water, hiking a trail, basking in the view from a mountain or simply sipping a glass of red wine while sitting on her backporch. She lives in Georgia with her wife, son and furbabies. She always enjoys hearing from readers and can be followed at www.cdcainauthor.com.

www.ingramcontent.com/pod-product-compliance
Lightning Source LLC
Chambersburg PA
CBHW020245180626
46810CB00006B/2375